THE GIRL IN BLACK PAJAMAS

BY CHRIS BIRDY

DISCLAIMER

This novel is a work of fiction. Names, characters, places and incidents are products of the author's imagination or used fictionally. Any resemblance to actual persons, living or dead, events, or locales is coincidental.

TEXT COPYRIGHT 2014 CHRIS BIRDY

ALL RIGHTS RESERVED

ISBN- 13: 978-1500335397

ISBN-10: 1500335398

Library of Congress Control Number: 2014911966

CreateSpace Independent Publishing Platform

North Charleston, South Carolina

DEDICATION

To: Abi

Some have a muse
I have amuse-ment
After all this time,
You still make me laugh.

1

ALL THE WORLD'S A STAGE

BOSTON

A gigantic man lumbered down the street. The strong wind blew his straight platinum hair away from his head, but he was too distracted to notice. At eight-thirty on Sunday morning, Tommie Jurgenson approached a storefront building on Lincoln Street. Businesses in the downtown area were closed as was the one with the blackened windows sporting "R&B Investigations" in gold lettering. Tommie gripped his laptop firmly in his left hand, punching in numbers on a keypad panel with his right. Just as he was about to press the last key, a car pulled up to the curb. Tommie glanced over his shoulder and saw a man wearing a George Bush Halloween mask and a cowboy hat get out of the car. Before Tommie could react, George Bush took a gun from his pocket and shot the big man four times in the back.

Tommie dropped to his knees, then fell face down on the ground.

"You friggin hacker! Now that other shithead will crawl out of his hole," the gunman muttered.

Tommie lay on the stoop bleeding while the would-be-assassin tried to roll him over. The gunman pushed him, but Tommie's three hundred and fifty pound bulk wouldn't budge. When the shooter looked up, he saw the alarm lights blinking. "Damn you! You elephant!" George Bush yelled before he ran back to his car.

☞

SOUTH FLORIDA

Over a thousand miles away, a slim blonde with a three hundred dollar, chopped haircut and large breasts stood next to the green and white sedan with "Sheriff Palm Beach County" emblazoned on the door. Zoe's wrists were cuffed in front, and her red painted lips curled slightly, showing off her pearly white teeth. She batted her false eyelashes and pleaded, "Oh, Officer, isn't there something I can do so you won't arrest me?"

A dark haired man, wearing a blue police uniform, moved his hat at a rakish angle and leered at the blonde while he unzipped his fly.

Hands free, Zoe Ziegler was on her knees as she performed oral sex on the cop. The sucking sounds were accompanied by a close-up shot of the distended penis sporting red lipstick marks all over the shaft. After the policeman ejaculated over her face and chest, Zoe smiled, pretending to enjoy it.

Sarah Thomas, a buxom brunette holding a Canon Vixia HF G10 camcorder, watched the small screen intently then yelled, "That's a wrap! In the next shot JJ will walk in, then you'll both do her." As Sarah bent her head, blood poured from her nose. She placed her index finger across her nostrils and muttered, "Oh, shit!" then put down the camera and dashed away.

Bored, Zoe Ziegler sat on the hood of the cruiser, cleaning cum off her face and chest with Johnson's baby wipes while the two men set up the next scene. Zoe called out to another blonde sitting in a folding lawn chair. Zoe raised and wiggled two fingers indicating that she wanted a cigarette. Tiffany Gallagher, wearing a school girl's uniform with a micro mini pleated skirt and no underwear brought over a pack of Marlboro 100's and a BIC lighter. Tiff's long blonde hair was braided into two pigtails. The women relaxed and smoked, enjoying the peace and quiet of an early Sunday morning in Palm Beach.

ᐤᏆᏆᏆᏇ

South Florida (Elsewhere)

The family sitting around the breakfast table at nine in the morning might have been posing for an ad in *Parents Magazine*. The tanned man with gray hair was Bogie McGruder, the *B* in R&B Investigations. He smiled as his redheaded wife tried to feed a piece of banana to their baby son. The blonde baby pushed her hand away, sealed his lips, and squeezed his eyes closed. Their four-year-old daughter, a miniature of her mother but with her father's ice-blue eyes, giggled then yawned. Bogie studied his daughter. As he opened his mouth to speak, little Isabella said, "I'm fine, Da-Dee! Yawning is good for you."

"Thank you, Isabella, I'm glad you're such an authority on yawning," Bogie said dryly.

Isabella smiled. "That's because I Googled it. I love Google! It's very educational."

Bogie nodded slightly as Isabella tried to stifle another yawn. Isabella turned away, picked up a small piece of banana from the baby's highchair tray and asked, "Do you want this, Hankster?"

The little boy covered his mouth with both hands and quickly shook his head. But as soon as his sister popped the piece of banana in her mouth, he started screaming. "No! Sissie, no!" When the baby started crying in earnest, Isabella looked at her father. "May I be excused?"

Bogie nodded. "Don't forget we're going to the cookout this afternoon."

Isabella considered this, then asked, "Aren't we visiting Grandma today?"

"We'll stop over there first then go straight to Mandie's house."

As the child left the room and ran up the stairs too quickly, Bogie turned to his wife, who was cleaning up the baby. Bailey held the Hankster on her lap. Her green eyes blazed, and her mouth tightened. "I swear she does things like that just to torment him! I think this jealousy bit has gone on long enough. He's almost a year old. When's she going to understand that he's here to stay?"

Bogie shrugged. "The child psychologist—"

"Pleeease!" Bailey interrupted. "I think Dr. Jane is a waste of space! She's having a great time playing chess with Isabella then sending out a bill at the end of the month. As far as I can tell, she's never dealt with Isabella's losses or the fact that Isabella killed another human being. If that woman's made any breakthroughs, she's kept them to herself. I repeat, sending Isabella to that shrink is a waste of time and money!"

Bogie nodded. "I still think her losses are the issue. The kill was righteous."

"*Righteous*! She's not a commando! She was three when it happened."

Bogie sighed. "Okay, we'll give Dr. Jane till the end of the month, but only if she stops pushing that damn private school. She acts like she's getting a referral fee from them. If Isabella's that gifted, living with her family isn't going to reduce her IQ. You can only imagine how she'd react to being shipped off to school at the age of four. Anyway, I'm worried about her. She seems awfully tired lately. Do you think she might be coming down with something?"

Bailey shook her head. "I think she's spending too much time on her computer."

Bogie considered this. "She sends out her email in the morning then she's busy doing other things for the rest of the day."

"Exactly! When did she have time to become a Google aficionado? I think she's on that damn laptop at night when she's supposed to be sleeping."

"Should we make her leave it down here when she goes to bed?"

Bailey shook her head. "Good luck! I can just imagine the scene, the high drama and the tears! She's as single-minded as you are."

Bogie raised an eyebrow. "What is it you're trying to say?"

Bailey smiled. "I just said it."

∽✺∽

As her parents discussed her sleep habits, Isabella pulled her laptop out from under her bed. She plugged in her ear buds, pressed a key and continued watching her new favorite movie, *Kill Bill Volume 2*.

> *The Bride was sealed inside a coffin and buried alive. While trapped underground, the Bride punched through wood from inches away, a technique she learned while working with Pai Mai. She made a hole in the coffin and clawed her way to the surface.*

After watching this scene, Isabella paused the movie, yanked out her earbuds, and carried the laptop to her desk to prepare her daily email to friends and family who anxiously awaited reports of all the minutiae in the McGruder household.

∽✺∽

BOSTON

For the first time in five years, Rose Jones - the *R* in R&B Investigations - had gone out bar-crawling on a Saturday night. Coco, her transgender friend and employee, had just finished the last step in the costly and painful process of physically becoming the woman who dwelled inside her six foot, one-inch frame. They had celebrated Coco's liberation until three-thirty in the morning.

At five minutes after eleven, Rose Jones was awakened by the persistent ringing of the phone. More than half asleep and unaccustomed to receiving calls on her land line, Rose grabbed the receiver and mumbled, "Hello" without checking the caller ID. As she listened, her eyes opened wide. "Oh, good God!...Is he?..." She continued to listen then asked, "What time did this happen?" When the caller answered, Rose yelled, "Why wasn't I called before this?" As the person on the other end responded, Rose impatiently bounced the side of her fist on the nightstand. "What hospital was he taken to?"

After hanging up, Rose tried to absorb the information. Her hands moved through her mass of black curls until they joined at the back of her head. Her plan of action formed as she rifled through the nightstand drawer and found a crumpled pack of dry Winstons. She took one out, straightened and lit it, then inhaled deeply. Although she coughed from the harsh taste, she took another drag. Her one month smoking cessation program was now over.

Rose grabbed her BlackBerry, checked schedules and speed-dialed a number. "Jesús, get back to the shop *now*! Tommie's been shot, the place is open and the cops are there. You know *nothing*! If they ask any questions, give them my card. I'll try to be there in a half an hour. I've got to get Tommie's laptop and modems out of his apartment in case the cops decide to check them."

"Is Tommie——?" Jesús began to ask.

"No. He's at Mass General. He's in surgery. That's all I know now."

"Where did he get shot?"

"At the shop."

"Then why Mass General?"

"I don't remember, something about a church roof collapsing in the South End and them diverting him to Mass General." While speaking to Jesús, Rose quickly typed a 911 email to the staff from her laptop. "COME HOME!"

After she hurriedly showered and dressed in a black tee shirt and custom fitted black pants, she pulled up her black silver-studded motorcycle boots. Rose Jones took a large suitcase from the guest room closet and started emergency evacuation procedures. She grabbed an envelope from a sealed Tampax box in the guest bathroom. Rose ripped open the envelope, took out a key, and studied the alarm code.

Rose disarmed her alarm and carried the suitcase next door. She unlocked that door and turned off the alarm. Rose looked around the condo that was supposed to be a twin to hers. Fast food wrappers, pizza boxes and Coke cans were strewn over the living room. Computer equipment surrounded an extra-large recliner. She looked at the super-sized TV screen/ monitor on the wall in this man cave and shook her head. Rose disconnected three modems and carried them to the front door. She looked around for a laptop but couldn't find it. After hurriedly flipping through stacks of grease-stained paperwork, she walked into the bathroom and opened a drawer to the vanity. Rose removed a sealed box of Trojans from a drawer and stuffed it in her pocket knowing Tommie would no longer need an emergency key to her apartment.

While listening to telephone messages, Rose pulled a nightgown out of the suitcase and hung it on a hook on the back of the bathroom door. She placed women's toiletries and a toothbrush in the bathroom to give the illusion of having an intimate relationship with Tommie.

Rose returned to the living room and wrapped the modems in pillow cases. She was able to fit two in the suitcase and carried the third. Not too bad for the short trip next door.

By the time Rose placed the equipment in her spare bedroom closet, it was time to leave. She went back into her black and white, chrome and glass living room and moved the dial to open the sun shades. She looked out over Boston Common and smiled. Rose loved this city. Every time she chastised herself for paying three quarters of a million dollars for this place, she remembered the years of hard work that had brought her to this point. Rose could look out over Boston and feel like she owned it.

As she drove toward R&B Investigations, Rose didn't know whether to cry or scream. Why Tommie? Of all the people in her employ, he was the last one she expected to be shot. Tommie didn't even carry a gun. He may have been a genius, but he didn't understand the meaning of the word discretion. Had he played the fool and helped somebody set their sights on R&B Investigations?

2

THE DAY OF REST

SOUTH FLORIDA

As Bogie drove down Forest Hill Boulevard, he glanced in the rearview mirror. A red Toyota Corolla moved behind him and stayed with him until he parked his white SUV in front of the apartment complex. Isabella studied her father from her bumper seat in the rear. She stretched her neck to take another look at the red car.

Bailey glanced at the glass front doors of the main building and asked, "Why didn't you park in the lot around the corner?"

"As soon as the tenants see the SUV, they'll be on me like white on rice. They'd rather badger me on a Sunday than call the office and leave a message. Even God got a day off; I think I deserve one too."

The McGruder family walked through the main building and entered the gated pool area. The large swimming pool, surrounded by umbrella tables and lounge chairs, was the centerpiece of the property. Bogie waved to a few tenants who were sunning on chaise lounges while the family made their way around the fence to Bogie's stepmother's apartment.

An attractive woman with dark brown hair opened the door and tried for a brave smile, but her sad brown eyes glistened. "Elizabeth! The children are here!" Margarita called out to the slack faced old woman sitting in a wheelchair.

Elizabeth McGruder looked up and smiled as Isabella kissed her cheek and said, "Hello, Grandma." As usual, Elizabeth complained that the child should be wearing a lacey dress instead of white pajamas. Isabella sighed, tired of explaining that her clothes were warrior's clothes, not pajamas.

Bailey took the blonde baby out of his pouch and handed him to Elizabeth. Bailey kissed Elizabeth's cheek and asked, "How are you feeling today, Mother?"

Elizabeth stared at Bailey's lovely oval face studying it without seeming to comprehend what she was saying. She looked down at the small blue-eyed boy in her arms and bent her head to kiss him. "Oh, Bud," she said softly. "You are so beautiful! What a good boy you are." The baby grinned, showing off his four teeth.

Isabella walked to the bookshelf across the room and retrieved a book. "We're on chapter three now, Grandma." She opened the book and started reading *Tom Sawyer* to her grandmother.

Bailey touched Margarita's arm and asked, "How are you doing?"

A tear spilled down Margarita's cheek, and she brushed it away then pushed her dark hair behind her ear. "I'll live," she said softly.

Bailey hugged her and wiped a sympathy tear off her own cheek, consoling Margarita over her breakup with Carlos Aragon.

Bogie watched the women, then walked in the kitchen to make a cup of tea. His wife, the lawyer! She wasn't heartless enough to be a good lawyer, but she was a great wife and mother. Her brother was right; she should have been a social worker.

Carlos Aragon, Bogie's right-hand man and construction manager had finally popped the question to Margarita. He'd made quite a show of proposing to Margarita while they were on the dance floor at Bogie's older daughter's wedding. Margarita accepted. After sharing her bed with Carlos for five years, she believed they were meant for each other. She was in love with Carlos, and Carlos was in love with Carlos. Margarita had caught him cheating six times, but when he put the diamond ring on her finger, she forgave all and assumed he was ready to settle down.

Then came Yazmin Flores' paternity suit. It shook them up, but Margarita stood by him. Carlos swore he never touched the girl, Yazmin was lying. DNA tests proved she wasn't. Carlos was the father of Yazmin's baby.

Another liar filed suit three weeks after that.

Drunk at his sister's wedding, Carlos bragged that at least those two women gave him sons. Margarita smashed a bottle of Jose Cuervo across his face.

When Carlos came to work the following Monday with two black eyes and a broken nose, Bogie showed him no mercy. Bogie was angry for several reasons. He liked Margarita and didn't care for the way Carlos treated her. Not only had Carlos participated in another public fight with Margarita; but he also impregnated Yazmin, a distant relative. Yazmin Flores had been hired to take over Margarita's former duties since Margarita was now Elizabeth McGruder's primary caregiver. Carlos' inability to keep his pants zipped caused an uncomfortable situation in both apartment complexes. Bogie couldn't ask Yazmin to leave since she was doing a decent job and needed the money to support her baby. But her presence caused Margarita considerable pain. Bogie decided that the best he could do was ban Carlos from the large apartment complex where Margarita lived and worked. Bogie told Carlos that if he found him there, he'd fire him.

Carlos was angry because he thought that Bogie sided with Margarita in a personal matter, but he was clever enough to keep his mouth shut, knowing that Bogie could be a dangerous man.

As Isabella read and Elizabeth smiled and stroked the baby's cheek, Bogie motioned for Bailey to take Margarita for a ride. Although Margarita initially protested, she perked up when Bailey led her to the family's Cadillac. Bailey didn't worry about leaving the children with Bogie. He had more experience with kids than she did, as he raised his now twenty-year-old daughter Amanda himself. The Hankster loved to be held and fussed over, and Isabella enjoyed reading, especially to Grandma. And Grandma didn't mind Bogie being in her apartment since she no longer remembered who he was.

After an hour of family bonding, Isabella's throat was dry, the Hankster's diaper was full and so was Grandma's. When the women returned, Bogie stood up and gently took the baby from Elizabeth McGruder's arms, telling her he needed to be changed. As he handed the Hankster to Bailey, he turned to Margarita, "Somebody else needs a change. I'll help you."

"No, you don't have to—"

"It's too much for you to handle yourself," Bogie said as he lifted Elizabeth out of the wheelchair and carried her to the bathroom. The Alzheimer's was bad enough, but after Elizabeth fell and broke her hip, she required nursing care as well as a companion. "What time's the nurse supposed to be here?" Bogie asked. At that moment, the doorbell rang, and he called out, "Don't answer the door, Isabella!"

The child turned to her mother as Bailey got up to let the nurse in the apartment. Isabella knew her father's fears were well-founded. A year earlier, she had been abducted by a monster who came to the door and shot her bodyguard. Isabella killed that monster with her Bokken sword, but it had never been replaced. No matter how much she begged, pleaded, and cajoled, her parents refused to buy her another sword. She would have one... someday. Isabella knew it would only be a matter of timing and planning.

After they left the apartment, Bogie looked down at the front of his clothes. "We need to stop in the office. I have to take a shower and change my clothes."

Bailey opened her mouth to speak, but just said "O" as she looked at his white polo shirt. The strange relationship between Elizabeth and Bogie

McGruder always baffled Bailey. Bogie was not Elizabeth's son, she never treated him like a son, and she didn't like him. Bogie came into Elizabeth's life when she was married to Baxter McGruder, Bogie's father. Elizabeth, Baxter, and their two children lived happily on Beacon Street in Boston until Boghdun Uchenich, Baxter's illegitimate thirteen-year-old son, was thrust upon them when his mother died in Pittsburgh. Every day, Elizabeth and Baxter made sure the boy knew he was unwelcome. Bogie was a brilliant kid who thrived at Boston Latin School when he wasn't in trouble or getting into fights.

Bogie's salvation was Baxter's partner on the police force, Darryl Jones. Darryl liked the boy and felt sorry for him. He let Bogie live with him and his family for a couple of summers while Bogie worked off debts incurred through his misdeeds. Bogie then became part of Darryl's family and looked up to Pop as the only father figure he ever needed. Pop's daughter Rose was Bogie's best friend.

Although Bogie was forced to change his last name to McGruder, he never considered himself part of their clan. Bogie and his half-brother, Bud, detested each other. The only McGruder bond he formed was with his younger half-sister, Ann.

When Bogie's first marriage ended, he left the Army and returned to the Boston area with his baby daughter, Amanda. Bogie raised her with the help of Pop and Rose. One day, Baxter McGruder showed up at R&B Investigations with an unusual proposal. Baxter offered Bogie the deed to a Palm Beach property valued at more than two million dollars. All Bogie had to do was marry Baxter's Russian girlfriend. The Immigration and Naturalization Service was getting ready to boot Olga out of the country because she was out of status. Baxter would have dumped Elizabeth and married Olga, but the timing was off. Elizabeth was the one with the money, not Baxter, a Boston cop. Elizabeth had deeded the Florida property to him years earlier, but the payout on a large annuity Elizabeth purchased on his retirement from the police force wouldn't mature for another two years. He knew that if Elizabeth found out he was leaving her for his young, pregnant girlfriend, she'd make sure he never got the big payday. Being greedy, Baxter wanted everything. He believed he could convince Bogie to marry Olga using the property as bait and then scam it back. If Baxter had taken the time to know his son, he would have realized that Bogie was smarter than Baxter could ever hope to be.

Bogie got the property and sold it immediately. By the time Baxter, Olga and baby Barbara were killed in a car accident two years later, Bogie's daughter Amanda had grown uncomfortable with their whole living arrangement. The relationship Bogie started with Bailey while he was legally married to Olga imploded.

After almost four years of change and upheaval, Bogie and Bailey reconciled, and Bogie finally got to meet his three-year old daughter, Isabella.

When Elizabeth learned of the deception perpetrated by Baxter with Bogie's assistance, she started a downward spiral into dementia. When Bogie returned for Bud's funeral and saw this once proud woman reduced to a state of confusion, he felt he was partially to blame. Bogie provided Elizabeth with an apartment in the complex he owned while his sister Ann, the recipient of Elizabeth's fortune, paid for her companion and nursing care. All Elizabeth had were her fantasies. She believed that Isabella was her long-dead granddaughter, Jennifer and that the Hankster was her son, Bud, as a baby.

Bailey sat on one of the sofas in the reception area playing with the baby while Bogie went into the office. Bogie unlocked a door behind the desk that led to the bedroom that was once his, then theirs before they moved into a large, four bedroom home he had renovated. While Bogie showered, Isabella took a key from the middle drawer of the desk, went down the back hallway and opened the door to a room that was once her sister's bedroom but was now her practice room, complete with mats. This was where she received lessons from Master Lim and practiced kung fu and other martial arts while her mother or father worked in the office.

When Isabella heard the shower stop, she ended her routine and returned to the front office. She placed the key back in the desk drawer and glanced out the window. The red Toyota that had followed them turned around in Grandpa John's driveway.

By the time the family was back on the road, they were already forty-five minutes late for the cookout at Amanda and Randy's house. Isabella sat in the back frequently checking out her window. Finally, she asked, "Is that red car still following us, Da-dee?"

"What red car?" Bogie asked.

"The one that drove behind us from our house. It turned around in Grandpa John's driveway, and I don't think he's home. His car's not there."

Bogie checked the rearview mirror and said, "I don't think so."

Bailey scowled at him and whispered, "She's becoming as paranoid as you are."

"No, I'm not," Isabella said from the back seat.

⸾⸾⸾⸾⸾

When the McGruders arrived in North Palm Beach at the enormous stucco house, Amanda McGruder Carpenter greeted them with "You're late! Where the hell have you been? You're the last ones here!"

As Bogie opened his mouth to tell his older daughter to go to hell, Isabella spoke up. "Da-dee had to take a shower and change his clothes. Grandma had a poop accident and Da-dee had to pick her up and carry her to the bathroom and then he got poop on his clothes and then..."

"Thank you, Isabella," Amanda finally said. "I'm sorry. I apologize." She waved her hand to include the group. "The baby had me up most of the night."

Bogie put his arm around Amanda's shoulders. "Other than keeping you up all night, how is Riley Rose?"

"You'll see for yourself. John has her, and she's sound asleep in his arms. How's the Hankster doing?"

Bailey motioned with her chin at Henry in his pouch, his eyes drooping. "He's a little night owl, too. He'd rather sleep in the afternoon and keep us awake at night."

Randy, Amanda's husband, appeared behind his raven-haired wife. The muscular man smiled and tipped his head. "Bogie, Bailey, Izzy and Hankster, welcome to our house!"

After admiring one more room that Amanda had professionally decorated with expensive furnishings, they walked out to the back lawn. The two young men manning the industrial-sized grill were Randy's friends from the sheriff's office, Billy Ray Marcel and JJ Johnson. Both had short brown hair and wore Oakley wraparound sunglasses. They were dressed casually but had beepers, cell phones and other equipment attached to their clothing. Amanda's blonde girlfriends, Zoe and Tiffany, sipped unidentifiable drinks and watched the men until they spotted Bogie and Bailey. The young women stood up and walked over to Bogie and kissed his cheek. They greeted Bailey, but not with the same display of warmth.

"How are you doing with your acting classes, Zoe?" Bogie asked. Zoe smiled and nodded. Bogie turned to Tiffany. "How's Burger King treating you?" he asked.

When Tiffany scrunched up her freckled nose and shook her head, Bogie questioned her, "You don't like working there?"

Tiffany continued to shake her head, saying, "I quit! It sucked!"

Bogie's eyebrow lifted. "So what are you doing for work?"

When Zoe glared at her, Tiffany shrugged one shoulder and quickly said, "I'm between jobs right now."

Bogie glanced at Bailey, and she gave him one of her *mind-your-own-business* stares.

Bogie and Bailey turned to face a large semi-circle of older men and women. Several of them were huddled together, but a portly man holding a sleeping baby sat off by himself. Bogie tagged behind as Bailey re-introduced herself and Bogie to three men sitting together, officers in the PBSO. They smiled and checked out the stunning redhead as they nodded toward her husband. Two of the men were Billy Ray's father and grandfather; the third was JJ's father.

The ladies with dyed brown hair were Billy Ray's and JJ's mothers. The silver-haired woman was Billy Ray's grandmother. Billy Ray Marcell's mother held a chubby African-American baby on her lap and spoke to JJ's mother in a stage whisper. "I hope JJ's not getting too serious with Tiffany. That girl comes from a very troubled family."

Billy Ray's grandmother brushed her hand over her sun-dried, leathery face and said, "I thought her father was a lieutenant in Palm Beach."

"Riviera Beach," Billy Ray's mother corrected her. "It's Dee Dee who has all the problems. She's in detox again."

"Dee Dee Gallagher?" Billy Ray's grandmother asked.

Billy Ray's mother nodded.

"She's been in detox a couple different times in four or five years," the grandmother noted.

"Yes, and this time she's at Lukens," Billy Ray's mother said.

Grandma Marcel looked surprised. "How can they afford that place?"

"Dee Dee's a Page. The family has big bucks." Billy Ray's mother rubbed her fingers together to stress her point.

Tired of listening to these women gossip, Bogie walked toward the lone man sitting at the end of the semi-circle. The corner of Bogie's mouth flickered into his version of a smile as he watched the big man holding a beautiful baby with large black curls. Bogie almost felt sorry for John Carpenter,

Randy's father. Even though he was moving up the ranks in the PBSO, the other cops still treated him like a poor relation. "I see you're hogging the baby so I don't get a chance to hold her," Bogie said to him.

John Carpenter smiled. "You've got enough kids to hold." He nodded at Bogie then Bailey. "Where's my little girlfriend?"

"She's still in the house bringing Mandie up to date on all the trivial details of our lives. I don't need a telephone with her around. I have nothing to tell anyone that Isabella hasn't already shared with the world." Bogie smoothed the tips of his fingers over Riley Rose's cheek. "She looks just like Amanda when she was a baby."

When her parents walked out into the backyard, Isabella stayed in the kitchen watching Amanda moving food from white cardboard containers onto decorative serving dishes. "May I help you?" Isabella asked.

Amanda shook her head. "There's nothing to do. I'm just putting the food into bowls."

The child studied her older sister. "Will you have time to show me some moves today?"

Amanda shook her head. "We have guests, you know," she said irritably. "Besides, you can ask Mr. Lim to show you."

Isabella frowned then said, "Master Lim is teaching me kung fu. He said not to mix up too many martial arts. He wants me to do one at a time."

"Aren't you the one who chose to study kung fu?" Amanda asked.

The child nodded. "Yes, because my legs are very short for kick boxing," Isabella said as she pointed down. "Look at your legs then look at mine!"

Amanda glanced at Isabella and smiled. "You're not always going to be little. You know, someday you'll be as tall as I am."

Isabella shook her head vigorously. "Da-dee said *no!* He said your mother had long legs. Mommy's shorter than you are."

Amanda considered this then said, "You never know. Dad's tall. Maybe you'll be tall like him."

Isabella shook her head. "Da-dee said *no*."

"From his lips to God's ears," Amanda muttered as the child walked out into the backyard toward the group of people she considered to be her personal friends, Zoe, Tiffany and their boyfriends.

Excited to see the young women, Isabella greeted them by kissing each one on the cheek and asking if they had been receiving her daily emails. After they assured her that they had, Isabella smiled believing herself to be part of the inner circle. Billy Ray and JJ grinned as they studied Isabella's white martial arts outfit.

Isabella left the group and introduced herself to the Marcels and the Johnsons shaking hands with each one. She kissed the little toddler as he sat on Mrs. Marcell's lap. He kissed her back. "What's your name?" Isabella asked the small boy.

He grinned at her but didn't answer.

Isabella smiled. "Aren't you going to tell me your name?"

The toddler looked at her and laughed. The woman holding him said, "His name is Bobby Joe."

Isabella said, "Hello, Bobby Joe."

Bobby Joe studied her then made a farting sound with his lips. When Isabella and his grandmother laughed, he did it again.

Isabella moved over to John Carpenter. She kissed the gray-haired man on the cheek and said, "Hi, Grandpa John. I haven't seen you for a long time." Although Isabella was John's daughter-in-law's little sister, Bailey believed the child should give John a title in deference to him being Riley Rose's other grandfather.

John Carpenter smiled. "I've been working a lot. And I've been visiting Riley Rose." He studied Isabella as she smoothed the sleeping baby's black curls and then looked up at him. "You shouldn't forget about me just because there's another child in the family."

John nodded not wanting to explain to Isabella that he was Riley Rose's grandfather, not hers. After a few minutes of watching Riley Rose sleep while the Hankster was being removed from his pouch, Isabella traded more kisses with Bobby Joe then wandered down toward the grill where her friends, Zoe and Tiffany, were sitting. "Would you like to see some of my new moves?" Isabella asked expectantly. The women nodded and Randy's fellow deputies also nodded.

When Isabella started her performance, a full figured woman with bobbed hair walked toward the group from the side of the house. Sarah Thomas, Billy Ray's sister and little Bobby Joe's mother, stood next to the grill, ignoring Isabella. But when Sarah saw Randy, she quickly adjusted her large breasts in her bikini top, grabbed a hamburger off the grill and moved toward him. Sarah held it up to his mouth. "Take a bite," she insisted, pressing against him. The more he protested, the closer Sarah came. Randy finally relented and took a bite of the hamburger. With a mouth full of food, Randy turned toward the house where he saw his wife glaring at him. Randy looked back at Sarah, unsure if he should swallow the hamburger or spit it out, disgusted by the blood dripping from her nostrils.

JJ left the grill and handed Sarah a roll of paper towels. He walked away with her and muttered, "Why don't you snort a little more coke?"

"Fuck you!" Sarah said, taking a seat near Zoe and Tiffany. The three women huddled together in a conversation that was animated and private. They ignored everyone else around them, including Isabella and her performance.

Bogie studied the young women and tried to understand their love story. Zoe and Tiffany with Billy Ray and JJ, four people who had been in Amanda and Randy's wedding party, had all fallen in love at the wedding. Not only was Bogie troubled by who was supposed to be in love with whom, but by the feeling they didn't seem to even like each other very much.

Seeing Bailey sit down with the Hankster on her lap as she tried to make polite conversation with the Marcel and Johnson women, Bogie decided he, too, should socialize. He picked up an empty chair and parked it next to John Carpenter. It wasn't that he and John were close, but Bogie couldn't stand the other self-important cops.

John Carpenter studied Bogie then said, "I guess the Palm Beach social season is about to begin."

"How do you figure that?" Bogie asked knowing he and John Carpenter weren't even on the fringes of Palm Beach society.

"Well, Henry will be a year old in a few weeks, the kids' first anniversary is coming up, and then there's Thanksgiving, Riley Rose's birthday...then Isabella's birthday followed by Christmas."

Bogie studied John without expression then said, "I'm sure you've got a point in there somewhere."

John smiled. "I was just wondering if you've invited someone special to share those grand events."

The corner of Bogie's mouth twitched. "Aha! It's becoming clearer. I believe you're trying to find out if Rose is planning a visit anytime soon."

John grinned. "Well, is she?"

Bogie shrugged. "I have no idea."

"I thought the two of you talked every day," John commented with a slight impatience in his voice.

"We're online working, conducting business. If you want to know what Rose's social plans are, just give her a call."

John shrugged. "I hate calling. I never know what to say."

"You're shy all of a sudden?" His phone vibrating in his pocket, Bogie went to pull it out when he noticed Isabella moving into her Tiger Claw stance directly in front of the brush at the edge of the property. With the phone still vibrating, Bogie stood up, pulled something from his New Balance sneaker and took two long strides toward Isabella.

The little girl stared at him when he said firmly, "Don't move!" Isabella stood frozen with her arm raised and her knee bent as Bogie pushed his thumbnail against a small button on the side of his switchblade. The phone continued to vibrate as Bogie focused behind Isabella. He moved his right arm back slightly and flipped his wrist, sending the knife to a point on the ground behind Isabella. As the others watched in stunned silence, Bogie lifted Isabella into his arms and walked back to his chair. Only Lieutenant Johnson was aware of what was happening and had almost retrieved a gun from his ankle holster, holding off when the knife was embedded into the Burmese python's brain.

While the other adults walked over to look at the dead snake, Bailey and John Carpenter sat frozen in their seats, holding the babies. Bailey's phone rang as Bogie sat down with Isabella in his arms. Her hands shaking, Bailey checked the caller ID and passed the phone to Bogie. He took the phone and held Bailey's hand. "It's over. There's nothing to be upset about now."

Bogie listened as Rose spoke at double speed in a loud voice. Bogie's face became solemn. There was a slight tremor in his hand as he listened intently. Finally, he asked, "What can I do?" After a while, he said, "Keep me posted."

As he closed the phone, Bailey squeezed his arm. "Are you okay?"

He shook his head. "Tommie's been shot."

When she heard this, Isabella screamed. Tears rolled down her face as she lamented, "No! Tommie's my friend! Not again!" Bogie held her tight and soothed Isabella as she continued her heartbroken cry.

Bailey cried as she remembered Isabella's losses a year earlier. As Bailey and Isabella wept, the Hankster, too, cried. With all the noise around her, Riley Rose opened her eyes and wailed in her grandfather's arms. Bobby

Joe observed all the crying as his grandmother carried him back to her chair. His lips quivered then Bobby Joe joined in. Soon they had a full crying choir.

The host, hostess and other guests were relieved when the McGruder family made their excuses and piled back into their SUV for a return trip home.

3

A CALL TO ACTION

Boston

Twenty men and women dressed in black were packed into the conference room, some standing, some sitting. Rose Jones stood at the end of the long table and said, "As you already know, Tommie was shot coming into the building this morning. It was not a robbery; it was personal. The cops are being about as forthcoming with information as we are, so we know very little. I want coverage at the hospital twenty-four/seven. Tommie just got out of surgery and is in the Intensive Care Unit. I can't get anything out of them over the phone." She pointed to a blonde Amazon wearing a black, form fitting jumpsuit that showed off her vulva as well as her firm breasts. "Coco, I need you to go to the ICU posing as his mother. We'll make up an ID and give you his data sheet. The hospital will be so glad to get his insurance information; they shouldn't give you any trouble. And dress down! You're supposed to be from a Minnesota farm, not Broadway!"

The tall woman rolled her eyes then looked at Rose. "What if his real mother shows up?"

"She won't. She's dead. Tommie has nobody; we're all he's got. Only immediate family in the ICU so make sure whoever goes in has some kind of ID. No one other than hospital staff should go near Tommie. I need you to be on the lookout for Tommie's laptop. It's not around here, so he must have had it with him. We've got to get it back. He's got passwords and data on it!"

A heavily muscled man with an olive complexion and a black mark on his cheek said, "How do we know that the shooter didn't take it?"

Rose looked at Jesús Hernández. "We don't. That's a possibility - a very ugly one - but it's there. All I know is that Tommie wasn't robbed, and he was probably shot before he knew what hit him. And if the shooter took the laptop, you'd think he would have turned it on by now. The computer's not on or we'd be able to pick up the GPS signal."

Jesús gave her a curt nod as he remembered his cousin Angel who was shot in the face when he opened a door while protecting Bailey and Isabella.

Rose sat down and opened her laptop. "Let's get everybody coordinated." As she started bringing up the scheduling program, she received *SERVER IS BUSY* messages. She held her head in her hands. "Fuck!"

Rose opened her cell phone and speed dialed Bogie's number. When Bogie answered, she said, "Somebody's fucking with the computer system."

Although they were only a few blocks from home, Bogie pulled over to the side of the road and got out of the SUV to talk. "Bring the server down."

"We can't work if the system's down!" Rose said frantically.

"Rose, you can't work with it up! It sounds like somebody's trying to hack in. Bring it down. I'll call you in about fifteen minutes. I've got to get Bailey and the kids home, then I'll call you back. I'll see what I can do from here. Any word on Tommie?"

"He's out of surgery and in the ICU. I'm sending Coco over to Mass General posing as his mother so we should get more information soon."

"Coco? How's she—?"

"She'll be fine."

"Whatever! What are the cops saying?"

"They said Tommie was shot in the doorway coming into the office."

"Robbery?"

"Four in the back? And nothing was taken?"

"What about his laptop?"

"It's MIA right now."

"Jeez! He had to have it with him. I don't think he goes to the bathroom without it. Why was he coming in on a Sunday? I thought he was working on his thesis."

"The last time I talked to him was Friday. He was trying to get ahold of his professor. Something wasn't balancing with an equation. That's all I know. He was obsessing about it."

"What's he working on for us?"

"He's been doing the IT work on the system but nothing special. I told you, he's been distracted, and I tried to cut him some slack."

"So why was he coming into the office?"

"I have no idea."

"What did the surveillance camera pick up?"

"A guy – probably - wearing a plastic mask and western hat."

When Bogie came back to the SUV, he smiled at Bailey but her face was tight and pinched. "What?"

"We'll talk later," she said robotically.

"Da-dee! How's Tommie doing?" Isabella asked from the back.

"He's out of surgery and in the ICU. Some of the members of the team are heading over there."

"What's a ICU?"

After explaining the Intensive Care Unit to his daughter, Bogie watched as she thoughtfully nodded. Bogie glanced at Bailey, and she turned away.

As they pulled into their driveway, Isabella asked, "Is a Burmese python deadly?"

Bogie shook his head. "It could do a lot of damage, especially to a child, but its venom isn't deadly."

"Not like the black mamba," Isabella said nonchalantly as she walked into the house.

When they entered their large living room, Bailey turned to Bogie and icily said, "I could use some help getting everyone settled for their naps."

Bogie studied her for a moment then said, "I'll take him, you take her." He hurriedly walked up the wide, carpeted staircase, carrying the baby and looking at his watch.

Bogie cleaned Henry, gave him a bottle and rocked the baby in a large, upholstered glider while he fell asleep. Bailey glanced in the room but said nothing and walked away.

When Henry was asleep, Bogie laid him down in his crib and raced down the stairs. He went into his home office and called Rose. "Bring it back up, and I'll see what I can do." He put on his half-glasses as his laptop booted up. He stared at the screen in complete concentration while typing in commands. Bailey walked by the door twice, but he didn't seem to notice her. Finally, he said, "Someone's definitely trying to break through the firewalls. I can't do anything from here." After Rose moaned, he asked, "Is Walter out yet?"

After a long pause, Rose said, "Yes. But I don't know where he is."

"Pop will know. Tell him we need Walter yesterday. In the meantime, shut down the system. I'll be there tomorrow." After he ended the call, Bogie looked down, dejectedly resting his forehead on his fist wondering how his life had turned upside down so quickly. Bogie never believed he'd have to depend on the largesse of Walter Beck, the hacker king, to get out of any mess.

"Did I hear you say you were going to be there tomorrow? When did you decide that?" Bailey asked as she stood in the doorway.

"Right now. We've got a serious problem."

"And no one in the world can handle it but *Bogie the Hero!*"

Bogie stared at her then said, "We need to talk." He took off his glasses, came from behind the desk, and led her into the living room. He sat on one tan couch and gestured for her to sit on the opposite one. He said, "Okay, you first."

"I hate it when you close me out. There was no reason for you to leave me sitting in the SUV with the kids while you talked to Rose," Bailey said in a raised voice.

He said softly. "Yes, there was. I didn't want Isabella listening and repeating the conversation. I'm more than happy to tell you everything that was said."

"It's not just that! You're second guessing every penny I spend while Amanda..."

Bogie thought carefully before he spoke, reminding himself not to bring up the protection detail and legal fees a year earlier that cost him over two hundred thousand dollars, spent because Bailey lied to him. He also nixed the idea of mentioning that although Bailey filed for bankruptcy before they got married, he was repaying her student loans from law school since he was her cosigner. All he asked was, "The crib?"

"Among other things. There was no reason why we couldn't have bought..."

Bogie began to tune Bailey out as he recalled the argument over her purchase of a crib for the new baby. Amanda had bought a seven thousand dollar *cradle to grave* bed for Riley Rose before she was born and convinced Bailey that she owed it to her son to have a similar crib. Bogie made the mistake of laughing at her when she mentioned it. Bogie didn't mean to mock her, but the whole idea seemed ludicrous to a man who slept on an old Army cot outside a bathroom for the first thirteen years of his life. He apologized for laughing at her but was adamant that such an extravagance was unreasonable.

Bailey ended her speech with "If we could afford to pay Amanda's taxes, you know we could afford a fancy crib. Is it because he's not really yours?" When she saw the flash of anger in his ice blue eyes, she stopped.

Bogie looked at her sadly and said, "My daughter is spoiled and a spendthrift. Since we create our monsters, I can only blame myself for it. Even if we could afford to pay Mandie's taxes, we're not going to pay them. I had no crib when I was baby, and if you had one, I doubt it was seven thousand dollars. Isabella didn't have such a crib. I bought Mandie's crib for twenty-five bucks from a guy in my unit. Who are we trying to impress?"

When she didn't answer, he said, "Money's tight and there are a lot of mouths to feed. The economy is still in the toilet, and I'm dealing with it every day. I'm renting out apartments to people who are doubling up and taking in roommates. I can either look the other way or have an empty unit. It's the same in the new complex. And that's just here. I don't know if you realize it, but most of our income comes from R&B Investigations." She shook her head, and he continued, "We have more than twenty-two employees on a very high-end payroll and sometimes we have to brow beat clients to get paid. People don't do the kind of work we do so they can be screwed over at the end of the week and told to wait for their paychecks."

Bailey looked down. "I'm sorry. I didn't realize..."

"Let me finish. The life's blood of our agency is the computer system. That's my job. Someone is trying to get into our system. If they succeed, they'll put us out of business. If the government gets involved, Tommie and I could end up in prison."

Bailey gasped. "What? What are you talking about?"

"By now you must know. We're hackers. That's illegal. We don't steal or scam, but we grab information. If the Feds got either one of us, we'd be spending a long time in a dark hole with no computers."

"Don't talk like that! You're scaring me!"

"You couldn't be half as scared as I am. Someone is trying to get through our firewalls and take over our network. If that happens, they'll destroy us."

"Is that why you need to go to Boston?"

Bogie nodded.

"What are you going to do there?"

"Try to work with Rose's uncle Walter, if we can find him."

"Walter! Whatever happened to him?"

"The last I heard, he was in Lompoc."

"Where's that?"

"In California. It's a Federal prison." Bogie watched as Bailey's face turned ashen. "I don't mean to upset you with this shit. I'm sorry if I seem tightfisted with money, but I worry about you and the kids. Face it Bailey! I'm a lot older than you. I've had a heart attack and gone through heart surgery."

"But you're fine! You're in great shape! You're in better shape than men half your age," she protested.

"But inside I'm still almost fifty years old with some patched up parts. The odds are good that I'm going to die long before you. I don't want to leave you and the kids worrying about where your next meal is coming from."

She covered her face and sobbed. He went to her, sat down and put his arm around her shoulders. Her tears slowed, and she said, "I thought because he wasn't really yours. I'm so sorry."

"He *is* mine," Bogie said softly. After a while, Bogie asked, "Are you pregnant?"

She nodded.

"I thought we weren't going to keep secrets from each other anymore?"

"I just did the test last night. How did you know?"

"I missed the signs the first two times. I wasn't going to miss them again."

Bailey looked at him and smiled then raised both hands and bent her fingers as she repeated, "*The signs*. What signs?"

Rather than mentioning the mood swings, cranky disposition and crying jags, he said, "Look at those boobs; they're almost as big as Zoe's!" as he waggled his eyebrows.

She touched her swollen breasts and laughed.

4

FIRST WORLD PROBLEMS

BOSTON

Jesús looked at Rose Jones and asked, "How long we gonna be without service?"

Rose shrugged. "Bogie will be here tomorrow." She didn't mention that her uncle, Walter Beck, was also flying in from Las Vegas. "The cell phones will be okay but not the BlackBerries. We can't use the internet so no emails." Rose looked up to see a huge, bald, black man walking through the back door. She went to him, and they hugged wordlessly. Rose wanted to cry but didn't want to seem weak and badly in need of a hug from her father. Darryl Jones asked, "How's Tommie doing?"

Rose held her fist to her mouth then took a deep breath. "He's messed up pretty bad - spleen, liver, kidney damage - but the worst is the bullet near the lower spine." She took another deep breath. "If he makes it, he might not walk again."

Darryl softly said, "Lord, have mercy on that boy," and held his daughter tight. "Crime scene guys finished here?"

"I guess so. They made a mess then disappeared. I'm waiting for the locksmith. We've got to change the combinations. Anybody on the job you can talk to?"

"I'll ask around."

After bumping fists with Jesús, Darryl shook hands with George and John Washington, two retired BPD cops, then moved on to do a complicated homie handshake with Ken Nguyen, a small Cambodian man. Darryl walked over to two young guys wearing double shoulder holsters. He stretched out his arms for a group hug with Benjamin and Rodney who tried to look like badasses with their CZ75 automatic pistols and extra clips. Since they were Darryl's protégés, they moved quickly toward him.

Darryl worked the room, greeting more of the staff, then asked, "Where's Coco?"

"She's at Mass General, posing as Tommie's mother."

Darryl looked at Rose, then started laughing. He roared as he imagined Coco and her outrageous costumes at MGH; soon everyone joined him.

☙❧

South Florida

The two blondes walked through Bloomingdales in the Gardens Mall. Zoe picked up a Hugo Boss Black Label bright blue silk blouse. She held up the low cut top and turned, "Does this show off my eyes?"

Tiffany nodded and moved her long blonde hair off her shoulder. "I wonder if they have it in pink."

"You don't *have* to wear pink all the time. You can wear another color!"

"I know, but it's my signature color. Besides, it looks so good on me," Tiffany said, checking her lipstick in one of the long mirrors.

Zoe smirked and reached into her small Louis Vuitton shoulder bag. She took out a white envelope and handed it to Tiffany. "Pay day! Billy Ray asked if you had a chance to talk to Mandie."

"You know I didn't. Riley Rose and the other kids were screaming and crying. When was I supposed to talk to her? Billy Ray acts like he's Simon

Cowell! If he's such a talent scout, why doesn't he talk to her? I still don't understand why Billy Ray or JJ doesn't just talk to Randy."

"Billy Ray said that Randy's too much of a boy scout; he'd only go along with it if Mandie did it."

"But why would she? Why would they?" Tiffany asked.

Zoe shrugged. "They've got that big expensive house—"

"Which the fathers paid to finish," Tiffany interrupted. "They bought that place for next to nothing with Mandie's money."

"Yeah but the taxes and insurance on the house are going to kill them. Billy Ray said Randy was complaining that the electric bill for July was off the wall. Keeping a place that size air conditioned has to be expensive."

Tiffany scrunched up her nose. "I don't care one way or the other. All it means is that we'll have to split with two more people."

"Billy Ray said we'll make a lot more so there will be more for everybody. But then again, Billy Ray talks a lot of shit. Sometimes I don't know whether to offer him a piece of toilet paper or a breath mint." Zoe took her BlackBerry out of her bag. "Let's see what we have for tomorrow."

Tiffany and Zoe looked over their schedules: workouts with personal trainers, massages, waxing, facials and fillers for their acrylic nails. Being *in the business* wasn't the cake walk common folk thought it was.

5

THE LONG GOOD-BYE

SOUTH FLORIDA

The room was dark, and Bogie's eyes opened slowly as he felt her body wrapped around his. Bailey was warm and soft as she pressed against him, moving her hands down his back. She kissed his neck and licked the stubble on his cheeks. Bogie grabbed her and rolled over with her underneath him. His kiss was tender, then grew rough as his tongue prodded hers. Bogie's hands glided over her swollen breasts, and he felt her nipples harden. As he moved down, her breathing quickened. Bogie parted her legs, and his tongue massaged her clitoris. Bailey fisted his short hair as she writhed and moaned with pleasure. They continued making love until they were sated and drifted off in each other's arms.

When Isabella awoke, she got out of bed and quietly walked to her parent's bedroom. She tapped on the door, then quickly opened it hoping to find them in one of those strange positions again. But as soon as the door opened, Bogie sat up and pointed at her. She closed the door and went back to her own room.

With Bailey laughing beside him, Bogie smiled. "She's a piece of work! She's always afraid she's missing something!"

"Weren't you the same way as a kid?" Bailey asked.

Bogie nodded and glanced over at the clock. "Guess it's time to get up." As he started to roll away, Bailey grabbed him by the waist.

"No morning kiss?"

"You got that an hour ago, and then took advantage of me."

She playfully pushed his back as he got out of bed and headed for the bathroom. As soon as the shower started running, the bedroom door opened again, and the little redhead appeared in the small opening. "I'm finished sleeping. May I get up now?"

Bailey smiled and nodded.

When Bogie came back in the room wrapping a towel around his middle, he saw his daughter standing at the foot of the bed. "Didn't I send you back to your room?"

Isabella nodded. "But Mommy said it was okay to get up." After a pause, she asked, "Why aren't you running, Da-dee? You didn't run yesterday either."

Bogie smiled. "I twisted my ankle on Saturday and need to give it a few days to heal."

"Did you hurt it running?" Isabella asked.

Bogie shook his head. "I slipped on food that Henry tossed on the floor."

Isabella scowled at Bailey as though the accident were her fault. She sighed and asked Bogie, "Do you know what day it is?"

"It's Labor Day."

"No, not that! It's Monday, Cocoa Puffs day!" Isabella exclaimed. As part of an ongoing battle to get Isabella to eat healthier, Bogie negotiated items with her. Before Da-dee was in her life, Cocoa Puffs was her standard breakfast food. Isabella enjoyed chips, fast food, ice cream and chocolate, but Da-dee tried to change that. Every day, Bogie encouraged her to eat healthy foods. He knew it was tough to break the habit of eating those tasty, greasy, artery-clogging goodies, but he was determined that she quit before she, too, had a heart attack.

As they ate breakfast, the Hankster sat in his highchair, spitting oatmeal back at Bailey while Isabella chased and collected Cocoa Puffs swimming in her cereal bowl. Bogie finished his juice and glanced at his watch. "Call me if you need anything."

Bailey looked over at him. "Aren't you going to pack?"

"Not now. I have some things I have to take care of this morning."

Isabella stopped fishing for Cocoa Puffs and looked at her father. "Are you going somewhere, Da-dee?"

He nodded and thought he should have escaped about a minute earlier. "I have to fly to Boston today."

She grinned. "I'm so glad! We'll see Tommie and..."

Bogie looked from Isabella to Bailey. "I've got to go. Do you want to tell her?" he asked as he dashed out the door.

Bogie drove to the new apartment complex and parked his black Dodge Ram 1500 near the front door. The complex was a smaller version of the main one but without a swimming pool. Bogie walked toward the office, and knocked and opened the door at the same time.

A sturdy Latino man looked up from behind the desk where he was listening to telephone messages. "Hey, bro, que paaaasa?"

Bogie pointed at Carlos Aragon then sat down. "This is it, mi amigo!" When Carlos studied him, Bogie continued. "I know the Rodriguez brothers have been courting you and making all kinds of promises. I just want to know if you're staying or going."

Stunned, Carlos pushed back his black hair with both hands then asked, "Well, Boss, what do you say? You want to match them? They made me super offers. More money, new car..."

Bogie reached in his pocket and took out a slip of paper. "Call these guys and ask them about the Rodriguez brothers."

"Now?"

"Why not?"

After two upsetting telephone conversations, Carlos put down the phone and stared at Bogie. "How did you know they were just cranking me?"

"The housing market is the worst it's been in fifty years. It'll take a decade to recover. Do you think two guys who no longer have a pot to piss in or a window to throw it out of can afford to have an executive manager on a construction crew? Use your head, Carlos! They're going around making promises then telling guys to go out and get the jobs so they can manage them. They're just sucking contact information out of people hoping to hook up with someone who has real money."

Carlos' face turned pale. "Hey bro, why'd you tell me? You could have just let me go."

"Because I didn't want to lose you. I know you think I took Margarita's side in your domestic war, but if you remember correctly, I just told you I was finished with your public fighting." As Carlos opened his mouth to object, Bogie continued, "I know your battle didn't start in the apartment complex, but I knew that sure as the sun was going to shine, that's where round two would take place. If that happened, I'd have to fire you. I can't fire Margarita - she works for my sister now. And I really didn't want to fire you. We've come a long way since the days it was just the four of us."

Carlos smiled, remembering when Bogie and Amanda were living in the main building surrounded by a large, empty, three-building apartment complex badly in need of a complete overhaul. Bogie looked older then and walked like somebody had kicked the crap out of him. He'd just gone through open heart surgery, so they brought in Margarita to cook and keep house. Slowly, Bogie's health improved, the apartments were renovated, and Amanda blossomed into a lovely young woman.

Carlos looked at him. "I'm sorry."

Bogie reached over and bumped his fist. "Me, too. Now that the niceties are out of the way, I need you to keep an eye on things. I'm not real thrilled with the crew on the new job site. Hire or fire whoever needs it. I've got to go back to Boston today. One of our men was shot."

Carlos crossed himself. "It's a dangerous business."

"This guy worked in the office. He didn't even carry a gun."

"And he was shot in the office?"

"The doorway...when he was coming in."

"Robbery?"

Bogie shook his head. "Now our computer system is acting up. I think somebody is trying to put us out of business."

"You better start checking your enemies list."

"That's what I intend to do."

"Bailey and the kids going with you?"

"No. I'm going alone."

Carlos raised an eyebrow.

"It's tough traveling with a baby. He's got all this equipment to lug around. And, besides, Bailey's pregnant again."

Carlos laughed. "Hel-lo! You don't waste any time."

Bogie smiled. "Anyway, I'd appreciate it if you'd keep an eye on them, see if she needs anything." He paused then said, "Besides a man in her bed."

⁓⁕⁓

After leaving Carlos, Bogie phoned Amanda to make sure she was home.

As he pulled into the wide driveway, he marveled at the excess and ostentation of this house. The pink stucco mini-mansion almost drove its first owners to the poorhouse. Bogie feared it might take the present owners for a ride as well.

When Amanda opened the door, Bogie said, "It's my turn to hold the baby. John hogged up all the holding time yesterday!"

Amanda laughed. "Sorry, but she's sound asleep, and I'm not waking her up."

Relieved that the baby was sleeping in her seven thousand dollar crib, Bogie said, "Then you can offer me some tea, and we'll sit down and talk."

Fearing *a* lecture was the reason for the visit, Amanda moved toward the kitchen jammed with state-of-the-art appliances and an enormous sub-zero refrigerator.

"I have to go back to Boston this afternoon, and I wanted to talk to you before I left."

"How's—?"

"Tommie. He's holding on, but he's in rough shape. I can't do much for him, but we're having problems with our computer system. I think somebody's trying to break in."

"Why?"

"Probably to destroy us."

"Why?"

"Why not? I'm sure we've made a number of enemies over the years."

"Bailey and the kids going with you?"

Bogie shook his head.

"Izzy's okay with that?"

Bogie just shrugged.

"I'm here because I'm concerned about you."

"Why?"

After a moment Bogie sighed and then started. "You're spending money like..."

Amanda stood up. "I don't believe this!"

Bogie pointed a finger at her then said in a raised voice, "Sit down!"

She glared at him, but sat back down, sulking.

40

"I've watched you pissing away money month after month and kept my mouth shut. Each time I hoped that the latest over-priced thing you bought would be the last one. But it just got worse. That check I gave you was supposed to be used to buy a house and have a safety net. John and I finished this house so you kids would have a fine home with a cushion in the bank. Instead of saving money, you burned through it buying crap to fill up this place." As she started to interrupt him, he held up his hand. "I know how much money Pop, Rose and Ann gave you for your wedding. You could have bought another house with all that money! Instead, you bought more expensive, needless shit. I told you that as soon as the house was finished, the property would be reassessed. You wouldn't listen to me. And now you've got a tax bill that would choke a horse and think it should be my problem. That was really cute, sending the bill to me. I'm not paying it. If you can't afford to live in this house, do something about it!"

"Like what!?" she screeched and started to cry.

"Get out or get a job."

"And do what with the baby?"

"You can take her with you. I told you before that you could take over the office at the new complex."

"I already explained to you that I have pilates and yoga classes—"

"You used to swim in the pool and get exercise. Now you need some fancy workout programs?"

"It's not just exercise. It's like social networking."

"What, are you running for public office?"

"Nooo! It's just that I want Riley Rose to grow up with a better class of people."

"You're delusional. Who do you think you are, some heiress or trust fund baby? We're working people."

"I don't have to stay *working people!*"

"Right now, you don't even qualify as working people. You don't work."

As her eyes filled with tears, Amanda angrily said, "Now that you have a new family, you don't care about me."

"I don't have a new family!" he yelled. "I have one family, and you're part of it. You've been acting like a spoiled child for way too long. Shape up!"

"You don't know what you're talking about!"

"Yes, I do," he said sadly. "I've watched you pouting every time Randy didn't do back-flips over your many, many purchases. I never thought I'd be feeling sorry for my son-in-law, but I do. That poor bastard is working day and night so you can blow away everything he makes. You used to help out in the office. You used to work as a life guard. Now all you do is spend money and take up space. You're turning into your mother."

Amanda gasped. "That's the meanest thing you ever said to me! I hate you!" She jumped off her stool, ran from the room, and dashed up the main staircase.

Amanda grew up knowing that her mother left them without looking back when Amanda was two years old. Amanda was never told that Madeline eagerly gave her up for ten thousand dollars and a boob job so she could make her way to Hollywood and become a star. Amanda was sixteen years old before she saw Madeline again. Being a contrary teenager, Amanda insisted that her father locate Madeline so they could reunite. The reunion in Las Vegas was not a Hallmark moment. Her mother was a heavily painted, seasoned showgirl who introduced Amanda as her younger sister because Madeline was trying to pass for twenty-five. Amanda returned from Vegas disillusioned but glad she had a father who cared about her and didn't try to set her up on dates with old men in their thirties.

Bogie tossed the envelope holding the property tax bill on the counter, looked at his black Suunto Core watch, then left the house.

As he backed out of the driveway, he saw a Palm Beach County Sheriff's patrol car coming down the street. Not in the mood to stop and chat, he waved as he drove away.

6

BYE, BYE - I NEED TO FLY

South Florida

Randy waved to his father-in-law as they passed each other on the road, but something about Bogie's demeanor was troubling. They used to be neighbors, and Randy recognized the aura consistent with violence that surrounded Bogie whether he was trying to be intimidating or not. Today, though, something was different. Randy pulled into his driveway wondering what was going on.

Walking to the back door, Randy started muttering; she left it unlocked and the alarm disabled–again! When Randy opened the kitchen door and saw the envelope on the counter, he picked it up. The envelope was addressed to Bogie at the apartment complex office. It had obviously been opened more than once, so he looked inside. As Randy stared at their tax bill, he felt sick. How could she do this to him? He worked his ass off so they could make this house, this marriage work. Randy stood numbly holding the bill when she came down the back stairs.

"What are you doing home?" Amanda asked.

When Randy finally believed he could speak without crying, he said, "You goddamned liar!" He ran up the stairs and got to work gathering duffle bags, suitcases and clothes as his wife sat on the expensive inlayed stone kitchen floor sobbing.

∽♾∾

44

Since Zoe decided to have a pedicure while they were at the salon, Tiffany sat in the reception area taking tiny sips of the cheap champagne the salon provided to its upscale clientele. She took out her BlackBerry and updated her Facebook status.

"Being in the business isn't all glitz and glamour. Zoe and I had tough workouts with our trainers this morning. Got to keep the bods in top shape. Had a Brazilian wax. Ouch! Ouch! Now I really look like a clam. Shooting again tonight. It'll be indoors so we won't have to worry about bugs and mosquitoes. Love and kisses from the movies in Palm Beach."

༄

When Bogie returned home, he was greeted by Isabella's wailing. She was stretched out on the living room floor crying. Her face was red and blotchy and she screamed, "No! No! No! You can't do this to me!"

Bailey stood holding the baby who was clinging to her as he watched his sister throwing a tantrum. Bailey looked at Bogie. "Talk to her!" she said, then turned and walked to the family room with the baby.

Bogie sat on the leather couch and patted the seat next to him. "Come here, Isabella! Sit down."

The little girl wiped tears off her face with both hands. Her shoulders still quivering she said, "Tommie is my friend, my best friend! You can't leave me here while he's in the hospital!" Isabella protested.

"He can't have visitors now, Pumpkin!"

"They'll let me see him. I'm his best friend!" the little girl argued.

"I'm sorry, Isabella."

The child stared at him with fresh tears rolling down her cheeks. she put her hands over her ears and wailed again. When Bogie cringed, she screeched, "And everybody misses me! Uncle George, Uncle Jack, Pop Pop,

Aunt Rose, Jesús, Ken...they all miss me. They want to see me! They don't want you to leave me here when you go to Boston!"

Bogie stood up and walked to the family room as Isabella cried out after him, "You don't love me anymore! Mommy doesn't love me either!" As the crying continued, Bogie watched Bailey as she sat on the floor with Henry. The baby had a worried expression on his face as he touched a tear rolling down Bailey's cheek. At that moment, Bogie realized he couldn't leave Bailey alone to deal with her pregnancy, Isabella's histrionics, and Henry's needs. When Bailey looked up at him, Bogie tried to smile then said, "That went well, don't you think?"

Bailey shook her head. "When she gets like that, she just breaks my heart! Remember her birthday party when she didn't get a sword?"

Bogie nodded. "See if Jack and George are willing to put us up."

Bailey beamed. "I'm sure that won't be a problem. After all, it is your house."

Bogie half-laughed. "We'll just knock on the door and tell them to move over, we're coming in."

On hearing this, Isabella dashed into the family room and wrapped her arms around Bogie's legs wiping her dripping nose on his khaki trousers. "I love you sooo much, Da-dee!"

"I'm glad at least one of my daughters loves me." When Bailey glanced at him, Bogie shook his head and said, "If you get her packed, I'll get her a ticket and throw some things in a suitcase. Maybe you and the Hankster can give us a ride to the airport."

"I'm busy, but he'll be glad to drive you," Bailey said making Isabella giggle.

7

A STAR IS BORN

SOUTH FLORIDA

Wearing dark glasses and an unflattering, gray, shirtwaist dress, Linda Traiger drove a red Toyota Corolla into the Alamo lot on Belvedere Road. After assuring the attendant that everything was in order, she retrieved a black Prada soft-side suitcase from the trunk. She walked to a bench in front of the building and sat down, waiting for the next shuttle bus to the airport. Linda flipped open her phone and speed-dialed a number. Less than a minute into the conversation, Linda's hands shook and she became defensive. "I told you...he didn't go running...he wasn't alone after that. You said no witnesses...It's in my suitcase...No, I can't take it on the plane." She lowered her voice and whispered into the phone, "I'd like to see you get a garrote through security. You have my flight info...Yes, he'll be on the plane...I'll try then."

෴

As they settled back in their wide seats, Isabella smiled. "I like these seats. They're gargantuan!" When Bogie raised an eyebrow, she added, "I like that word, but I so rarely have an opportunity to use it in a sentence."

Bogie studied her, wondering where she was acquiring her new vocabulary. Rather than worry about it, he decided to sit back and enjoy the trip. As soon as he closed his eyes, he heard the *ka ching* sound repeating in his head as he added up the cost of the first class tickets. Bogie wanted to enjoy these little extravagances, but the faces of the people who depended on him for a living flashed through his mind, and he went back to worrying. Bogie glanced over at Isabella who was wearing the lovely pink dress she wore to their wedding, Amanda's wedding, and her own birthday party. Isabella had gotten taller but thinner, so she was able to wear the dress as part of her travel disguise. The child hated dresses but knew she had to concede to her father's wishes and not bring attention to herself. The dark glasses were her idea. "I think you can take the glasses off now, Pumpkin. We're in the air."

"May I use my kindle?"

Bogie nodded as he handed her the kindle. "Are you still reading *Sherlock Holmes?*"

Isabella nodded. "They use funny words so it takes a while."

"Like *gargantuan?*"

Isabella shook her head and giggled.

Sitting across from them, Linda looked over at Isabella and smiled. When she saw Bogie watching her, Linda removed her sunglasses. Her brown eyes looked dead as she said, "She's adorable!"

Bogie gave her a quick nod and looked away before Linda could start a conversation.

As they de-planed in Atlanta, Bogie cursed under his breath. For all the money the tickets cost, he still couldn't get a non-stop flight to Boston. As they sat in the terminal waiting to board, Isabella opened her laptop and booted it up. She grinned as she read her emails. "Mommy said hi and you should call her. She thinks your phone is turned off."

Bogie took the phone from his pocket, turned it on, and walked to the window. When he reached Bailey, he asked, "You miss me already?"

"Of course. But I also wanted you to know that John stopped by the office. He said that Randy moved back in with him."

"What?!"

"Randy came home this morning and found an envelope on the kitchen counter with the tax bill. He and Mandie had a fight. I guess she was supposed to be putting money aside each month for the taxes but was spending it. He didn't take it well when he realized she hadn't paid the taxes and sent the bill to you. I'm assuming that was the same bill she sent to the office?"

"Yeah. I told her this morning I wasn't paying it. We had some words, and I left it on the counter. Poor bastard!"

"Who? Mandie?"

"No. Randy. He's been taking on extra shifts trying to prove he can handle that house on his own and, meanwhile she's out there burning through money faster than he can make it."

"Oh, God! I'm sorry for both of them. She's just a kid."

"No she's not! She's twenty years old. It's time for her to grow up!"

"That's probably exactly what you said to her."

"Yep. And it's true."

"Do you want me to talk to her?"

Bogie smiled. "No. Let them be." He glanced at Isabella who was chatting with the woman from the plane. When Isabella pointed to something on her computer screen, the woman's eyes opened wide and Bogie knew what Isabella was doing. "I've got to go. Isabella just blew her cover." As Bogie shut off his phone and returned it to his pocket, Linda Traiger touched the side of the laptop and attached a tiny red heart sticker to it.

Bogie sat down next to Isabella and listened while the woman exclaimed, "So that's you? The Girl in White Pajamas!"

Isabella nodded proudly.

Bogie glanced at his watch hoping they would be boarding in the next few seconds.

"Your daughter is amazing! And she's only four years old?" she asked.

Bogie nodded.

"You were all over the news...you rescued her and she killed her abductor," she added.

"We don't like to talk about it," Bogie deadpanned as Isabella continued to chatter about her Bokken sword. First class boarding was announced, and Bogie jumped up. "We've got to board!"

"I'm going too...back to Boston," the woman said.

As they entered the plane, Isabella begged to sit on the aisle, and Bogie's attempt to remind her that she wouldn't be able to see out the window was no deterrent. She found a new friend and could chat with her all the way to Boston. Bogie sighed and sat in the window seat. He thought about Isabella's uncles, Jack and George, and how they presented her with the laptop. Bogie wasn't overjoyed, believing she was too young for it. And he distinctly remembered the horrible day that Isabella discovered Google. But that was small stuff compared to the newest computer problem - some unknown cyber enemy trying to ruin them.

Descending into Boston, Isabella was still talking. "And Da-dee and I buy our underwear in Walmart. Mommy buys hers at Victoria's Secret. Da-dee said she's sexy without them." Bogie groaned, but Isabella continued. "We get the Hankster's diapers at CVS..."

As they emerged from the jetway into the gray and white terminal, Isabella continued to chatter, telling Linda about her martial arts training. After they rode a long escalator down to an area below ground, Isabella stopped when her father did not step on the moving sidewalk. "Why don't you get on, Da-dee?"

Bogie shook his head. "I'll walk next to it. I need to exercise my ankle. I've been sitting too much."

Isabella tapped Linda on the arm. "I'm going to walk with Da-dee. I'll see you at the end."

She smiled and nodded, then took out her phone and began texting.

As they stood watching the luggage carrousel, Linda reached in front of Bogie and grabbed her black Prada bag. Bogie felt a tingle up his spine but couldn't figure out why. He turned to look at her and found himself facing a man with hair so black it looked painted onto his scalp. The shiny hair was pulled back into a tight ponytail at the base of his neck. The stranger wore black rimmed glasses that matched his hair and goatee. Bogie realized that the man was wearing make-up. As if to confirm Bogie's suspicions, the man touched the red print ascot at his throat. Linda immediately introduced him as her husband, Stephen Traiger.

He grinned broadly showing off his perfect, white teeth including the back molars. He held out a business card that identified him as the president of Black Hat Elite Entertainment saying, "Linda told me about Isabella. What a charmer! Linda thinks Isabella could outshine Honey Boo Boo! We produce several reality shows. Give me a call, and we can talk about having your family on TV." Bogie accepted the card without comment and reached out to grab their suitcases. When he turned around again, the Traigers were gone and Rose Jones was walking toward him.

Rose wore her black tee shirt, tailored cargo pants and silver-studded motorcycle boots. As other men took surreptitious glances at the buff beauty, Bogie grabbed her and gave Rose a big hug. "I'm going to put a muzzle on this kid!" he mumbled.

Rose smiled at Isabella, picked her up and twirled her around. "You're getting so big! And you're so beautiful!"

"You recognized me, Aunt Rose?"

"I'm afraid I did. I remember that pink dress, and the glasses didn't fool me." When Rose noticed how dejected Isabella looked, she added, "But you know I'm a detective."

Almost placated, Isabella nodded. "How's Tommie doing?"

"He's about the same, Sweetheart."

"Is he conscious?" Bogie asked.

Rose shook her head.

Rose took Isabella's hand while Bogie carried the luggage. As they walked toward the exit, Bogie asked, "Did you happen to notice that couple standing next to me? He had black hair—"

"Yes," Rose answered quickly. "Strange!"

"So it wasn't just me," Bogie said.

Rose shook her head. "The woman was dressed like a field mouse but had a suitcase that cost over two grand. The guy looked like central castings version of a Hollywood movie producer. Is there anything I missed?"

Bogie shook his head and watched the black R&B Escalade pull up to the curb. He turned and asked, "Who's Honey Boo Boo?"

When she finished laughing, Rose said, "Reality TV—" Bogie's upheld hand let her know that was enough information. She squeezed his arm and said, "Now tell me all about my beautiful namesake, Riley Rose, and don't leave out any details!"

The Traigers huddled together in another doorway and studied the departing group. Stephen's genial facade was gone. He glared at Linda. "You were supposed to take him out on the plane."

"He never ordered a drink, and the kid was with him all the time. She never shuts up."

"Thanks to you, Bogie the Booger and his fat friend are still alive. They were supposed to be eliminated yesterday." When she said nothing, he sighed. "On to Plan B."

8

EMPEROR OF THE INTERNET

BOSTON

As soon as Isabella saw Jesús driving the black SUV, she began to cry. Jesús was identical to his cousin Angel except he had a dark scar on his cheek. Isabella was with Angel a year earlier when he was shot. She cried as they traveled from the airport to Lincoln Street in downtown Boston where R&B Investigations was located.

Bogie cringed when the group entered the building. It looked like the command center for a futuristic army with its stark black-and-white décor. A wide, black lacquer desk had been added to the reception area which was already filled with black cubes that served as tables and seats.

Several men dressed in black came forward to greet them. Isabella did a hand slide with Ken Nguyen, who looked like an adolescent compared to the other men. While Isabella was swallowed up in the rush of old and new friends, Bogie and Rose walked back to Rose's office. Bogie took out the black enameled business card that Traiger had given him. He handed the card to Rose and said, "They're interested in doing a reality show with our family. That's just what we need! We can air all our secrets on television, especially the ones Isabella hasn't shared with the world yet!"

Rose laughed and tossed the card on her desk where it joined stacks of papers. "That child is either going to keep you young or make you old very fast."

"I think it's the latter."

While they talked, Rose glanced at the surveillance monitor. She saw Darryl Jones walk through the back door with a man half his size whose grayish complexion matched his gray ponytail. Rose walked to the smaller man and hugged him. "Uncle Walter! Thanks for coming."

Walter held her while Bogie and Darryl Jones embraced. Darryl said, "I heard Isabella was coming with you." When Bogie shook his head in disgust, Darryl asked, "What's the matter? You couldn't bring her?"

"I brought her. Now I wish I hadn't. She just won't stop talking! She's told our life story all the way from Palm Beach. And now that she has her computer, she's Googling herself and showing off her news clippings."

Darryl laughed. "No more martial arts?"

"Get serious! She still practices every day. She's just broadening her scope to include the internet."

As Darryl laughed, Walter grabbed Bogie's upper arm. "Boghdun!" Bogie wrapped his arms around the only person who called him by his real name. "I wouldn't recognize you. You're thin and tan with light hair. You look good!" Walter exclaimed.

Bogie wanted to tell Walter he, too, looked good, but they'd both know he was lying. "Valter!"

"Hey, vat?!" They both laughed at the old joke they shared. When Bogie was seventeen, he first met Walter. Bogie was spending another summer in Dorchester with Darryl, Gretchen and Rose. Gretchen was ill, and the fear of a family facing terminal cancer was palpable. But when Walter came to visit his younger sister, he brought a ray of hope, if only in the form of a diversion.

Walter flew in from Germany and spoke with an accent. Bogie was thrilled to have someone he could razz about talking funny just as people in Boston had ridiculed him and his Pittsburghese for years.

Although Walter lived in Germany, he was an American citizen; whereas his younger sister lived in the U.S. but retained her German citizenship.

Walter was born in the slums of Detroit to Walter Smoukowski, a Polish factory worker, who brought Hilda Buchmaster to this country as a German war bride. After two pregnancies, one miscarriage and beatings every Saturday night at the hands of her drunken husband, Hilda returned to post-war Germany believing it was a step up from the slums of Detroit. She divorced Walter's father and eventually remarried, changing Walter's last name to Beck.

Walter and Bogie immediately recognized a kindred spirit in each other. If Darryl was the father figure Bogie needed, Walter was the unscrupulous uncle who would help him get into trouble. In Walter's case, he showed a very bright boy a strange new thing called the internet.

"How goes the battle?" Bogie asked.

"I'm not retreating, just advancing in the opposite direction."

"You out on parole?" Bogie didn't need to ask any more, since they all knew Walter had been doing time for designing a program that grabbed credit card information from millions of TJ Maxx customers.

Walter shook his head. "I'm finished with them and don't have to bother with that parole shit. But don't think for a second that they're not watching me."

Bogie nodded. "Can you help us?"

Walter laughed. "I like that, Boghdun, you get right to the point! You think I could say no to my Rose? She looks like Gretchen, but with his black hair...when he had any." Pointing to Darryl and laughing at his own joke, Walter continued, "Rose is my godchild. Of course, I'll help her. But I thought I taught you enough..."

"Let's just say I never fine-tuned my skills the way you hoped I would."

Walter shrugged. "How's Amanda?"

"All grown up with a husband and a baby."

"And I heard that now you have a new little daughter and a son?"

"Yeah. I married the redhead, the one you said was always chasing me."

"And I guess she caught you."

"What were you doing in Las Vegas? Do you live there?" Bogie asked.

"Oh, hell no! Who wants to live there? I was the guest speaker at a DEFCON Convention."

"Where do you live?"

"I'd tell you, but then I'd have to kill you. Darryl said you live in Florida now."

Bogie nodded. "Where are you staying?"

"We decided it would be better if I stay with Rose since she's not far from here."

"But you know there are security cameras all over that building and the cops will be going through the other condo—"

"I know," Walter said. "It's like hiding in plain sight. Rose is my niece, I'm visiting. I'd stay with Darryl, but the commute to Dorchester with all the traffic would waste too much time. Sooo...You think you can afford me?"

"Can we afford not to have you?" Bogie asked.

Walter grinned. "Right answer! You win the prize, Boghdun!"

9

YOU OUGHT TO BE IN PICTURES

SOUTH FLORIDA

Amanda and Riley Rose cried as Zoe opened another bottle of wine. "I hate him! It's all his fault, you know. If he had paid the bill and shut up, none of this would have happened. Now my whole life is ruined because of him!"

Zoe opened her eyes wide. "Randy?"

"No, my father," Mandie said angrily.

Zoe studied her wine glass and then checked her long nails for chips in the polish. She lifted her foot to make sure her pedicure was intact. As Zoe continued to appraise her beautiful self, she said, "I know how you can get money...lots of it. You and Randy."

Amanda sniffled and studied her. "How?"

"You could be in movies. Me, Tiff, Billy Ray and JJ make movies."

Amanda stared at Zoe trying to comprehend what she was saying through the wine haze. "What kind of movies?" she slowly asked.

"You know...like...stag movies. We sell them on the internet. We get paid in cash. You and Randy could..."

Amanda studied Zoe with shock and horror. She got up, looked away, and carried the baby upstairs while she and Riley Rose cried together.

Randy sat at his father's kitchen table pouring more Vodka into his glass of orange juice.

John Carpenter looked at his son. "Instead of sitting here drinking alone why don't you go out with your buddies and have a few brewskies?"

Randy stared at his father. "I don't have any buddies."

"Sure you do! Give Billy Ray and JJ a call."

Randy made a sour face. "Just because you work with their fathers doesn't make them my friends."

John studied his son. "They were in your wedding party."

"So what? I would have rather had Alex and Rob. We played football together and were friends all through high school. You were the one who kept pushing me to have Billy Ray and JJ. You were afraid your buddies would think my friends were hicks from Dayton. What was that you said? *They'd probably show up wearing bowling shirts and white socks with dress shoes.*"

"You moved here to start a new life, not to drag Dayton, Ohio here with you," John said sharply.

"I moved here because there were no jobs in Dayton," Randy said. Watching his father's face turn crimson with anger, Randy quickly added, "But don't think I don't appreciate you getting me into the Sheriffs."

John nodded curtly, then asked, "What do you have against those guys? They seem nice enough."

"There's something weird about them. I can't put my finger on it, but there is." Randy took a gulp of his drink then stared at the glass.

"What's weird about them?"

Randy thought for a few seconds then said, "They're the only guys I've ever met who are tanned all over...and I mean all over."

"So what?"

Randy shrugged, then added, "They shave the hair around their dicks."

John glared at him. "What the hell are you looking at other guys' dicks for?"

Knowing his father's homophobia was palpable, Randy said, "I wasn't studying them, but you know how guys change in the locker room...I noticed because it was strange to see guys who are all tanned and seem to have their pubic hair styled."

John laughed, knowing there was no privacy among cops since they were the worst gossips on the planet. He'd heard remarks about Randy being hung like a horse and felt a certain pride in that.

"Do you think they're queer?" John asked conspiratorially.

Randy shook his head. "That's what's so weird. They're full of themselves for sure with plucked eyebrows and expensive haircuts, but they don't seem gay."

"And aren't they dating Mandie's friends?" John asked.

"That's another thing that's odd. They don't seem like two couples. Whenever I see them, Zoe and Tiff are together and Billy Ray's with JJ. They're more like four people who are hiding something."

"Whatever it is, stay away from it. You have enough of your own problems."

"Is this where I hear 'I told you so'?" Randy muttered.

John shook his head. "I'm too sad for that. I'd have to work my way up to that."

♒

As her friends were getting drunk, Tiffany read a text message from her cousin Rhonda in Jacksonville.

"AYT. I thot u were gonna get me a part in ur movie. 2 good 4 me now?"

Tiffany answered:

"WRKG ON IT. LAK FROM MOVIES PB. B4N."

10

MI CASA ES TU CASA

QUINCY, MA

Bogie drove down Hancock Street, the main thoroughfare in Quincy, and glanced in the rear view mirror. Isabella was sound asleep, her head almost resting on her shoulder. Bogie smiled as he looked at the sweet cherubic face surrounded by red curls that had been shortened, a necessity in the Florida heat.

Bogie soon pulled into the driveway of a white-frame house he owned. Bogie allowed his brothers-in-law Jack and George to live for free in the rental property since they lost their home in Weston, thanks to Bailey.

Carrying the sleeping child up the porch steps, Bogie grinned at the two men in the doorway. They, too, had finally gotten haircuts. Jack's curly red hair covered his ears while George's hairstyle was short with indiscriminate dark spikes poking out around his head. "So you finally got haircuts! Sorry, we're so late. I have a feeling Isabella is going to stay where we put her. Too much activity for one day!"

When they settled Isabella into an upstairs bedroom, Bogie looked around the house and nodded. "You did a great job decorating this place, George. It looks better than ever. And, I'm sorry for barging in on you like this..."

"Stop it!" both men said at the same time. Bogie was grateful they didn't feel the need to remind him that the house was his. It had been Bogie's house for more than fifteen years, but he hadn't lived in it for several years. When Bogie and Amanda moved from Quincy into Boston so he could play his part in a marriage charade, Bogie rented out the house. Over time, the Irish complexion of the neighborhood changed to Chinese. The house remained a rental until the real estate market crashed and the economy circled the rim of the toilet. Young renters lost their jobs and moved back home with their parents. Chang, the neighbor, offered to buy the house for a fraction of its value, and Bogie refused. He believed that Chang discouraged prospective renters hoping to persuade Bogie to sell the house to him for short money. Their impasse was underway when the house in Weston, where Bailey, Jack and George previously lived, was foreclosed. Since the foreclosure was mainly Bailey's fault, Bogie felt he should try to make it right with the men until they could recover from the financial loss. Like his twin sister Bailey, Jack was a lawyer. But unlike Bailey, he enjoyed practicing law and had a flare for it. With his paralegal and husband George by his side Jack was building up a solid practice.

When the three men sat in the living room filled with overstuffed floral patterned chairs and a couch, Bogie closed his eyes and sighed. "It's been a very long day!"

"How's Tommie doing?" Jack asked.

"He's still in ICU, still unconscious. We've got people over there watching—"

Jack interrupted. "In the ICU?"

Bogie nodded.

Jack shrugged and asked, "Have the police come up with anything?"

"Not as far as we know, and that leads us to some other problems. We'd like to retain you to represent us."

Jack studied him. "Who's 'us'? Represent you for what?"

"Us is R&B Investigations. We want you to act as our representative and interface with the police and possibly the Feds."

"What the hell have you done?" When Bogie only stared at him, Jack asked, "So you want me to act as consigliere for your illegal activities?"

"Exactly! Just like the Mafia," Bogie answered.

Jack and George glanced at each other, then at Bogie and laughed.

Finally Jack said, "I'd rather represent Tommie and sue you for lack of security."

"Tommie's an employee. You could get him a pittance with workman's comp, but that wouldn't make either of you happy."

"You don't pay him very much?"

"Not on the books. Tommie's a grad student at MIT. He got a grant to pay for his tuition. Tommie's like a big kid. He's about as discreet as Isabella. To avoid too many people noticing a large income stream, we have him live in the condo next to Rose's. We give him a low salary on the books, cash under the table, and fill up debit cards for him."

"I'll take his job!" George offered.

Bogie smiled. "Are you a computer whiz? Are you a hacker?"

"No, but I could learn."

Bogie took a check from his pocket and handed it to Jack. "This is your retainer. Draw up the paperwork, and we'll sign it tomorrow."

Jack stared at the check. "I can't take this—"

"It's not a charitable gesture, Jack. You're good, you're smart, and you're family. I have a feeling that by the time this tsunami passes, you'll earn every penny of it."

Twenty minutes later, Bogie squeezed into a twelve inch sliver that Isabella left unoccupied as she lie spread eagle over the guest room bed. Accustomed to sleeping alone, Isabella stretched out, moving and kicking in her sleep. A knock on the face or ribs wasn't so bad, but a kick in the balls was always an eye opener.

⌒⊃⊂⌒

It seemed like Bogie had just closed his eyes when he heard Isabella laughing. Bogie opened his eyes. The sun was up and Isabella was downstairs, chattering with her uncles. Bogie rolled out of bed and looked at the clock. Without shaving or showering, he hurriedly put on shorts and a tee shirt. He wrapped an ace bandage around his ankle and foot, laced up his running shoes, and ran down the stairs and out the front door yelling, "Good morning!"

Bogie moved at a slower pace through the suburban streets until he reached Quincy Shore Drive. With Wollaston Beach to his left, he sprinted at full speed to the end of the beach, then turned and ran back. Bogie didn't slow down until he was on the side streets heading back to the house. He dashed up the porch stairs, opened the door and stood panting. "Lucy! I'm home!"

George walked into the living room, made a sour face, and waved his hand in front of Bogie. "Okay, Ricky Ricardo. Take a shower or something!"

11

GETTING TO KNOW YOU

BOSTON

Entering R&B Investigations, Bogie carried packages and Isabella shouldered her computer in a small black messenger bag. Isabella's kindle was in a new black backpack. Rose grinned. "Have we been shopping in Chinatown?"

Isabella nodded. "We bought new clothes. Da-dee said my other ones were getting washed to death. Wait till you see what I got, Aunt Rose!" She took a bag from Bogie and ran to the back practice room.

"How's Walter making out?" Bogie asked.

"He's been waiting for you. He said someone tried a Denial of Service attack, so it's a good thing we shut the system down." When Bogie said "I told you so," Rose ignored him and continued, "Uncle Walter said we need a couple of fixes to patch up vulnerabilities. He also thinks he can strengthen the firewalls."

Bogie considered this, then looked up as Isabella ran from the back room wearing her new black martial arts outfit with her yellow belt tied at the waist. Bogie and Rose laughed as the little warrior with red curls came toward them. "You look wonderful, Isabella!" he managed to say.

"And dangerous," Rose added.

"Good. Where can I work?"

Rose brought Isabella to a small office that was once occupied by Bogie when he worked in Boston. Rose placed books on a chair so that Isabella could sit down and work at the desk on her laptop. With her kindle next to the computer, the electronic age child was all set.

Bogie stood in the doorway. "Isabella, please email Aunt Ann and tell her we're in town?"

The child nodded.

As Bogie and Rose left Isabella in the small office, Rose said, "I'm surprised she doesn't have a cell phone to go with her other electronics."

"I don't want her texting. I hate that! Can't people just type out a message without all the abbreviations and misspellings? That's the only reason I let her have an Outlook account. She's forced to write out words without those cutesy abbreviations. It slows her down, too. Her little fingers get tired faster than her jaw."

Bogie and Walter worked for four hours without taking a break. They only spoke to occasionally repeat lines of code back and forth. The silence was interrupted by red curls peaking at the door, a sure sign Isabella had gotten bored. Walter looked up and smiled broadly. "You must be Isabella!"

She nodded. "What's your name?"

"I'm Walter...Uncle Walter."

The child stretched out her hand to shake his. She studied him as he studied her. They held each other's hand rather than shake, then smiled. "I heard you were a very intelligent little girl, Isabella."

She nodded. "Mommy says I'm a smart little cookie."

Walter laughed. "I'm sure! Do you like computers?"

Isabella nodded. "I have my own computer over there." She pointed to the doorway.

"Well, Isabella, why don't you bring your computer in here so we can all work together? Wouldn't you like that?"

She nodded.

Bogie put his hands over his face and roughly moved them downward.

Exasperated, Isabella asked, "Why not, Da-dee?"

Bogie stood up and stretched. "I have a better idea. How about you practice some of your moves for a while?"

"Will you practice with me?" she asked, dejected.

"I will," Jesús said as he walked up behind her. "I want to see if you've learned any kung fu or you're just shining me on." He tossed a plastic water bottle in the air and winked at Bogie when Isabella quickly grabbed it with the fingers of one hand as it started its downward path.

While Isabella and Jesús practiced, Bogie and Walter concentrated on their computer screens until Bogie's phone vibrated. He looked at the caller ID. It was Ann McGruder. She was Bogie's half-sister. After their brother Bud died, Bogie brought the lonely woman and her mother, Elizabeth McGruder, to Florida. As Elizabeth slipped further into her demented world, Ann was no longer obliged to spend her life as Elizabeth's companion. When Ann met Dolores, John Carpenter's sister, they struck up an immediate friendship. Ann was wealthy but never learned to enjoy herself; Dolores knew how to live well but had no money. It was a perfect match! Ann and Dolores were often mistaken for sisters. They were both petite with light brown hair, but they were more. They had become a couple, and the only one who seemed unaware of this was John Carpenter, Dolores' homophobic brother.

"Hey, Ann, what's up?"

"What's up with you? Isabella emailed that you were in Boston. What are you doing here?"

Concerned about the slight edge to her voice, Bogie asked, "What? This town's not big enough for the two of us anymore?"

Ann laughed. "I'm sorry. I didn't mean to sound so harsh, but I just wondered what you were up to?"

"One of our guys got shot, and somebody's trying to break through our computer system."

"So what are you doing?"

"Trying to stop them."

After a pause, Ann said, "Mandie called me today."

"Oh, Jeez! I don't believe her! Did she ask you for money?"

"Yes."

"Don't do it, Ann. Please! She's got to learn—"

"She said you wouldn't help her..."

"And when was the last time I denied her anything?"

After telling his sister the story of Amanda and the tax bill, Bogie said, "I know she's pissed off and hurt, but bailing her out isn't the answer. She's got to figure this one out for herself."

After a long silence, Ann said, "Do you want to meet for lunch or dinner?"

"Yeah, sure. How's Dolores doing?"

"Fine. We're both fine."

"When do you want to go out? Today? Tomorrow?"

"How about tomorrow? I'll make reservations at Scampo's for seven-thirty."

Since that time basically ruled out a child-friendly meal, he said, "It'll just be me. I'll leave Isabella with Jack and George." When she didn't object, Bogie asked, "Where is this place?"

While Bogie was talking on the phone, he heard Jesús yell, "No! No suh!"

Walter got up, stretched and walked out of the room to find out who was yelling.

After he hung up, Bogie returned to his computer and stared at the screen trying to block out all thoughts of Amanda and her childish behavior and his sister and her strange attitude.

By the time Amanda finally got married, she was eight months pregnant. She had been so focused on her engagement party and then wedding shower that she couldn't plan the wedding. Then she was pre-occupied with wedding gowns and flowers, food and music that Bogie wondered if Amanda was going to have the baby before the wedding, thereby upending all her plans for yet another party, a baby shower. But Ann and Dolores stood by her, giving her advice and support.

After the wedding, baby shower, and birth of Riley Rose, Ann and Dolores quietly left Palm Beach on an extended vacation. When it ended, they didn't return to Florida. Ann sold the Beacon Street brownstone, and then purchased an over-priced condo in the South End of Boston where she and Dolores lived.

More than half an hour went by before Walter returned to Rose's office, holding Isabella's hand and carrying her computer. "Isabella was showing me the news articles. I didn't realize you were such a hero, and a *hot hero.*" Walter was referring to the news photographs of Bogie carrying Isabella down a ladder wearing nothing but his boxer shorts and work boots. "And the Girl in White Pajamas!" Walter laughed. "Now she's The Girl in Black Pajamas! You are very special, Isabella!"

Bogie looked at Isabella and asked, "Are you tired, Pumpkin?"

Isabella smiled and shook her head. Of course not, she'd found a new admirer.

For dinner, the group ate pizza while Bogie had a large salad. Rose nibbled on her usual one slice of pizza while Jesús and two other men ate hungrily. When Bogie asked how their martial arts practice had gone, Jesús and Isabella glanced at each other then at Bogie. Jesús gave a slight nod. Isabella watched him and did the same. Walter looked at Isabella's paper plate and grinned. Bogie had placed one small slice of pizza on it with a large helping of salad. Bogie and Isabella drank orange juice while the others drank Coke. Remembering the days when Bogie would have inhaled half that greasy pizza and washed it down with a liter of Coke, Walter nodded his approval.

As the R&B group enjoyed their dinner break, the man known to them as Stephen Traiger leaped through the air with Rudolf Nureyev, the world renowned ballet dancer. Rudolf Nureyev performed Tchaikovsky's *Sleeping Beauty* on the flat screen TV while Traiger, wearing a matching leotard, awkwardly imitated his moves. Traiger no longer had black hair with matching glasses and a goatee. His almost bald head was covered by a knit cap.

Linda Traiger, whose hair was now ombré with brown glowing to bright red tips, listened to the aimless banter of the R&B team. Hopefully, they'd learn a lot more now that Walter had moved the kid's computer into the room where they were working.

As the dance ended, Stephen Traiger tapped the remote, and Rudolph Nureyev returned to the nether world. Breathing heavily, Traiger said, "I'm a better dancer than he ever was. I could have been famous if I wanted to be."

His wife made no response. She was still shaken after he shoved her against the living room wall twice for not having done a proper surveillance on Bogie McGruder. Linda should have known Bogie wouldn't run on Sunday. If he had been killed on Sunday morning like they planned, Tommie could have been eliminated as well. As it turned out, Traiger only filled Tommie with lead so that Bogie, the real trouble-making hacker, would return to Boston to protect his precious network. Getting that laptop would have been a coup d'état; Traiger would have gotten their passwords and found all kinds of goodies before he took their network down. Now the fat turd Tommie was in the hospital, and no one knew where the laptop went.

Linda looked up and asked, "Who's Walter Beck?"

Traiger looked at her and asked, "Why?"

"He's there. He's helping them with something."

He pumped both fists in the air. "This is going to be my finest hour...the clash of the Titans! Walter Beck's only famous because he got caught. I'm the best, and I'm going to prove it!"

She nodded. "It's just like you said! They can't be that stupid!"

"But they are, my dear, they are!" Stephen said, doing a poor imitation of W.C. Fields. "And this guy thinks he's Father of the Year and doesn't have a clue what his kid is watching on her laptop...Numb nuts! They're all going down...Daddy Dearest and the whole gang. And now Walter Beck...he's going right with them!"

12

NUMBER ONE IN THE RATINGS

SOUTH FLORIDA

Almost a mile away from the PBSO on Gun Club Road, two Palm Beach County Sheriff's cruisers were parked in front of the Subway shop in the Pine Trail Square strip mall. One of the cars faced the Subway shop while the other had its rear to the strip mall so the deputies could speak to each other. The dark-haired deputies wore their wraparound Oakley sunglasses. JJ Johnson bit a hangnail on his thumb then asked, "I don't understand why you're so anxious to bring in Randy and his wife. Any other couple would be glad to do it."

Billy Ray Marcel looked at him then said, "Sarah said she's been studying other sites to see what people are looking for. She thinks a blonde guy with a big package is a good contrast. Throw in the wife with the black hair and you get a more diversified group. With more players we'll attract a bigger audience."

JJ stared at Billy Ray without speaking. Finally he asked, "So this is her version of the Nielsen ratings? Or is it Sweeps Week on the porn sites?" When Billy Ray didn't answer, JJ said, "Save that bullshit for the girls! Tell me the truth or don't say anything!"

When Billy Ray didn't speak, JJ quickly backed his cruiser out of its spot and drove down Military Trail.

Billy Ray stared at the car disappearing into traffic as he replayed the argument he had with his sister Sarah the night before. He went to her house and confronted her. Sarah finally admitted she might have a bit of a problem with nose candy, but she had a lot going on and needed that extra boost. When she got over this crazy spot, she'd wean herself off the cocaine. She admitted it was getting too pricey, but she refused to tell Billy Ray how much she was spending.

When pressed about why she was pushing so hard for Randy and his wife to join them in making skin flicks, she gave him the same bullshit story he'd repeated to JJ. His reaction was the same as JJ's. Only after Billy Ray threatened to quit the movie business did she tell him the truth.

Billy Ray Marcel left Sarah's house realizing his sister was a drug addict who talked him into a get-rich-quick scheme that was sure to blow up in their faces.

13

CIRCLING THE WAGONS

SOUTH FLORIDA

Bailey locked the office, went into the bedroom, and lifted Henry out of his Pack 'n Play. The smiling baby grabbed fistfuls of her red curls then said, "Ma ma." Bailey kissed his chubby red cheeks. "'Ma ma ma' to you, too!" After cleaning him, she carried Henry through the glass sliding doors overlooking the swimming pool.

Margarita was waiting for them in the doorway of the apartment. She whispered, "She's asking for them. What do I tell her about Isabella?"

"We'll tell her she's at summer camp and will be back in a few days."

As Elizabeth held Henry and kissed the top of his head, she looked at Bailey and asked, "Where's Jennifer?"

"She's at camp. She'll be back at the end of the week."

The old woman considered this. "She's too young for camp, but no one consults me." Elizabeth then stared blankly at Bailey and turned her attention back to the baby.

Bailey whispered to Margarita, "Is it okay if I leave him here for about an hour?"

"Of course." Margarita gathered her thick black hair and secured it in place at the back of her neck with a red scarf. "Are you going to talk to Amanda?"

Bailey nodded.

When Bailey arrived at the enormous house, she was glad to see Amanda's truck in the triple garage. There was no answer when she rang the bell. Bailey went around to the back of the house and found the door unlocked. She called out, and no one answered, so she went inside. There were two glasses and two empty wine bottles on the counter. As Bailey listened, she could hear the baby crying. Bailey slowly moved up the stairs and found Riley Rose crying in her expensive crib. Her face was red and her lips were dry as she wailed. Bailey quickly moved to the master bedroom and opened the door. Amanda was passed out on the bed snoring. The room reeked of stale, second-hand booze.

Bailey went back to the nursery, lifted Riley Rose, and carried her down to the kitchen to get a bottle. While the bottle was warming, Bailey took the baby to the family room and quickly cleaned her and changed her clothes.

The hungry child greedily sucked at the bottle, and Bailey had to pull it away twice to give the baby a chance to calm down so she didn't get sick. After the baby was nourished, Bailey carried her back upstairs and rocked and soothed her until she fell asleep.

With the baby asleep, Bailey walked into the master bedroom, grabbed the wastebasket, dumped the contents on the floor, took it into the master bathroom and filled it with cold water. Bailey carried it back into the room and poured the water over Amanda's face.

Amanda sputtered and flailed, then jumped off the wet bed. As she glared at Bailey through bloodshot eyes, she started to speak, but ran in the bathroom and threw up. Amanda threw up again and again until she was dry heaving and crying.

"Take a shower and put on some clean clothes," Bailey said coldly. "I'm packing some things for Riley Rose. You pack your own clothes."

"What!?"

"You're coming home with me." Bailey pointed a finger at Amanda just as she had seen Bogie do. "Don't say another word. You're coming home with me!"

"You're not my mother," Amanda mumbled weakly.

"Nor do I want to be," Bailey said. "While you were passed out drunk, the house was unlocked, the security alarm was off, and the baby was neglected. If someone else walked in here, they'd be calling the Department of Children and Families and carting that poor child away."

Amanda held her mouth and started sobbing.

"Stop feeling sorry for yourself! Get cleaned up and packed."

After filling up the Escalade and Amanda's truck with Riley Rose's paraphernalia and Amanda's one suitcase, Bailey ordered Amanda to lock up the house, set the alarm and follow her in the truck to Palm Springs.

When Bailey returned to Elizabeth's apartment, Margarita held Henry as he fussed. Margarita looked up and smiled at Bailey as she carried Riley Rose into the apartment. "Somebody here just had enough loving for one day. Did you bring Amanda?"

"She's at our house, sleeping."

As the women spoke, Elizabeth looked up and smiled. "Oh, Amanda! You are so sweet!"

Bailey held Henry while he helped her hold his bottle, and Elizabeth held Riley Rose as she kissed and rocked her. Margarita looked at Bailey and whispered, "How's Amanda doing?"

"She's broken up. Not handling things too well. I thought it was better for her to have family around."

"Bogie's not going to—"

"Well, he's not here. I am, and I'm running the show now!"

❦

The thin blondes walked down Worth Avenue and entered Neiman Marcus. They wore pastel halter top dresses that ended mid-thigh. Zoe's dress was yellow and Tiffany's was her signature pink. Zoe wore tan and yellow Botkier four-inch strappy heels while Tiffany chose pink and gold Juicy Couture wedges for their shopping excursion. As the pair walked through the store, Zoe didn't remove her Versace sunglasses. When Tiffany glanced over at her, Zoe said, "Mandie and I got shwasted last night. I had to bump a line this morning just to take the edge off."

Tiffany studied her. "Why didn't you call me?"

"I was doing you a favor! She called me crying because she and Randy had a blowup, and he moved out."

"Really? What happened?"

Zoe tried to remember then said, "I think she was supposed to pay the taxes and spent the money instead. Randy got pissed and they had a fight."

"Is it serious?" Tiffany asked.

Zoe shrugged as they checked the dresses on the rack. She held up a Roberto Cavalli asymmetric white jersey dress that had been reduced from $1,135 to $691. She turned to a clerk. "Do you have this in a size two?"

The tall, thin woman checked the rack and reported, "I'm sorry, we just have the size ten"

Zoe sneered at her. "Do I look like I wear a size ten?"

The clerk shook her head. "Absolutely not! We do have a Robert Rodriguez here in your size, and I believe it would look stunning on you." The saleswoman held up a white jersey wrap dress that covered little more than a bath towel.

As Zoe exited the dressing room wearing the Rodriguez gem that was a steal for $565, Tiffany and the sales clerk lauded her and exclaimed that the dress was made just for her. It showed off her breast implants to full advantage while the crisscross bottom almost gave a peek at her bikini underwear as she walked.

Zoe handed the sales associate an American Express card. She was really going to zing it to her father today! He had badgered her again about meeting that old Jew from New York. Who cared if his family had money? Just because the guy was a rich old Jew, Martin Ziegler was pushing him on her. Just to mollify him and that bitch Annette, Martin's current wife, Zoe agreed to meet this turd. Anyone related to that douche bag Annette had to be worse than a sack of shit. Two weeks was a long way off. They could all be dead in two weeks, so there was no harm in making empty promises. But when her father had the audacity to suggest she might slow down on her spending since Floridians were still punishing him for the BP oil spills and staying away from his gas stations in droves, he crossed the line. He whined about how it wasn't his fault BP caused the worst ecological disaster in the history of the Northern Hemisphere and that people should get over it already. Zoe gave him one of her famous pouts and started to shed a tear. Then Martin Zeigler back-pedaled and told her not to worry as he handed her another check to pay for her acting classes. Just to punish him, Zoe topped off her shopping with a white origami-strap camisole top from Versace. That, too, was another steal at almost half its original price of $995.

As they sat in a café sharing a small salad and sipping sweet tea, Tiffany asked, "Did you talk to Mandie?"

Zoe nodded.

"What did she say?"

Zoe considered this as she slowly chewed her salad. "Not much. She's thinking about it. Since they're having money problems, I think they'll do it."

"Billy Ray will be happy to hear that," Tiffany offered.

"Fuck him!" Zoe said with contempt. "I don't know what he's trying to pull. He's really getting on my nerves! He's so hot to bring in two more people! But no matter what he says, it's just going to make smaller slices of the same pie. I thought he was being straight with us, but this morning the prick called and told me that Sarah is going to issue 1099 forms to us at the end of the year."

Tiffany looked confused. "What are you talking about?"

"What I'm talking about is that we're going to have to pay tax on all that money. At first, Billy Ray said we'd be paid cash, and now he's saying we have to show income or the IRS is going to be all over us."

"I don't want to pay taxes," Tiffany said petulantly.

"Then don't."

"What'll happen if I don't pay them?"

"You'll go to jail."

"This whole thing is starting to suck ass! Did you ask him about my cousin Rhonda?"

Zoe nodded. "He said no way. Billy Ray said she looks like a cow and nobody's going to pay to see a cow getting fucked unless they're into animals." Zoe looked at the check then threw a bill on the table. "I'm still hungry. Let's go have a smoke."

The women sat in the yellow Volkswagen Beetle smoking while the air conditioning blasted. Tiffany asked, "So what's next? Is Mandie supposed to get back to you or what?"

Zoe shrugged. "I don't remember. I was super trashed. I'll drive by later and drop in. If Randy's not there, it doesn't really matter when I go."

⌾⌁⌾

Amanda came downstairs wearing a white tee shirt and print pajama pants, watching as Bailey fed both babies. Riley Rose sat in Henry's Eddie Bauer high chair and Henry sat in Isabella's chair with a booster seat. Bailey had attached him to the chair with a belt from a terrycloth robe. Amanda smiled as she studied the happy babies and Bailey as she fed each a spoonful of mashed vegetables while she sang along with Adele. Each time Adele sang "rumour has it," *Bailey* tapped a wooden spoon on the table to accompany the drumbeat in the background. The babies held their small spoons and joined her. She pointed her wooden spoon toward the stove. "I have some soup there for you."

Amanda nodded, kissed Riley Rose on the top of the head, and walked to the stove where a small pot of chicken noodle soup was waiting for her.

After the babies were cleaned and placed on the carpet in the family room, Amanda watched as they crawled over to the baskets loaded with soft toys and emptied them. She smiled. "I'm surprised Dad doesn't mind having toys all over the floor."

Bailey looked at her then said. "He doesn't care as long as we pick them up when we're ready to leave the room. It works out to about five minutes for emptying the baskets, five minutes of play and fifteen minutes of cleaning up."

"Is it worth it?"

"Sure. Henry enjoys himself and I get exercise."

"Doesn't Dad help?"

Bailey shook her head. "Why should he? He works all day, then he's on the computer every evening. All he asks is that we don't leave a mess. Isabella's very neat, so Bogie expects Henry to be the same way."

"Henry's a baby and, besides, Isabella's his clone."

They both laughed knowing there was truth in that statement. Isabella had inherited her father's obsession with order and cleanliness.

Bailey studied Amanda's pale face and noticed the dark circles under her eyes. "Are you okay?"

Amanda shrugged. "My life is over, but other than that, I'm fine."

"Your life is far from over; you've just hit a rough patch. Pick yourself up and move on."

"How?"

Bailey considered this. "The first thing you might want to do is get a job."

"How can I get a job? I have the baby—"

"Leave her with me until you get settled. Bogie gave you until Labor Day to decide if you wanted to take over the other office. Labor Day is here and gone, but I'm sure the offer is still open. You can start there. I'll be glad to watch Riley Rose while you get organized."

"How much is he paying?"

Bailey laughed. "Talk to your father. I know you won't make enough to pay the taxes, but at least it will be a step in the right direction."

☙

JACKSONVILLE

Rhonda Gallagher, Tiffany's cousin, stood in her two piece bathing suit, studying her reflection in the long mirror. She was giddy over the twenty-six pounds she'd already lost thanks to the diet plan she'd seen on TV. Rhonda had to order ninety days' worth of the meals in order to get a good deal. When the first month's supply arrived, Rhonda sat down for her first tiny meal and started to eat. Childhood memories of making and tasting mud pies tickled her brain. Those were followed by the feeling she was eating cardboard food. It all tasted like cardboard, no matter what it was. Having spent her hard earned money from working the counter at Chick-fil-A on this dreck, she was determined to follow the diet and eat every tasteless morsel. Rhonda almost retched every time she was hungry, thinking of what awaited her, but she stuck to the plan.

Now twenty-six pounds lighter and down to one hundred and sixty two pounds, she thought she was ready for a tan from the salon down the street. Rhonda believed that Tiffany's movie guy would recognize her star potential and overlook a few extra pounds. She figured if Gabourey Sidibe got a starring role with her weight, Rhonda Gallagher should be a shoo-in for at least a small part.

She was so excited, she emailed her cousin Tiffany.

"Am I getting the part or not?"

Tiffany answered:

"No. The boss said N 0.

Love and kisses from the movies in Palm Beach."

Forty-five minutes after her dreams of a movie career were dashed, Rhonda Gallagher consumed a half gallon of heavenly hash ice cream while eating a family-sized package of Oreo cookies.

Feeling bloated and sugar-charged, Rhonda searched the internet for answers or revenge, whichever came first. She emailed pictures of Tiffany to twenty-five friends and relatives asking for information on her movies in Palm Beach.

14

ALL IN THE FAMILY

BOSTON

At seven-forty, Bogie entered the restaurant, looked around, and walked over to a small woman who was sitting at the bar. He greeted her, saying, "Sorry, I'm late. I had to get Isabella over to Jack's office."

Ann McGruder hugged him. "It's good to see you. I'm sorry I didn't invite Izzy, but I wanted to talk to you and—"

"I figured that! It's fine! She'll have a fun evening with her uncles and be the center of attention. We all know how she loves that. How's Dolores doing?"

"Okay, I guess."

When they were seated, Bogie looked around at the exposed brick wall of the restaurant and asked, "Have you seen James or Trudie lately?"

Ann shook her head. Although Ann purchased Bogie's condo for the family servants after selling the Beacon Street house, she did not believe that their forty plus years of service warranted her keeping tabs on them in their Allston apartment.

Bogie made a mental note to visit the old couple. "Elephant Ear Walking! Give me a break! That's a nice name for a fancy piece of bread."

Ann's mouth twisted with disapproval. "Sorry, I thought you'd enjoy something a little different."

Bogie continued to look around. "You know this building was once Chucky's Place."

Ann looked at him and laughed. "I haven't heard anybody call the Charles Street Jail that for years. This is where father always said you'd end up."

"And here I am!" Bogie said. "What's going on with you, Ann? And don't give me that 'nothing' crap. You seemed happy the last time I saw you, and now you're down and edgy."

She shook her head, but when Bogie continued to stare at her, she said, "Dolores. I really have feelings for her, and now she's having second thoughts about us. I'm looking for a commitment, and she's thinking that maybe we just got together because we were lonely and down on men."

After giving their orders to the waiter, they stared at each other. Finally, Bogie said, "Maybe that's true. People get together for lots of reasons. You were alone way too long. Dolores was divorced a couple of times, so she could be down on men. She's got grown daughters and grandkids, so maybe she's reluctant to commit to anything and have to deal with the blowback from her family."

"And what about my family?"

"I'm your family, and I don't give a shit. If you're happy, I'm happy. Is she talking about moving out?"

Ann shook her head.

"Then what?"

Ann shrugged. "She just wants to keep things quiet. I think that's insulting to me."

"Why don't you just give her time to adjust? Dolores is a reasonable person. She's led a fairly ordinary life, and it's probably tough for her to make that final leap."

"And me? I'm just supposed to sit and wait?"

Bogie smiled. "What's your hurry, Murray? One thing I learned is that the more you try to force something, the less chance you have of it happening. Maybe if you just sit back and enjoy the ride, you'll both be happier. Whatever happens, happens! Your pushing isn't necessarily going to make it go your way."

Ann grimaced. "That's not quite what I wanted to hear."

"But it's the truth, and you know it. If you care about each other, nothing else matters," Bogie said.

As their dinners were placed in front of them, Ann studied Bogie without looking at her food. "Did you care about her when you were lovers?"

"I told you before. We were friends who had sex, not lovers," Bogie answered as he eyed his dinner.

Ann studied him as he started to eat. "I think she thought you were more serious, and you tossed her aside when you and Bailey got back together."

"That's bullshit!" Bogie said incredulously as he put down his fork. "We never loved each other, and she and I weren't even talking to each other when I got back together with Bailey. To tell you the truth, all we had was occasional sex. It was no great love match!"

"That's how you saw it?"

"That's how we both saw it...I'm sure. It's not real romantic when your partner is only giving you instructions on what to do. 'Move this way, move that way, grab this, touch that.'"

Ann looked at him and burst out laughing. Regaining her composure, she said, "That's her! That's Dolores!"

They both started laughing.

Bogie looked around at the other diners to see if they were being watched. "I can't believe we're having this conversation!" He laughed again then said, "Well, if it doesn't work out with her, at least you'll be better for the next one. You'll have all the right moves in place."

Ann laughed so hard tears rolled down her face. Finally she asked, "Did she make you a better lover?"

"I think so. I'm happy, Bailey's satisfied, so I guess that's what counts." Bogie picked up his fork again and pointed to his dinner. "This is pretty good!" he said and nodded.

Ann smiled. "When did you realize you were in love with Bailey?"

Bogie considered and chewed then said, "When she was eighteen years old."

Ann's eyes opened wide. "Are you serious? You were with her when she was eighteen years old?"

Bogie shook his head. "No. That's when she graduated from high school. I had a little celebration dinner for her and Jack, and afterward she came to me and told me she loved me and wanted to sleep with me."

"And you did what?" Ann asked.

"Shot her down! I told her she was waaaay too young for me. The next day I went out looking for a two bedroom condo for them. That's when I got the condo in Allston. They were both going to B U that fall, so I just wanted to speed up the moving process. I knew then that I was in love with her."

"Did you tell her so?" Ann asked.

Bogie shook his head again. "I knew I loved Bailey and thought if she really loved me, she'd still love me in a few years when she was all grown up. I didn't want her to confuse gratitude and love."

"So you waited till.. when? Once she had finished college or law school?

"When she finished college, it was the same thing. Bailey told me she loved me and wanted us to become lovers. I told her she was still too young, and she got pissed off. When Bailey was in law school, I told her I married Olga. She punched me in the mouth and didn't talk to me for a year."

Ann looked at him sadly. "Did she know the marriage was just a sham?"

Bogie shook his head. "That was one of the conditions. I couldn't tell anyone. But when Bailey graduated from law school, I took her out to celebrate. She made it clear that was her last pitch and I was on the old 'three strikes and you're out' rule. I caved in!"

"Didn't it bother you thinking Bailey might be with younger men all the time you weren't together?"

"Nope. I always knew I wasn't the first. I just wanted to be the last!"

"How'd you know that?"

"Bailey was sexually abused by her uncle when she was a teenager."

Ann looked at him in horror. "The one she worked for?"

"No. His brother Stanley. He took over all the kids' money when their parents died. Stanley shipped Jack off to a military academy and had Bailey stay in his house in Newton where he was abusing her. That's how I met her."

"She came to you?"

"No, Stanley did. He hired us to find her. Bailey was a sixteen year old runaway. Stanley didn't want the cops involved. When I found Bailey, she went to pieces and begged me not to take her back. Rose and I talked to her, and I started doing some digging. Bailey was telling the truth. That ass-hole took over all the money from their parents' estates. I made that son-of-a-bitch pay for their upkeep and education. At first, I had Bailey and Jack transfer into Phillips Academy. They boarded there. Jack liked it, Bailey hated it. So I put her in Thayer Academy in Braintree. The problem was that Thayer didn't have boarding, so Bailey lived with me and Amanda in Quincy. It was great for babysitting, but even then she made me uncomfortable with the way she looked at me."

"Oh, you poor baby!" Ann teased. "So you were with Bailey when you were married to Olga?"

Bogie nodded. "I should have told her the truth, but I didn't." He shook his head. "I never told her until after they were killed in that car accident. She didn't take it well...said I made her feel like a whore. When I pointed out that she was the one who seduced me, Bailey went nuts. That's when I learned a valuable lesson: Trying to win an argument with a woman is like baptizing a cat. The results are ugly!"

Ann laughed. "Yeah, but when you're both women, that doesn't work. So you're happy now?"

Bogie nodded. "We're happy. We have two great kids and another on the way."

"What! Are you serious? Bailey's pregnant again?"

Bogie nodded.

"I thought she was getting ready to take the Florida Bar exam."

"She is. I just don't think Bailey's that anxious to get back in the game. Isabella's a handful and the Hankster is crawling and pulling himself up, so he'll be walking sooner rather than later. With a new baby in the mix, it should be a real three-ring circus."

Ann smiled. "And you're loving it, aren't you?"

Bogie nodded.

As their plates were cleared away, Ann said, "I guess I should ask about Mother, but from what I can glean from Isabella's emails things are about the same."

"Slightly downgraded. Her general health is deteriorating."

"Do you think I should come back?" Ann asked.

Bogie frowned. "For what? She doesn't even know who you are any more. And besides, I'm her favorite child now."

Ann started choking, knowing that her mother had always detested Bogie. When she was able to catch her breath, Ann said, "Amanda!"

Bogie closed his eyes.

Ann continued, "I've given this a lot of thought, and this is what I've decided to do. I'm going to lend her the money to pay the taxes, but I'll tell her I expect her to pay me back."

"And how do you propose she does that?"

"Like you said, get a job!"

ᘒᛔᛔᘒ

After leaving Ann, Bogie walked down Cambridge Street to Mass General Hospital. The horseshoe shaped driveway on Fruit Street was barricaded down the middle with the construction of yet another building going up. Bogie walked up the crowded pedestrian walkway on the right side toward the front entrance and called Coco. "Any change with our boy?"

"I guess you haven't heard. Tommie's conscious but confused and in a lot of pain. He didn't even recognize me!" Coco exclaimed.

"Coco, I know you like to get into character; but, remember, you're not his mother."

"In my heart I am. My poor Tommie is really hurting."

Bogie realized that Coco sounded off, and asked, "Is there someone in the room with you?"

"Yes. I appreciate your kind words, pastor," Coco said.

"Cops?"

"Absolutely."

"I'm downstairs. Call me when it's safe to come up. I'll wait outside."

Bogie stood in the shadows with a small group of people waiting near the front door. He watched two large men wearing oversized jackets that concealed weapons exit the building. He made them for cops before his phone vibrated.

ᘒᛔᛔᘒ

As he walked toward Tommie's bed, Bogie felt a profound sense of sadness. There were tubes protruding in and out of him with monitors keeping track of various bodily functions. An IV drip ran from a pole to a bandaged site on top of Tommie's hand. His once clear blue eyes were sunken with dark circles. Although still enormous, he looked diminished in the bed.

Bogie touched Tommie's arm and looked at his unshaven cheek. "You look like shit!"

Tommie smiled. "That's just how I feel, for sure."

"Do you remember what happened?"

Tommie smiled again. He knew Bogie would not waste words on pleasantries and instead get directly to the point. "I was working on this equation, and I knew something was wrong. I couldn't get it to balance. I tried to get ahold of my professor and left him a message. I fell asleep waiting for a return call. When I woke up, it came to me. It was like a revelation! Once I stopped thinking about it, I was able to work it out. Since I had all my data on our network, I went to sign on. I started getting "Server is Busy" messages. I knew that was impossible and started freaking out. All my work was on the system."

"Why didn't you have it on the MIT network?"

"I had some of it there, but I couldn't be sure that someone wouldn't try to steal it or use my notes and data. I've learned a lot about intellectual property rights and felt more comfortable with it on our system. Anyway, I went in to find out what was happening. I remember punching in the code then I felt this burning pain inside. It was like hot pokers were moving through me. I remember falling to the ground."

"Did you see anyone? Hear anything?"

Tommie shook his head then said, "I don't remember. Everything was going black, but I'm sure I heard someone say 'Hacker'. That's it! What's going on?"

"I'm not sure, but I'm going to find out. Where's your laptop?"

Tommie's mouth opened and he bit his bottom lip. "I don't know! Where is it? I had it with me—"

"Don't get upset, Tommie. We'll find it. We'll get it back." Bogie turned to the tall, blonde woman standing next to the bed. "Coco, go to the nurse's station and ask them where they have Tommie's belongings."

Wearing a shapeless black dress and no makeup, Coco nodded slightly and left the room.

Tommie moaned. "All my work!"

Bogie put his hand on Tommie's shoulder. "Don't do this to yourself. I promise you, we'll find it." Trying to calm Tommie down and change the subject he said, "Isabella's been very worried about you. She flew to Boston with me to see you."

Tommie smiled and looked around. "I don't think they'll let her—"

"You get a little better, and we'll find a way."

Tommie stared at him with tears in his eyes. "I hurt for sure, but my legs aren't doing anything..."

Bogie squeezed his shoulder. "You were shot four times. You know how you talked about having that bypass operation to lose weight? Well, consider this a quadruple bypass with your liver and kidney clipped along with a lot of your guts."

Tommie looked at Bogie and grinned. "Thank you, doctor! You think I'm going to lose a lot of weight now?"

"That I guarantee, especially when they're feeding you like this!" He pointed to the IV drip.

"But what about my legs?"

Bogie sighed. "One of the bullets did some damage near the lower spine. Listen, Tommie, I'm not a doctor; but I'm being straight with you. I don't have the answer; the doctors don't have it either. They'll keep running tests on you, but no one will know for sure what's going on until a lot of the swelling goes down. So before you go on eBay and bid on a wheelchair, wait and see what happens. In the meantime, we're all pulling for you. We've got you covered here, and we're going to get your computer and find the asshole who did this to you."

Tommie furrowed his brow. "Did he get into the system?"

"No. And you're sure it was a man who spoke to you."

Tommie nodded.

"We don't know if it's somebody working alone, but there have been attempts to breach the firewalls. We brought in Walter."

"Walter! The Walter? I've always wanted to meet him. He's the greatest—"

"Yes," Bogie added quickly. "I'll see if he'll give you his autograph."

"Don't toy with me! He's sure a superstar, he's—"

"I'll ask him to come over to meet you."

Tommie sighed and held his hand to his heart, reminding Bogie of a teenage girl about to meet Justin Bieber. Realizing the depth of Tommie's immaturity, Bogie said, "You know what your story is as far as pay and the rest?" When Tommie nodded, Bogie added, "And you and Rose..."

Tommie laughed. "You bet. Like anybody'll believe that!"

Dragging her feet in black oxford shoes, Coco came back into the room. "His clothes are gone. They had to cut them off. His wallet, keys and things are with the cops. No one knows anything about the computer. It wasn't brought in with him or his belongings."

As the small amount of coloring in Tommie Jurgenson's face drained away, Bogie said, "Go out and demand a copy of his admission paperwork. Tell them *he* wants to see it. Make sure you get the ambulance sheet. If they tell you everything's in the computer system, tell them to print it out." Bogie turned to Tommie. "The server was not compromised. Your work is protected. That doesn't mean we don't care about your laptop. We do, and we'll get it!"

Tommie made a feeble attempt to smile then asked, "What about the GPS?"

"Whoever has the laptop, hasn't turned it on yet. Once they do, we'll be able to track it. Any messages for Isabella?"

Tommie smiled broadly. "Sure. Tell Izzy she's my greatest friend!"

Although Bogie knew how bizarre it was for a four year old child to have friends between the ages of twenty and fifty, he only thanked Tommie and promised to pass the message along to Isabella.

15

BAGGED

It was almost eleven o'clock when Bogie returned to the white-frame house in Quincy. Standing on the porch, he looked in the front window and saw Jack asleep on the couch and George sleeping in the chair with the TV on. Bogie tapped on the window until George opened his eyes. George smiled, slowly got off the chair, and opened the door. "Why didn't you ring the bell?"

"I wanted to limit the number of people I woke up." Bogie grinned. "Jeez, you guys are exciting! You're just like an old married couple."

"That's because we are."

"Thanks for babysitting. I assume she's sound asleep."

George stretched and nodded. "I wish I had half her energy. She just goes on and on—"

"Are you okay? Health-wise I mean?"

"Oh, I'm fine. When I went off the Avonex and started the Copaxone, I felt better in a week. The only nasty part is that I have to give myself injections every morning. Half the lower shelf of the refrigerator is full of boxes of medicine."

Bogie grimaced. "I'm not too crazy about needles. I don't know if I could do that every morning."

"You do what you have to do," George said, then turned away, not in the mood to dwell on his Multiple Sclerosis.

Bogie yawned and bid George a good night. He gave a two finger salute to Jack, who was just opening his eyes.

Jack grunted as he slowly made his way off the couch while George checked to make sure the alarm was set. As they walked toward the staircase, Bogie hurriedly came down carrying a laptop and a white, plastic, supermarket bag. When the men saw the look on Bogie's face, they knew somebody was in trouble.

⟋⟋⟍⟍⟍⟍⟍

Bogie went into the guestroom finding Isabella asleep holding her laptop. The computer was on, and she was still wearing her ear buds. Bogie removed the buds from her ears and lifted the laptop. He studied the screen:

> *Elle Driver and the Bride were fighting. Elle went into a tiger stance and charged at the Bride, who had been knocked to the ground. Elle lunged toward the Bride with her leg in the air. The Bride grabbed Elle's leg and flung her with such a force that Elle crashed through the wall behind them. The women continued their vicious fight and Elle Driver warned, "And now I'm going to kill you, with your own sword, no less, which in the very immediate future, will become my sword."*

> *The Bride responded: "Bitch. You don't have a future."*

⟋⟋⟍⟍⟍⟍⟍

As Bogie re-entered the living room, he showed Jack and George what Isabella had been watching on her computer. They shook their heads as Bogie typed in commands and studied the history. "She's watched *Kill Bill 2* forty times," he said angrily.

"Are you sure?" George asked.

Bogie nodded. "She's seen *Kill Bill 1* twenty-two times. Oh, and look at this, two Jackie Chan movies on twelve occasions."

"How did she get them?" Jack asked.

Bogie continued typing and scrolling through the screen. "She bought them on Amazon."

"How?" George asked.

Bogie typed, he studied the screen then said, "I'll be damned!"

"What?" Jack and George asked together.

"She set up an account using Bailey's debit card information."

"How'd she get the numbers?" George asked.

Bogie shrugged. "Bailey could have them written down somewhere. She likes to shop online. That little twerp probably watched her and figured she'd do some shopping too."

"And Bailey doesn't know the difference?" Jack asked.

Bogie shook his head. "Because of her bankruptcy, she can't get credit cards so I load up a card for her every month so she doesn't have to keep asking me for money. These weren't large charges and not made at the same time. Obviously, Bailey's not checking the small stuff."

"That little sneak!" George said, then started laughing. "She's so damned smart!"

"She's too smart!" Bogie retorted. He cupped his hand over the top of his ear and asked, "And who bought her the computer?"

"It was supposed to be educational," Jack answered defensively.

"And quite the education she's received. Not only is she now an expert on *Kill Bill 1 and 2*, she's a whiz at Googling and is now dabbling into identity theft. But above all she's broadened her sex education." Bogie opened the white, plastic bag to show the men two black, diamond-shaped, rubber devices each attached to a rubber base. One of the butt plugs was covered with a condom. Several condoms lay in the bag. Some were outside their packets while others had obviously been removed then replaced by pushing them back inside with the small pencil lying in the bottom of the bag. Bogie handed the bag to George.

Bogie started laughing as he watched Jack's and George's faces flush with embarrassment.

"She was rifling through our drawers!" George exclaimed.

"I didn't think you gave her this stuff to play with," Bogie said before he started laughing again. "We'll have a chat with our little angel in the morning if you don't throw us out before then."

⟨⟩

SOUTH FLORIDA

It was almost midnight when the yellow Volkswagen Beetle pulled into the triple driveway of the enormous house. Zoe knew before she got out of the car that the house was empty. The lone light in the front window subtly announced that Randy, Amanda...and Elvis had left the building.

16

MEAN MEN

As the three men sat around the table staring at her, Isabella studied them, then asked, "What?"

Bogie reached under his chair and brought out Isabella's laptop. She smiled then said, "I was worried about that! Where was it?"

But the men continued to stare at her. With his jaw tight Bogie said, "So this is why you're so tired all day! You've been watching stolen movies at night!"

Isabella puckered her lips and shook her head. "They're not stolen. I bought them."

"With what? You don't have any money!"

"Mommy has a Mastercard. I just typed in all the information."

Bogie studied Isabella. "That's stealing! Using someone else's credit card is stealing."

"But I don't have one of my own," Isabella said, her lips quivering.

When the tears started, Bogie pointed to the computer and said, "You won't be using the laptop today. And we'll figure out how you will repay your mother for stealing her money to buy the movies you *used* to have on this computer."

Isabella gasped and her hand shot to her mouth. Tears flowed as she shook her head in horror.

Jack and George studied the little girl. It was George who took the white Stop & Shop bag off the counter and showed the contents to Isabella. She glanced into the bag, wiped the tears off her cheeks with her fists then glared at the three men. "You're all being mean to me! I'm a small child!" She pointed to George. "And you're not wonderful anymore!" She sighed, looked at the men again then said, "Excuse me!" Isabella walked out of the kitchen and stomped up the stairs.

The men looked at each other and shrugged. George was the first to speak. "Honey, I love that child to pieces, but I'm glad you're the one raising her and not me."

"Ditto," Jack added.

"Thank you...I think," Bogie said.

⌒◯◯◯⌒

SOUTH FLORIDA

The portly deputy walked through the open door and sat down in front of the large desk. He smiled at the woman studying a book while two babies bounced in their seats on the floor. "Are you running a daycare now, Counselor?"

Bailey looked up and smiled at John Carpenter. "Just lending a hand." As the baby with black curls bounced and laughed at the sight of her grandfather, Bailey said, "I think one of them recognizes you."

John reached down and picked up the happy baby. Her companion immediately started crying, and Bailey lifted the little blonde and cuddled him. "You're a troublemaker, John!"

"That I am! Where's her momma?"

"Working." When John raised an eyebrow, she added, "She started working in the other office this morning. It's quite a mess, so I told her to leave Riley Rose here until she gets the place in order. Carlos' organizational skills fall a bit short of the mark."

"Is she moving out of the house?"

"I hardly think so. She's just taking a time out. What about Randy, is he throwing in the towel?"

John just shrugged. "He's still licking his wounds. I got a call from Dolores last night. She said that Amanda called her and asked her to put in a good word for her at the country club. She said Amanda was trying to get a job there as a lifeguard. Dolores told her she'd make some calls. But Dolores gave up her membership months ago and doesn't know how much influence she has there anymore. What does Amanda plan on doing with the baby if she's working as a lifeguard?"

"I told her I'd keep an eye on her. I also told her that Riley Rose's father and grandfathers would be glad to pitch in when they could."

John smiled. "Just like the Waltons!"

"Exactly!"

"And the two of you are best friends now?" John questioned.

Bailey considered this, then shook her head. "Unfortunately, there will always be some strain between us. I've known Mandie since she was a child. We got along great when Jack and I were babysitting for her while we were in high school. Even after that, we were close. I always thought of her as a little sister. But when Bogie had the heart attack, she blamed me and turned on me with a vengeance."

"That's stupid! Why would she blame you for his heart attack?"

"In a way it was my fault. I was hurt and wrote him a nasty letter when he was coming here. I asked Amanda to give it to him so she handed him the letter when they were getting ready to land in Palm Beach. Bogie read it and had a heart attack. Once he was in the hospital, the doctor's found that his arteries were clogged from a lifetime of bad eating, smoking and drinking. That's when Bogie had open heart surgery. Since the letter precipitated all those events, she blamed me. Years later, when Bogie and I got back together, Mandie felt threatened. She was always the center of her father's universe and wanted to keep that position."

"That's really childish!" John said.

"She is a child, John. I know she's twenty, but she's a very young twenty. She's been coddled and sheltered most of her life. I think marriage, a baby, and a big new house all coming along in rapid succession overwhelmed her. But I believe that when all the snow settles down in her snow globe, she'll be fine."

"And Bogie agrees?"

Bailey gave John a withering look, and he laughed. "Bogie has spent years working on discipline and self-control. He doesn't believe in long adjustment periods. He thinks everybody should keep busy and make themselves useful. He doesn't adhere to the princess mentality."

"And yet he calls Amanda princess, I've heard him."

"I think he started that when she was very young, and he was overcompensating for her not having a mother. I'll bet he regrets it now! Notice her younger siblings are Pumpkin and Hankster."

John thought for a moment, rocking Riley Rose in his arms. "But even if she works day and night, she won't make enough money to pay the taxes on time."

"Amanda took care of them. She borrowed the money from Ann with the stipulation that she pay Ann back within six months."

"Will she? Or will she go out and spend more money?"

Bailey opened the diaper bag and retrieved two bottles. She handed one to John and answered, "If Amanda has any sense, she'll pay her back as quickly as possible. She knows she can't go back for more if she hasn't paid what she owes. Bogie won't give her the money, so Amanda's options are limited. Besides, working all day tends to reduce one's ability to go shopping."

John nodded as he fed the baby her bottle. "What's going on with Dolores and Ann?"

"I have no idea what you're talking about?"

John started to open his mouth then stopped. When he finally spoke, he said, "You know, after the wedding, they went on vacation together, then Dolores decided to move to Boston with Ann. Dolores' house is sitting here, and she's living in Boston. What the hell are they doing?"

"John, you're talking about your sister and Bogie's sister. I'm hardly a confidante to either of them. The only thing I know for sure is that Dolores isn't selling her house now because the market is deflated. Bogie sends men over to keep up the outside so it doesn't get overgrown."

"Randy and I have been watching the place, too, but I don't understand what her plans are. Her daughters live in Ohio, but she never mentions moving back there. What's the big attraction in Boston?"

"It must be the weather! Millions of people from all over the world come to Boston every year just to enjoy the brutal winters and sweltering summers."

After staring at Bailey with cop's eyes for an uncomfortable time, he asked, "Do you think they're queer?"

Bailey laughed. "John, I don't really understand what that word is supposed to mean. It's offensive enough but doesn't mean anything. Do you think that because my brother's gay I have gaydar? But, just for the sake of argument, let's say that these two middle-aged women are having a relationship. So what?"

"What? That's disgusting! I can't imagine how or why..."

"Then why are you going there? Why are you so concerned about them? They're adults. They're not hurting anyone."

"See! That's the problem with you liberals! Everything goes, and the next thing you know, the whole family structure is shot to hell!"

Now understanding why Carlos called John a cracker, Bailey said, "As soon as Mandie finds out if she got the lifeguard job, we'll work out a schedule. I'll give you and Randy copies so we can figure out who will care for Riley Rose and when."

"What about her other grandfather? Is he still in Boston?"

Bailey nodded. "Don't worry, he'll get his turn, too."

17

EVERYBODY'S BUST'N ON ME

BOSTON

With a scowl on her face, Isabella charged through the door of R&B Investigations before her father. Without greeting anyone, she marched to Rose's office where Walter had set up a makeshift workstation for her.

Sitting on top of the front desk, Jesús peered at Bogie. "Somebody wearing her Grumpy pants today?"

"She's wearing the whole outfit," Bogie answered.

Jesús twisted his mouth then motioned for Bogie to follow him to his small office. After they entered the crowded space, Jesús closed the door and said softly, "I feel like a scumbag for ratting out a little kid, but sometimes Izzy can be scary."

Bogie rolled his eyes and shook his head before he asked, "What's she done now?"

"Yesterday, I was working with her on her Tiger Claw. Izzy's wicked good, especially for a kid her age. Anyway, I told her she was doing great then she asked me to show her how to do the Five-Point-Palm-Exploding-Heart technique."

Bogie stared incredulously at Jesús and asked, "Where'd she hear about something like that?"

"*Kill Bill 2*. You might want to watch that movie just to see what's going through her little head."

"Fuck! That kid is going to send me to an early grave. Thanks, Jesús, and don't worry about it. I bagged her last night. She's been watching that movie so much that she probably knows the script as well as Quentin Tarantino. She downloaded it along with *Kill Bill 1* and some Jackie Chan movies onto her laptop!"

Jesús laughed. "Wow! She's a wicked smart kid!" But then he added, "But what's she so mad about? You're the one who should be pissed off."

"I won't let her use her computer today."

Jesús laughed. "That's cruel and unusual punishment! I think I might call the child abuse hotline!"

"Don't say that too loud or she'll be on the phone."

As Bogie walked back to Rose's office, he heard Isabella telling Rose and Walter "And Da-dee was very mean to me. He took these wonderful movies off my computer. They were *my* movies! I bought them!" When she didn't receive a sympathetic response from Rose or Walter, she asked, "Aunt Rose, would you please call Pop Pop and ask him if he'll take me to the park? He loves to walk to the park with me."

Bogie watched his daughter then looked at Rose, who was trying to keep a straight face. When Bogie glanced at Walter, the old man quickly stood up and walked out of the room. He could hear Walter laughing in the reception area.

"So you think you deserve to go to the park today?" Bogie asked Isabella.

"I have to go! I'm a child. I require fresh air and exercise. You tell me that all the time, don't you Da-dee?"

꩜

After Darryl and Isabella set out for their walk, Walter came back into Rose's office and studied Bogie. Looking up from his keyboard, Bogie peered over his half-glasses and asked, "What?"

"Why does she call you Da-dee? Is that some Ukrainian thing?"

Bogie shook his head. "I never got to meet Isabella until she was three years old. Bailey had this Cambodian woman watching her. I guess Kim was coaching her on what to say when we met. She started calling me Da-dee, just the way Kim said it and it stuck."

Walter nodded. "How old were you the first time you stole something?"

Bogie thought then said, "About seven or eight."

"She beat you!"

"She had no justification for what she did."

"And you did?"

"Yeah. I stole food because I was hungry." Bogie thought about his youth on the South Side of Pittsburgh when he was still Boghdun Uchenich.

When he was eight, Boghdun ventured further down Carson Street into Schwartz's Market. To him, it was a glorious super-duper store. Boghdun's mouth watered as he looked at the fresh meats behind the large glass case, but the butcher holding a cleaver was a deterrent. Instead, Boghdun concentrated on cans of Spam, baked beans, tuna and sardines. He'd stuff one or two items under his shirt and dash for the door. One day while 'shopping' a tall, half-bald man with black framed glasses grabbed Boghdun by the shirt and dragged him to the back office. Boghdun sat next to him as Schwartz dialed the Number 7 Police Station. Unable to reach the boy's mother, the police were about to take him away when Schwartz asked Boghdun why he kept stealing from the store. Boghdun looked at him and said, "Because I'm hungry."

Schwartz spoke to the police. Boghdun listened as Schwartz explained that he just wanted to scare the kid and get the parents involved. One of the cops laughed. "Good luck! The mother's a barfly and the father's long gone. We pick this one up every few weeks."

"For stealing?" Schwartz asked.

"No," the cop answered. "For playing hookie. It's always the same: We get a call from the nun at the Ukrainian school telling us he hasn't shown up for a few days; we go to that dump where he lives, and his mother's either drunk or out. Then we usually find him in the library just sitting there reading like he owns the place."

"The library!" Schwartz exclaimed and shook his head. "Why?"

"He claims school is boring. He learns more at the library."

When Schwartz returned to the office, he told Boghdun that he would give him some food every day, but he'd have to work for it. Every afternoon, Boghdun came to the store and sliced open cartons and filled shelves. He swept the floors in the store and back office. Each day, the boy was given food, and never stole from Schwartz again. Boghdun didn't have to pinch apples or oranges any more since the fruit Jews were related to the market Jews. They sent over bags of bumped apples or bruised oranges for him. Boghdun still found it necessary to boost soap and toothpaste from the Rexall drug store and occasionally some underwear and socks from Woolworth's. But all in all Boghdun, the street urchin, came to believe he was the prince of the South Side.

Walter said, "Even if I was blind, I would know she was yours. She is a little Boghdun, but even stronger! If I had that child for six months..."

"Then you could have adjoining cells," Bogie said sourly. After a pause he asked, "So how's your application for a new TJ Maxx credit card coming along?"

Walter glared at him then smiled and finally burst into laughter. "Who said you had no sense of humor? That was a good one, Boghdun!" Walter had been hit with Federal conspiracy charges for customizing a packet-sniffing program for the leader of a hacking group that stole over forty million credit and debit card numbers from the TJ Maxx computer system. When the Feds came knocking on the head hacker's door, he gladly threw Walter under the bus and even gave them proof that Walter had been waltzing around the NORAD and CIA secure sites. They all went down, and Walter got to enjoy a long stretch in Lompoc.

18

A WALK IN THE PARK

BOSTON

Dressed in a white martial arts outfit, the man known as Stephen Traiger stood near the large screen TV as *Kill Bill 2* played. He watched while Pai Mei met the Bride for the first time. Traiger imitated Pai Mei's moves as he disarmed the Bride and thwarted her attempts to use kung fu.

The phone rang. Traiger paused the TV and turned as Linda Traiger came out of the bedroom wearing a black pants suit and a white button-down shirt. She answered the phone, looked at him, then nodded. "The limousine's downstairs."

"Call me when you've secured the limo," he said. "I'll jog over to their building and let you know if any of them leave their hidey hole. Stephen Traiger turned around and resumed mimicking Pai Mei's moves, believing his own were superior.

෴

People walking through Boston Public Garden stole glances at the enormous black man holding the hand of a small white girl wearing a black karate outfit. But since the odd couple obviously enjoyed each other's company, no one commented. Isabella ran toward the large brass duck followed by its ducklings. "Do you know what that is?" Darryl asked.

Isabella studied him with those icy blue eyes. "This is the mommy duck and these are her eight ducklings. They came back here to make their home. It's a wonderful story. Uncle George used to read it to me when I was little."

Darryl smiled as the four-year-old recalled the days, long ago, when she was young.

As they approached the swan boats, Isabella squealed. "I love these, Pop Pop! We'll see all kinds of wonderful trees and flowers. And that man will tell us stories," she said pointing to the guide.

Darryl nodded. "I'm glad we made it here in time. They'll be closed in a few days."

"Why?" Isabella asked concerned.

"They put the boats away in the cold weather and then bring them back out in April."

"But it's not cold!" Isabella protested.

"It will be…very soon. As soon as Labor Day's over, you can feel the cold air moving into Boston."

"I don't like the cold. Da-dee doesn't like it either. It's always warm in Florida, sometimes it's even hot. Wouldn't you like to live there, Pop Pop? You could see me every day."

Darryl grinned. "Maybe someday."

Isabella listened intently as the guide pointed out the botanical wonders of the garden. Isabella's eyes sparkled as they floated under the small bridge over the lagoon. Watching the little girl, Darryl thought of how much like her father Isabella was with her insatiable thirst for knowledge.

As they walked along the path and saw signs of the leaves turning colors, Isabella suddenly stopped, her mouth opened. "Listen, listen, Pop Pop!"

Darryl recognized the dreaded sound of the ice cream truck with its music like the Pied Piper. He allowed himself to be led to the corner of Arlington and Boylston where the white truck stood ready to dispense sugar and hours of hyperactivity to all the children. He was about to make up an excuse until he looked down at that sweet little face pleading with him.

Walking down Boylston Street eating their chocolate ice cream cones, Darryl's movements became slower as he felt the burden of the extra pounds he'd packed on. Isabella bounced with each step, fueled by sugar and chocolate. Suddenly, Isabella stopped and studied the traffic. Glad for the short respite, Darryl didn't bother to question the child.

By the time they arrived at the Frog Pond in the Boston Common, Isabella was fully charged. She quickly removed her sneakers and black karate outfit and jumped in.

Grateful for the chance to sit down, Darryl took out his cell phone, snapped pictures of Isabella, and sent them to Rose and Bogie.

19

ENEMY MINE

"It's exactly what I thought!" Walter said. "I traced him through six bounce points and still haven't reached his real IP address. I'll find him, but in the meantime we need to scan through the files. I believe he will be in your records...somewhere."

As Walter, Rose and Bogie sat at the conference table, they established the parameters for the new program. They agreed they would look for X through records which were less than ten years old but more than six months old. X would be the subject of an investigation rather than the client. X would be someone either very cunning or intelligent. They decided to leave computer capabilities out of the program in case X was teamed up with someone who had computer skills.

Bogie and Walter wrote the code, going back and forth, agreeing, disagreeing, changing commands. When they finally finished the program, they ran it and waited.

After studying the results, they believed they'd found their enemy, Troy Mentor.

As Rose, Walter, and Bogie were about to review the information on Troy Mentor, Rose's phone rang and Bogie's phone vibrated. They each glanced at their phones to receive a message entitled 'Isabella at Frog Pond.' Rose laughed and showed Walter her phone, the corner of Bogie's mouth twitched as he looked at the picture of Isabella romping in the water. He cropped the picture until he was looking only at Isabella's face. Bogie showed his phone to Rose. "Look at her mouth. She's been eating chocolate. Poor Pop. She must be driving him nuts by now. I'd better have him bring her—"

"No!" Rose almost yelled. "Let him be. If he couldn't handle her, he'd let you know. Being out with her is the first exercise he's had since he retired."

"But her clothes," Bogie protested.

"I'm sure they're somewhere within reach. I'd be real surprised if he brings her back in her underwear."

Bogie shrugged. "Let's get back to work."

They returned to the printout on Troy Mentor. He had been the director of the server division of a large computer company. He made a lot of money during the dot-com boom and lived well until his twenty-year marriage blew up. A handsome man, Troy traveled quite a bit for his job. He couldn't help it if women threw themselves at him every time he was away from home. When he returned home with a STD and shared it with his wife, he confirmed what she had suspected for a long time, that he was a repeater cheater. If Troy was a cheetah, his wife was a barracuda. She knew that he diverted money to offshore accounts to avoid taxes but wasn't able to get proof of it.

Linda Mentor's attorney retained R&B Investigations and a forensic accountant to find the money.

Once either Tommie or Bogie hacked into bank sites, they discreetly passed on the information to the forensic accountant who showed that Troy had squirreled away sixteen point four million dollars in various accounts.

With the help of her attorney, Linda sucked Troy dry in the divorce, and then his real problems began. The IRS came down on him like a ton of shit and his employer, a publicly traded company, started their own investigation. The Securities and Exchange Commission jumped onto the pig pile as everyone scrutinized Troy's activities and associates to determine the true source of that hidden cash.

When the smoke cleared, Troy was convicted of insider trading, embezzlement and tax evasion. The fines and legal fees far exceeded his post-divorce assets. Under the Federal Guidelines, he was sentenced to twenty-five years in prison.

As the small group read on, Bogie exclaimed, "Holy shit!"

Rose and Walter looked up at him.

"He disappeared the morning he was supposed to report to prison," Bogie said. "How did I miss this? I usually have a good memory for these things."

Rose looked over the newspaper articles on her screen then said to Bogie, "How did you miss it? Look at the dates! He was arrested around the time your father, Olga, and the baby were killed. After that, the cops tried their damndest to get you indicted for involuntary manslaughter." She glanced back at her screen and scrolled down. "When he was on trial, you were on your way to Florida. After the heart attack and surgery, how long was it before you even followed the news?"

"Months," he said softly.

Rose nodded. "If you remember, we were sailing our ship at half-mast during that time. Pop helped out while I was in Florida with you and Mandie. For weeks, none of us was keeping up with Troy or his escapades. When I got back, I felt like Smokey the Bear. I was stomping out fires all over just to catch up and keep us afloat."

Bogie touched her hand. "If it wasn't for you and Pop, we would have gone under a long time ago."

"I know! So let's get moving and find this asshole before he causes more damage."

As Rose spoke, Bogie's cell phone vibrated. Looking at the caller ID, he stepped out of the room. When Bogie sat down at Rose's desk, he said, "I thought you called because you missed me. Now I'm finding out you're just concerned because Isabella didn't email you today."

Bailey laughed then said, "I miss both of you. It's just that I wanted to make sure..."

"I know. I wouldn't let her use her computer today." After telling Bailey the story of Isabella, her stolen, downloaded movies and her rifling through her uncle's possessions, Bogie explained how Darryl took her to the park.

"I'm surprised you let her go after...My God! Forty times! She watched that movie forty times? And my credit card! That little shit! And Jack and George must be mortified!"

"I thought it was better to have some space between us so I could remember how cute she is rather than worry how she's going to turn out." Bogie sighed then said, "I miss you. I really do! And I miss the Hankster and his four-tooth grin."

"I miss you, too. I love you."

After a long silence, he said, "What is it you're not telling me?"

"Mandie's staying with us."

"Why?"

"I don't want to get into it over the phone. She's fine, Riley Rose is fine. She's working in the other office and just got a job as a lifeguard at the country club."

"And where's Randy?"

"He's still at his father's house."

"Let me get this straight. She and the baby are at our house. Randy's at his father's house. Who's living in that big pink elephant?"

"Right now, nobody."

"Oh, Jeez! They really split up?"

"I don't know, they don't know. She got the money from Ann and paid the taxes. Now she's working to pay her back. I think Randy is still hurt and sulking."

"I guess I should say I'm sorry I didn't pay the taxes, but I'm not. She was spinning out of control. I'm sorry it's come to this. So who's watching the baby while she's working?"

"For now, I am. When Mandie has a firm schedule, I'll get Randy and John to watch her too. The little ones are enjoying each other. Even your mother is having a good time. She thinks Riley Rose is Amanda."

Bogie smiled. "And I thought I had it bad here. You must feel like a zookeeper."

Bailey laughed. "Have my baby call me after she wears out Pop. I just want to hear her voice."

"I love you!" Bogie said and hung up.

☙

While her parents worried about her future, Isabella and Darryl strolled down Tremont Street toward the theater district. As they walked, Isabella shared the wonderful story of *Kill Bill Volume 2* with Darryl. "And then do you know what happened, Pop Pop?" Darryl shook his head and Isabella continued, "She took her little girl away in her car. They were in a hotel room and the girl was watching TV while the Bride was on the bathroom floor crying and crying."

"Why was she crying?" Darryl asked.

Isabella thought then said, "Because she was happy. She said 'thank you'...'thank you' while she cried."

Believing he could show the child an example of God's mercy, Darryl asked, "And who was she thanking?"

"Pai Mei," Isabella answered quickly.

Stunned, Darryl asked, "Don't you think she was thanking God?"

Isabella shook her head vigorously. "No, Pop Pop! Pai Mei was the high priest who taught her the Five-Point-Palm-Exploding-Heart technique."

They walked in silence as Isabella studied the traffic. Finally, Darryl asked, "Don't your parents ever talk to you about God? Don't they mention him?"

Isabella nodded. "Sometimes Da-dee says 'God dammit, Isabella, why'd you do that'? Mommy says 'What in God's name have you done'?" Distracted, Isabella stopped and stared at the traffic.

Darryl watched her and asked, "What's the matter, Isabella?"

Staring at a black Lincoln Town Car, she pointed and said, "That car was watching us when we bought ice cream. It was there when we came out of the park with the wonderful pond."

"How do you know it's the same car? There are lots of limousines in the city," Darryl asked.

Isabella pointed to the dark car with tinted windows. "See the sleeve coming out the door?"

Darryl studied the Town Car and saw material protruding out of the bottom of the back passenger door. After having cleaned the streets of Boston, the white sleeve was only white on the area closest to the door. Darryl used his cell phone to take a picture of the vehicle as it tried to inch closer to them. As the Lincoln came closer to them, Darryl picked up Isabella and zig zagged through the traffic until they reached the other side of the street. When they got to the intersection with Stuart Street, Darryl carried Isabella quickly down the sidewalk against traffic. Just as they approached Jacob Wirth, an old-fashioned restaurant with large plate-glass windows and wooden doors, the dark limousine reappeared, driving toward them. The Lincoln's passenger side wheels were up on the sidewalk as it made its own lane of travel. A waiter opened the door and smiled at Darryl.

Without speaking, Darryl rammed into the waiter and knocked him to the floor. As Darryl, Isabella and the waiter lie in a heap, the thunderous sound of metal and glass colliding filled the air. Darryl held Isabella down but looked up in time to see a woman wearing a chauffer's cap fall out of the Town Car's driver's door. The woman stood up and looked around as Darryl snapped her picture with his phone. Then she ran. The mangled limousine had a parking meter stuck through the passenger side. The patio's black metal fencing remained cemented into the ground.

Isabella reached up and touched Darryl's chest. "Are we okay, Pop Pop?"

Darryl smiled and nodded as he helped her up. The waiter, who was no younger than Darryl, was shaken. Darryl helped the old man up saying, "I'm sorry, Bill."

The man adjusted his toupee and said, "No problem. Are you okay, Mr. Jones?"

"I'll be fine, nothing a little wiener schnitzel with an egg on top won't cure."

20

GERMAN SOUL FOOD

BOSTON

Bogie, Rose, and Walter searched the internet for every scrap of information they could find on Troy Mentor, his associates, and his ex-wife. As they compiled data, Rose's phone rang. Bogie didn't pay any attention to the call until he heard her ask, "Are you all right? No! Stay there! Someone will come and get you!" After a pause she said, "I don't know!" Frustrated, Rose held the phone to her side and asked, "Does anyone want German food?"

༄

Jesús walked into the building with Darryl. The large man carried an asleep Isabella. There was a collective sigh of relief. Jesús placed white shopping bags on the conference table while Darryl laid Isabella on a mat in the practice room.

Bogie stood beside him and said, "Congratulations, Pop! You wore her out!"

Darryl nodded. "And don't think for one second that it was an easy feat."

When they sat down in the conference room, Darryl told them how Isabella spotted the limousine. "I've got to make a call and find out about that Lincoln."

While they ate wiener schnitzel, potato pancakes, and bratwurst, John and George Washington came in. Both men had gray hair and were built like ex-linebackers. They were usually referred to as the Washingtons or Black and White, the moniker they brought with them from the Boston Police Department. Rose, who was sensitive to people being distinguished by their skin color, always made a point of calling them by their given names. John Washington was white and George Washington was black.

Rose smiled at the men. "Any luck?"

They nodded and sat down accepting the paper plates Rose offered. George Washington said, "We checked out both EMT's. They confirmed that they called it into Boston Medical Center but got diverted to Mass General. Both said Tommie was clutching the laptop when they turned him over. I guess that was a job and a half. Tommie's a big boy! Anyway, they said Tommie had a death grip on the computer, but things got fuzzy after that. The black guy lives in Dorchester, and the white guy lives in Brighton." He handed a slip of paper to Rose. "Here's their addresses. Did Ken pick up a GPS signal yet?"

Rose nodded. "As a matter of fact, Ken got it just before I sent him over to Mass General. I was waiting to see what you'd come back with before I gave him the go-ahead."

The Washingtons looked at her and shook their heads. John Washington said, "Ken Nguyen's a little too excited to do snatch and grabs. You sure he's not moonlighting as a cat burglar?"

"Have you got a better way of getting it?" Rose asked irritably. "Check the schedule to see when Ken's available, and put Coco back on. She's been released from active duty at the hospital."

When all the men stared at her, she said, "The cops pulled her in. They finally got around to checking Tommie's MIT records and questioned how his dead mother could be sitting at his bedside. Jack Hampfield's with her now. Tommie's coming out of ICU so he'll have lots of visitors. We'll do a schedule. In the meantime, I've got Ken floating around the hospital as a maintenance man."

After the group finished eating, all that was left was empty paper plates and the bags the food came in.

While the others discussed Tommie's security, Darryl sat in Rose's office and downloaded the pictures from his cell phone onto her computer. He punched in a number he knew by heart. When the phone was answered, Darryl said, "Hello, Michael!"

Detective Mike Wislowski clicked his tongue then said, "When you call me *Michael*, you either want something or I've pissed you off."

"Actually, I thought I'd call a veteran detective and ask him a question."

Mike Wislowski laughed. "You talk'n to me? You must be talk'n to me!"

Darryl smiled then continued, "About an hour ago a Lincoln Town Car crashed into the front of Jacob Wirth's."

"Don't tell me," Mike said. "You were in there eating and want to know what happened."

"Not exactly. I was there all right, but the driver was trying to run me down," Darryl said.

"No shit!" Mike Wislowski said. "I'll see what I can find out. Are you all right?"

"I'm okay, but I want to know who wanted to run me over."

"Everybody loves you, Darryl. Nobody would want to hurt you," Mike said lightly but knew it was mostly true. After all, Darryl was the man who looked out for him for many years on the force.

"Except the woman driving that limousine," Darryl said.

∞

It was six o'clock, and they were still sitting around the table compiling information on Troy Mentor. Bogie opened his mouth to speak when he saw a little redhead popping in the door. When he looked at her smiling face, he grinned and stretched out his arms. He lifted her onto his lap and kissed her cheek. "Did you have a nice nap?"

Isabella nodded and looked around. "Where's Pop Pop?"

"You wore him out. He had to go home and rest," Rose answered.

Isabella asked, "Is Tommie better? May I go see him now?"

Rose smiled. "He's improving, but not today, Sweetheart. Maybe tomorrow."

Bogie speed-dialed a number. When the phone was answered, he handed it to Isabella. Her eyes opened wide. "Oh, Mommy, I have so much to tell you..." She walked out of the room and toward Rose's office.

The group resumed their work, knowing that Isabella would be busy for at least an hour.

Walter was the first to speak. "He's good, he's on the cutting edge. He was selling cloud computing when most people didn't know what it was."

Rose looked at him. "I've just become acquainted with it in the past couple of years and still don't know exactly what it is."

"Cloud computing uses centralized shared servers rather than on-site servers. It's supposed to cut costs."

"Maybe we could share a server with the NSA; then we could read their emails instead of them reading ours," Bogie quipped.

Walter nodded. "If only!"

His eyes getting blurry, Bogie glanced at his watch. An hour and fifteen minutes was more than enough time for Isabella to bond with her mother. He got up, stretched, and walked across the hall. Isabella was not on the phone but staring at the monitor on Rose's PC while her small hand moved the mouse.

"What are you doing, Pumpkin?"

Still studying the screen Isabella said, "I'm making the picture bigger." She pointed to the screen then said, "I knew it! The lady who fell out of the car was the one from the airplane."

Bogie moved around the desk and studied the screen. "Oh, my God!"

21

A GARGANTUAN PROBLEM

BOSTON

Linda's head snapped back as the gentle-looking man punched her on the side of the face. Troy Mentor - alias of Stephen Traiger hit her again before she fell. As the woman lay on the floor, Troy Mentor kicked her repeatedly. "Who told you to try to hit him? Who? Who? You stupid bitch! I told you to follow him and report on his movements, not wreck the limo! You exposed us needlessly, you dumb cunt!" Troy Mentor screamed as he continued to kick Linda as she curled into a fetal position and sobbed.

⌇⌇⌇

Rose and Bogie studied the picture on the screen. Rose said, "Didn't you recognize her?"

Bogie shook his head. "I didn't really pay attention to her. She was mousey looking with brown hair. The woman I remember as Linda Mentor was a flashy blonde with heavy makeup."

Rose nodded in agreement. "I saw her, too, and it never entered my mind. All I thought about was how odd it was that this plain woman had such an expensive piece of luggage."

Bogie's phone vibrated. He sighed and answered it. "I know, I know... yes...of course...I love you, too," he said before disconnecting. When Rose glanced at him, Bogie said, "Bailey's concerned about Isabella's safety. Being the gentleman that I am, I didn't mention that she was the one who..." He ended his statement when Isabella stood looking up at him smiling.

Bogie smiled back and gave Isabella a reprieve. He allowed her to start drafting the next day's email on Rose's PC. As Isabella typed, the group sat around the conference table trying to assimilate the latest information.

Bogie's phone vibrated again, and he answered it immediately.

Darryl greeted him by saying, "I just got a call from my friend on the job. He said the car is registered to Downtown Livery. It wasn't reported missing, but they're still looking for the driver. He was supposed to bring it back at noon and never showed up. They're searching for him, but think there's a problem. The white sleeve Isabella saw hanging from the back door was part of his shirt. The guy always kept a clean, folded shirt in the front, just in case. We can only guess how the shirt ended up opened in the back with the sleeve hanging out the door."

After Bogie ended the call, he looked at Rose and asked, "Is my gun still in the safe?"

"No!" she said quick, and loud.

When Bogie and Walter stared at her, Rose said, "It's there, but it hasn't been cleaned for years. Surely, you're not going to take it out in front of her!" Rose said emphatically, pointing across the hall to her own office. "You never wanted that gun in the house with Amanda. How could you dream of having it in the same house as this child?"

Bogie half laughed. "Desperate times, desperate measures."

"That's not desperation, it's insanity! If you really think you need the gun for protection, take it into your old office and clean it. Then go out to the police range with Pop tomorrow morning. Squantum is close to your place. Pop can take you out to the range for some practice before you start feeling you're bulletproof. When was the last time you fired a gun?"

Bogie thought then answered, "About eight years ago."

When Isabella had a pee break, Rose went into her office and took Bogie's 9mm Smith & Wesson and his shoulder holster from the large safe. Rose opened a cabinet and pulled out two boxes of cartridges, cleaning materials and a roll of Necco wafers. She dumped everything on the conference room table in front of Bogie as Isabella walked back down the hall.

Bogie studied the loot then yelled out, "Did you wash your hands, Isabella?"

Her sigh was audible in the conference room. "Yes, Da-dee! I'm a big girl now!"

As Isabella continued composing her email, Bogie took the gun, oil, and cloth into the small office and started cleaning.

Returning to the conference room, Bogie grabbed his laptop and typed in commands. "I just thought of something while I was cleaning the gun." He studied the screen then said, "The airline listed her as Linda Mentor on their computer. She was in Palm Beach for a week. Her original reservation had her returning on Sunday afternoon, but she cancelled that on Sunday morning. She didn't make a new one until..." Bogie moved into another screen and shook his head. "I made my reservation at ten o'clock on Sunday night. She made hers ten minutes later." Bogie closed his eyes remembering the small red car that had followed him. He typed in commands and went into another site. "Linda Mentor or Traiger or whoever the hell she is, rented a red Toyota Corolla from Alamo and followed me around for a week...It took me six days before I noticed her."

Walter sighed and folded his hands. "Boghdun, you don't have time for self-recriminations. These two, if there are just two of them, are far ahead of us. They have a plan, an agenda. We need to find out what they want or we'll all be targets for them. We can't do this alone. I need to contact my people."

With his elbows on the table, Bogie held his head with both hands. "The Becks?"

Walter nodded. Some said they were an urban myth, others claimed to be a part of the group. The Becks were a group of hackers who boasted that they were more talented and better organized than Anonymous or WikiLeaks but never proved it. Where other groups published government secrets and emails on the internet then spent years fighting off incarceration, the Becks flashed messages across secure websites. The messages generally read: FREE WALTER BECK or a variation on that theme. Walter claimed he knew nothing about the group, that it was formed to honor him. But the truth was that Walter Beck was the driving force behind the Becks. The Becks had no political agenda. They believed all governments were corrupt. The Becks endeared themselves to the media and the public by pulling off amateurish pranks. Only Walter Beck knew the true purpose of the Becks. They were a band of thieves.

As Walter frantically typed messages, Bogie turned to Rose and asked, "Necco wafers? You think I'm that rusty?"

Rose shrugged. "We'll see!"

⌘

Quincy, MA

The black SUV pulled in the driveway next to the white frame house and parked behind the BMW. Rose was in the driver's seat with Bogie next to her with a shotgun across his lap. Walter and Isabella sat in the back. Sitting in her booster seat, Isabella shared the wonderful story of the Bride with Uncle Walter.

"Do you want to come in?" Bogie asked Rose.

She shook her head. "I've got to drop off...the stuff...with Pop then Uncle Walter and I are heading home. Ken Nguyen and one of the new guys are going to drive by here a few times tonight so warn Jack and George. We don't want them calling the cops." Rose turned to the back seat and looked at Walter. "You said you wanted good German food while you were here. Now you've had it."

Walter argued, "That doesn't count. I wanted you to make it."

Rose's laugh was full and hearty. Bogie smiled as he listened to her. She finally said, "I think the last time I cooked was in 1999."

"You're bad! Your mother was a great cook. Gretchen made—"

"I know," Rose interrupted. "But look who she was cooking for. If I cooked like that, Pop would probably weigh four hundred pounds."

"Are you saying he doesn't?" Walter asked.

✺

With Isabella bathed and tucked in bed, Bogie gathered up their laundry and headed downstairs. He grinned when he walked into the living room and saw Jack and George sitting on the couch staring at the TV screen.

> *Elle Driver sat reading from a small notepad while Budd lie writhing on the ground.*
>
> *"The venom of a black mamba can kill a human in four hours, if, say, bitten on the ankle or the thumb. However, a bite to the face or torso can bring death from paralysis within 20 minutes. Now, you should listen to this, 'cause this concerns you. 'The amount of venom that can be delivered from a single bite can be gargantuan.' You know, I've always like that word 'gargantuan'...I so rarely have an opportunity to use it in a sentence."*

Bogie glanced at the screen and started laughing. Jack pressed the pause button and stared at him. Bogie stopped laughing and said, "When we were

127

flying here, Isabella told me how she liked the seats on the plane. She said they were *gargantuan*. Then she went on to tell me that wasn't a word she got to use very much."

Bogie sat on the floor, and the three men continued watching *Kill Bill Volume 2* trying to understand Isabella's obsession with that movie. Isabella sat in the upstairs hallway listening since she already knew the scenes by heart.

While *Kill Bill Volume 2* played in Quincy, it was also airing in Boston. Rose and Walter sat on the chrome and leather couch in her condo and watched:

> Bill: *"Pai Mei taught you the Five-Point-Palm-Exploding-Heart technique?"*
> The Bride: *"Of course he did."*
> Bill: *"Why didn't you tell me?"*
> The Bride: *"I don't know...because I'm a bad person."*

Walter sighed. "She's incredible!"
Rose glanced at him. "Who, Uma Thurman?"
"No. Isabella."

22

LOCKED AND LOADED

QUINCY, MA

Bogie sat in the passenger seat as Darryl drove his gray Chevy Suburban on East Squantum Street. Darryl waved to the guard outside the shack on his left, and the corner of Bogie's mouth twitched into his version of a smile. "I remember the first time you brought me out here. I couldn't have been more than sixteen. And the look on the guard's face when you told him I was your son!" Bogie recalled that day so clearly because it was the first time in his life that he had felt like he almost had a parent. Bogie had spent his first thirteen years with a drunken, sullen mother. After his mother died, Bogie was thrown at his father, who considered him a nuisance and let him know it. But being with Darryl, Bogie believed he'd found a real father. That was the day he tried to call him Papa as Rose did - but Darryl's quick glance in his direction caused Bogie to shorten it to Pop. Darryl became Pop that day, but neither of them would have guessed that within a year, Rose, too, would start calling him Pop.

Darryl nodded thoughtfully. "You won't see that happening nowadays. Everybody's hung up on security."

"But who the hell would want to go to the police shooting range anyway?"

"You did."

Bogie smiled and shrugged.

"And you wonder who Isabella takes after!"

Darryl put on his right turn signal and drove into the Dunkin' Donuts at the intersection with Quincy Shore Drive. When Bogie looked at his watch, Darryl said, "Jack and George won't begrudge us ten minutes at Dunks to have a coffee or something."

Bogie smiled since he knew how much Darryl liked his Dunkin' Donuts coffee. "No problem. It's just that they have to get to work, and Isabella will wear them out before they start the day."

As they sat at the counter, Bogie drank orange juice and Darryl added extra cream to his large coffee. After he covered the entire surface of his toasted bagel with an inch of cream cheese, Darryl took a bite and made a "hmmmm" sound as he chewed.

"That stuff will kill you, Pop," Bogie said.

"Hasn't so far," Darryl said in between bites. He moved on his stool then winced.

Bogie watched Darryl and finished his juice. "Are you okay?"

Darryl nodded. "I think I wrenched my back when I pushed through the door at Jacob Wirth's."

"Did you call a doctor?"

Darryl looked at him, rolled his eyes, and said, "I don't need a doctor to tell me I'm hurt'n."

Bogie tapped his fingers on the counter. Darryl noticed his fidgety nature and said, "Rose is right. If you don't run, you get all jittery and wound up. Why don't you go for a run when we get back to the house?"

"How the hell can I do that? What am I supposed to do with Isabella?"

"I'll watch her."

Bogie shook his head. "I wouldn't enjoy it anyway. I'd keep thinking that somebody might take a shot at me or try to run me over. And I'm not going to run with a gun. By the time I got the safety off, I'd be dead."

Darryl laughed. "No, you run. Isabella and I will follow you in my Suburban."

Bogie considered this. "Thanks. That'd be great."

Darryl nodded. "Now that I'm doing something nice for you, you can spare me a few minutes of your time."

Knowing what was coming, Bogie rolled his eyes. "We've had this discussion before. Nothing's changed."

"I don't understand it. I brought you to church the summers you stayed with us. You used to let me take Amanda to services every Sunday when she was growing up, but now you're raising two children, soon three, with no spiritual guidance in their life."

"I told you, Pop. I don't care one way or the other. Bailey's got this hang-up about religion."

"Even she went with us on Sundays sometimes."

"I know. She was never religious, but somehow she's become anti-religious. When I try to talk to her about it, she goes ballistic."

"So you just let these little children grow up without God?"

"Bailey claims that's the way she was brought up."

"But wasn't her mother Jewish?"

Bogie nodded. "And her father was Evangelical."

Darryl chewed and covered his mouth to stop from laughing. Finally he said, "Now that's a winning combination."

"For them, the answer was doing nothing. Bailey and Jack were brought up without religion. I guess she wants the kids to follow that path."

"And you have nothing to say about it?"

"I go along to get along. I've learned to pick my fights."

"I know you think Bailey is perfect and—"

"She's close enough to perfect for me. And, you know, Pop, I'm not the easiest person in the world to live with either."

Darryl put down his coffee and grinned. "You? Come on now!"

"I know! Hard as it is to believe, Bailey thinks I always need to be in charge and that I'm too concerned with keeping things neat and clean. I try to tone down my bossy side because I know I'll never live with a mess."

❧

The morning was overcast with a slight drizzle, which pleased Bogie as he pounded down the sidewalk next to Wollaston Beach. He didn't care if it was high or low tide; he only wanted to work off the frustration and fear that had crept into his life. Running had become a way of life for him, but now he couldn't even do that without Pop following in that enormous vehicle. As Bogie ran, he tried to figure out the puzzle. Why was Troy Mentor so brazen? Was he that much of a psychopath? Why would Linda Mentor team up with the ex-husband she flayed to the bone during a divorce? If they were together, what did they want? They knew about Tommie, and they apparently knew about him. If they couldn't slip through the portals of their computer system, what was their alternate plan? Angry at the turmoil in his life, Bogie ran with a vengeance.

23

DRIVING MISS ISABELLA

QUINCY, MA

Darryl glanced around while he drove, making sure his Smith & Wesson 1911 was secure on the seat beside him. Darryl believed he was moving at a decent speed, but he was slow enough that motorists on their way to work honked or gave him the finger as they passed him. Isabella didn't mind. "I love this car...It's gargantuan! What is this called, Pop Pop?"

"It's called an SUV," Darryl answered.

"We have an SUV. Aunt Rose has an SUV. But none of them are this big. If you don't have little children or investi-greaters, why do you have such a big car?"

"I'm a big man, I like a big vehicle. Besides, I use it during the week and on Sundays to bring people to church."

"Why?"

"Some of them are old or can't walk too good. Some are sick."

Isabella nodded and thought. "So you bring them to your church. And what do they do there?"

"Well, Saturdays we have a community lunch so that those less fortunate can have a hot meal. Sundays we have services and pray."

After a long silence, Isabella asked, "What do you pray for, Pop Pop?"

"I pray to thank the Lord for my family, for the people I love."

"Like me?"

"Especially you."

Isabella smiled and nodded, then glanced out the window and watched a woman fast-walking on the sidewalk as a white dog on a leash ran ahead of her. "Look, Pop Pop! Look at that beautiful dog!"

Darryl glanced quickly to his right and grinned. "We used to have a dog like that. His name was Patzo," Darryl said as he remembered the shiba inu that Bogie brought home.

Patzo had been abused then tossed out of a truck window on Morrissey Boulevard. Bogie picked up the filthy, whimpering dog and carried him to the apartment where he was spending the summer with Darryl, Gretchen, and Rose. Walter was visiting and regaling Rose and Gretchen with stories of his travels. When Bogie came in carrying the animal, Darryl wanted to yell and tell him to get the sick dog out of there. But seeing the desperation in the boy's eyes, Darryl understood how he felt. Bogie was frightened of losing Gretchen and somehow believed that making the poor dog better would ward off Gretchen's death sentence. Patzo was bathed and brought to the vet where his paw was set. He was such a good natured dog that everyone loved him, but he especially attached himself to Gretchen and followed her everywhere she went in the apartment. At night, he slept at the foot of her bed. After Gretchen died, Patzo walked around the apartment looking for her. The dog didn't eat and continued to sleep at the foot of the bed. Feeling sorry for Patzo, Darryl brought the dog everywhere he went. When Bogie joined the Army and left Boston a few months after Gretchen's death, he knew Patzo was in good hands. Two years after he was gone, Bogie received a Christmas card with a picture of Darryl and Patzo wearing Santa Claus hats.

After listening to Darryl's shortened version of how Patzo came into their lives, Isabella thought. "Who named the dog?" she asked.

Darryl shrugged and then said, "Your father did, I guess. He was calling him Patzo when he brought him into our apartment."

"How did he know his name? Was Patzo wearing a collar?" Isabella asked, remembering her departed cat Fluffy and the collar she used to wear.

Darryl grinned and started to laugh.

"What so funny, Pop Pop?"

"You're a smart little girl! And to answer your question, no, Patzo wasn't wearing a collar when your father brought him home."

"But how else would he know his name?" Isabella persisted.

"That's a very good question," Darryl said. "Maybe you should ask your father about it."

Isabella nodded. "I will. Definitely!"

24

YOU HAVE THE RIGHT TO REMAIN

BOSTON

As the two men walked toward the lobby elevator in Tremont on the Common, Rose was already opening the front door of her twenty-fourth floor condo. Rose checked out the men, noting their ill-fitting, wrinkled, sport coats over polo shirts. The taller, salt and pepper haired man smiled at Rose and extended his hand while his partner with wiry gray hair studied her. After checking their ID's, Rose sighed and asked, "Do you want to come in?" Both nodded.

Entering Rose's apartment, the detectives noticed the chrome and glass, black and white décor. "Nice place," Mike Wislowski said. When Rose didn't respond, he asked, "Who is that?" pointing to Walter, sitting at a small table holding a china cup to his lips.

Rose smiled at Walter. "This is my Uncle Walter. He's visiting me. Uncle Walter, these are the cops."

Walter nodded slightly, put down his cup and resumed eating his breakfast.

When Mike Wislowski smiled at the old man, Brian Freeman looked at Rose and said, "We'd like to ask you a few questions."

Rose gestured for them to sit down. The two men sat on the couch, and Rose parked herself in a white leather chair across from them. She took out her BlackBerry, set it on the coffee table, and pointed to it. "My attorney is only a phone call away. Remember that when you're tempted to ask me stupid or personal questions."

Michael Wislowski said, "As you already know, we're investigating the attempted murder of Tommie Jurgenson. He works for you?"

Rose nodded.

"How long has he worked for you?"

Rose said, "About four years."

"Do you have the exact start date?"

"I'll get it for you," Rose responded.

"He works for you full-time, part-time?"

"Part-time."

"What does he do?"

"He handles our IT maintenance. Fixes any problems we have with the hardware, does the software installations."

Michael Wislowski studied her. "How many people do you employ?"

"Twenty-two."

"And you need an IT guy from MIT to work on your computers?" Wislowski asked.

Rose twisted her mouth. "No. We need somebody to do the IT work. Tommie happens to go to MIT. That has nothing to do with our business."

Wislowski continued, "Your firm does what? Security? Investigations?"

"Both," Rose responded.

"So how many of your people are working security, how many are doing investigations?" Mike Wislowski asked.

"It varies. It depends on the clients."

"Generally, just give me a ballpark number..."

"Maybe half and half," Rose responded.

"So if you have eleven people working on investigations, why do you need so much computer power?"

Rose shook her head. "I'm not sure what you're trying to ask me."

Wislowski yawned and covered his mouth. "Sorry, I've been up half the night trying to get some straight answers." He paused then sighed. "What I'm wondering is why a small business needs a resident IT guy."

Rose looked him in the eye and said, "We're in the twenty-first century, detective. Everything we do is computer-oriented." She pointed to her BlackBerry. "That's a computer! We have schedules on our BlackBerries. We're on the internet, and... we even talk on these!"

Brian Freeman jumped in. "Mr. Jurgensen lives next door?"

Rose nodded.

"How long has he lived there?" Freeman asked.

"About a year."

Although he already knew the answer to his question, Brian Freeman asked, "And he owns the condo?"

Rose shook her head then said, "Since your people already checked with me before they went through the condo, I believe we can stop playing that game. R&B Investigations owns it."

"How much rent do you charge him?" Freeman asked.

Rose looked at him incredulously. "And how is this information going to help you find the person who shot Tommie?"

"Every little bit helps," Brian Freeman answered.

Rose rolled her eyes. "Nothing."

Freeman twisted his mouth. "And why is that?"

"We bought the condo as an investment and as a safe house. Tommie knows that if we need to put up a client for a time, he'll have to vacate."

Freeman persisted. "Who's *we?*"

"My partner and I. It is R and B Investigations," she said as if talking to a slow child.

Freeman glanced at his notebook. "What can you tell us about Charles Chatsworth?"

Rose stared at Freeman. "Nothing!"

"He's one of your employees and you can't tell me anything about him." Brian Freeman persisted. "I'm sure you know we picked him up at Mass General. He was impersonating Tommie Jurgenson's mother."

Walter said, "Ahaaa!" so loud that Rose and the two detectives stared at him. Walter smiled, then excused himself and went to his room.

Rose sighed. "Charles Chatsworth is Coco Chanel. She had her name legally changed but apparently forgot to change the information on her driver's license."

Mike Wislowski asked, "So he...she is a transvestite?"

Rose shook her head. "Transgender M to F."

Wislowski smiled. "You know a lot about—"

"She's my friend," Rose interrupted.

"That doesn't explain what she was doing at the hospital with Tommie Jurgenson," Brian Freeman said.

Rose stared at him. "If you want to go down that road, call Jack Hampfield. He's our attorney. Otherwise, let's drop it. Coco didn't commit any high crimes or misdemeanors. All she did was sit next to Tommie's bed."

"Protecting him?" Mike Wislowski asked.

Rose tilted her head. "If you say so."

"And Darryl Jones," Mike Wislowski added. "Somebody tried to run him down."

Rose nodded as both detectives stared at her. "I hope you are actively looking for that person."

Finally, Mike Wislowski asked, "So you and Jurgensen are...involved?"

Rose nodded.

Wislowski looked at her and smiled. "Lucky guy!"

When Rose didn't comment, Brian Freeman said, "I have the feeling that you and your employees are hiding something. Care to share the big secret?"

Rose grinned. "Then it wouldn't be a secret anymore would it?

Brian Freeman glared at her.

Rose studied the men and pointed to Mike Wislowski. "God cop?"
Then pointed to Brian Freeman. "Bad cop? Is that how you guys play it?"

Brian Freeman shook his head. "You don't understand. We're both bad
cops."

⚬⚬⚬

When Bogie and Isabella entered the R&B Investigations office, Jesús was
at the black lacquered front desk. Isabella smiled at him. "Good morning,
Jesús!"

"Oh, today I get 'good morning.' Yesterday, I got jack!"

Isabella came around the desk and kissed his cheek, glancing at the
.45 Magnum resting in the open desk drawer. "I'm sorry, Jesús. I had a very
stressful day yesterday."

"That's okay, cupcake, - everybody has one of those once in a while,"
Jesús said winking.

Isabella winked back then turned to Bogie. "But you still haven't explained how you knew Patzo's name."

"I have to think about it," Bogie said as he walked down the hall.

"Are you going to tell me the truth?" Isabella asked as she hurried beside
him.

Bogie stopped and looked down at her. "Have I ever lied to you?"

Isabella shook her head. "But you still haven't told me how you knew
his name."

Bogie sighed. "You're not going to let it go, are you?"

Isabella shook her head.

"I think he might have been wearing a collar with his name on it."

"And you took it off?" Isabella asked.

Bogie nodded. "Whoever tossed that dog out on the road didn't deserve him."

Isabella grinned then moved to her makeshift workstation in Rose's office.

25

FOR YOUR LISTENING PLEASURE

BOSTON

Bogie, Rose and Walter sat at the conference table, each with an open laptop and a stack of printouts in front of them. Walter glanced at the time on the bottom of his computer screen. "We're about an hour behind schedule, thanks to the cops."

Bogie looked from Walter to Rose. "How'd that go?"

Rose made a dismissive wave with her hand. "Not even worth discussing."

Walter smiled then said, "Charles Chatsworth! Wait till I tell Coco."

Rose shook her head. "You're just like a bad child!"

Walter smiled and tapped his index finger against his stack of printouts. "My friends were able to get quite a bit of information on Troy Mentor and his divorce. It wasn't possible to get much on Linda Mentor. She moved to Baltimore and fell off the radar." Walter looked at Rose. "Since you sent Coco there, we'll just wait and see what she turns up."

Rose nodded.

Walter flipped a few pages of his printout and said, "Troy's divorce attorney, David Halper, is dead. He was fished out of the Charles River about a week after he disappeared. He had an office in Court Square and lived in Newton. Halper left behind a cryptic note on his office computer but nothing else. The river was an odd choice for a suicide since it was nowhere near his office or on his way home. He was wearing the suit he had worn to the office the Monday he disappeared. He had bills, but nothing outrageous. He was on his second marriage with two kids. He was forty-nine. The wife's been hitting the bottle since he died. His father had a massive heart attack six months after the suicide. Now he's dead too. His mother's in a nursing home with dementia. His brother was killed in the first Gulf war."

Rose looked at Walter. "And Linda Mentor's attorney?"

"Linda Mentor's attorney is also dead. He was an associate at Rubin and Rothman. Jacob Samuels was found dead of an overdose in a room at the Boston Harbor Hotel. Samuels was divorced with one kid. He did not check into the hotel. A woman using what turned out to be bad plastic was supposed to be the guest in that room. The maid found him in bed with a syringe stuck in his arm. The woman was nowhere to be found, no signs she had ever been in the room. The whole place was wiped clean. He had a hot load of pure heroin. The cops who worked it originally figured it for a bad date with a high price hooker, but nothing added up. The woman's ID was fake, the American Express Platinum card was stolen but at that time the owner didn't even know it was missing. The whole case smelled. Everyone who knew the guy said it didn't make sense, he was straight as an arrow. Yet he ended up dead in a five-star hotel room."

Rose thought about Jacob Samuels then asked, "Did you speak to Pop about this? I remember him getting involved in some way."

Walter nodded. "I talked to him when he got back from driving this guy around." He pointed at Bogie. "Darryl said that Troy Mentor ran off when you and Boghdun were in Florida. Darryl spent some time here then. A couple years ago when this Samuels was found dead, Darryl remembered his connection to the Mentors. By then, Darryl was retired, so he called his detective friend. And that guy talked to the cops who were handling the Samuels investigation. Eventually they got together with the cops who worked the Halper suicide. Everybody thought there was some connection, but they had no hard evidence. The best they could do was flag the files and note that Troy Mentor was a person of interest. A few months after that, this news lady, Catie Christenson, did a piece on Darryl about how he was a retired cop but 'Still on the Job,' that's what she called that segment. Anyway, Darryl said she made the whole thing sound more successful than it was. He got his five minutes of fame, and the big, blonde lady got higher ratings."

"That whore," Rose muttered.

Walter stared at her, but Bogie looked down at his printout, trying not to laugh. Rose went ballistic every time Catie Christenson's name was mentioned because they had both been sleeping with the same married man at the same time. Rose saw nothing wrong with what she did, but considered Catie a whore. Bogie, wisely, made no comment.

Rose studied Walter. "Does Pop think that's why that crazy bitch tried to run him over?"

Walter shrugged. "He said he'd say yes if Troy was the one who tried it. But her? Why?"

Walter cleared his throat and flipped more pages. "Anthony Anderson. He was the forensic accountant. Anthony went on a singles cruise about two years ago. He went ashore in Freeport for a look around the city then vanished without a trace. Anderson's family put pressure on the Bahamian Government to continue the search, but the authorities used their resources to keep the whole incident quiet...bad for tourism."

Bogie and Rose stared at Walter, but said nothing.

Walter continued. "The judge in the divorce case is dead. He went into cardiac arrest in his chambers. Considering his age..." Walter looked down at the printout. "He was almost seventy years old so there wasn't this great outcry about him checking out in his prime."

Rose looked from Walter to Bogie. "And all these people are dead!"

Bogie shrugged. "People die all the time. Their deaths didn't occur at the same time or in the same place. I think the monkey wrench here is that people on both sides are dead...not just his attorney or her attorney. I can't imagine those two reconciling to wipe out all the parties involved in their divorce. It doesn't make sense."

Walter sighed. "As far as we know, the defense team he used for the IRS and securities charges are all intact. The judge is still around. That doesn't mean they're not vulnerable. Maybe he just hasn't gotten around to them. He or they could be working their way up the food chain."

Bogie said, "Mentor's obviously changed his appearance. He's had a nose job and some work around the chin. There appears to be weight loss. But he can't appreciably change his height. Let's look into the fingerprints. Not only his but hers. There's something really off here. The only thing Linda Mentor had that he wanted was a big chunk of his money. He apparently got control of it."

"How do you figure that?" Rose asked.

"He had enough money to finance and stage murders. That took some cash. Tommie's attempted murder looked like a botched up job, but now I wonder if he wanted to smoke me out. All those shots, and not one above the waistline. He could have killed Tommie with one bullet in the head or the heart. And this Linda character bought her ticket after I bought mine. I think that my having Isabella with me screwed up some plan Linda had for me. Isabella's ticket was purchased at the last minute so she might not have known about her until it was too late." Bogie sat staring at the table then said, "They knew I was coming here and how I'd get here. Mentor threw down the gauntlet, and I was too blockheaded to pick it up."

Bogie stood up and went across the hall to Rose's desk, moved some paperwork around and retrieved a business card. He carried it into the conference room and tossed it on the table. "Look at this! Black Hat Elite Entertainment. This guy's full of himself! He considers himself a Black Hatter and Elite. He handed me this card thinking I was too dumb to get his inside joke. And...that bitch! She sat with my daughter, touched her computer..." Bogie suddenly stopped and ran in the other room. "Pumpkin, I need to borrow your computer for a little while?"

"But, Da-dee, I'm—"

"I know, but it's very, very important."

Isabella nodded, signed off and handed the laptop to her father as she took her kindle out of the backpack.

Bogie dashed into conference room, pulling a set of keys from his pocket. He took a small instrument from the keychain and opened up the casing of Isabella's computer. He and Walter checked it carefully. After he closed it again, he continued to check the outside. "He could have attached something to the outs—"

Walter ripped a tiny red heart off the side as they all stared.

Bogie picked up the black business card and rubbed it between his thumb and forefinger. Walter handed him a knife, and he sliced through the card. Two thin silver wires were inserted in the card and blended with the silver streak design over the black hat.

Bogie held the objects in his clenched fist then motioned for Rose to open the safe.

When the safe was closed and the laptop returned to Isabella, they sat and looked at each other, working to recall exactly what had been said while the bug carried their conversations straight to Troy Mentor.

⚭

Troy studied his equipment and laughed. "It took those idiots long enough to find the bug on the kid's computer. Who in their right mind would give a four-year-old a computer and an email account? They have that little chatter box convinced she's some kind of super hero. That kid is annoying! It will be a pleasure squashing that little buzzing bee!" If only Two Ton

Tommie hadn't fallen on the laptop, life would have been so much simpler. How brilliant was that turd? He put a public account on the same computer that held a secured system. "Dumb, de, dumb, dumb," Troy sang.

He could have gotten all the passwords and demolished their whole system before Bogie the Booger knew what hit him. But not to cry over spilt milk. They brought in Walter! Troy was up to the challenge: close a door, open a window. Hopefully, Walter hadn't lost his touch and the old man was still a formidable opponent.

Troy had wanted to surprise Darryl Jones with his own deadly accident. But now that this silly cunt tried to run him over and almost ruined everything, Darryl Jones would be waiting for them.

Not to worry, they were all going down. And while they were falling, Troy Mentor was going to add at least seven hundred million dollars to his piggy bank.

The programs were set to run. Now it was show time!

26

REVENGE IS A DISH BEST SERVED DRUNK

SOUTH FLORIDA

When Amanda answered the phone, Zoe asked, "Where have you been? I've been texting and leaving messages, but you haven't gotten back to me."

"I was working," Amanda said slowly as if speaking was a great effort.

"Doing what?"

"I've been working in the new apartment complex in the mornings and just started lifeguarding in the afternoon and evening."

"Why?"

"Because I have to pay the real estate taxes," Amanda said.

"Have your father pay them."

"He won't."

"That sucks! Why's he being so cheap? He's got lots of—"

Amanda cut her off. "It doesn't matter what he has. It's our house and we have to pay the taxes. Period!"

"Did you think about what I said...about making lots of money?"

"No. What are you talking about?" Amanda asked.

"The movies. Remember!?"

There was a long pause before Amanda finally said, "I thought that was a bad dream! You know, I was drunk! If you and Tiffany are doing that...

Oh, fuck! That's worse than, you know...being a hooker! It's like doing it over and over again while one guy fucks you and others jerk off watching. I can't believe—"

Zoe pressed a button that ended the call.

∽∾

JACKSONVILLE

In Jacksonville, a plump young lady sipped on a McDonald's chocolate shake while she browsed her emails. Rhonda Gallagher opened one, read it, and then read it again in disbelief. She brought up a website and watched as her cousin played the part of a naughty schoolgirl while taking it up the ass. Tiffany's lines were limited because another actor came into the scene, and she began to give him a blow job at the same time. "This is the movies in Palm Beach, bitch!?" Rhonda asked the empty room.

Rhonda could barely contain her excitement as she composed an email to her uncle, Lieutenant Paul Gallagher of the Riviera Beach Police Department.

∽∾

SOUTH FLORIDA

When the once handsome man sporting a purplish drinker's nose came home from work four hours past the end of shift, he carefully parked his wife's new, red Lexus in the carport. Twelve shots of Jack Daniels tended to dull the reflexes. Paul Gallagher walked an almost straight line to the kitchen door and unlocked it. The house was peaceful and quiet, no Dee Dee there to drunkenly accuse him of hooking up with other women. With her safely packed away in rehab, Paul was able to take a leisurely shower to wash the smell of his latest groupie's strong perfume off his body. Clean and totally buzzed,

Paul Gallagher fixed himself a double Jack on the rocks and went into the den. As he sipped his drink and read emails, he put down the rocks glass and read the email from his niece, Rhonda. Trying to concentrate, he copied and pasted a web address and brought it up. The first thing he saw was the Palm Beach County Sheriff's patrol car. Then he recognized the two deputies even though they were wearing some kind of blue uniforms that looked like Halloween costumes. The blonde with the short hair looked somewhat familiar, but he couldn't think who she was with the guy's dick in her mouth. Paul Gallagher was so excited he almost wet his pants. This was what he'd been praying for, this was a sign from God! He was ready to bring down the whole fuck'n PBSO and prove to the world they were unfit to take over policing Riviera Beach. Paul Gallagher composed a rambling email and sent it off anonymously to six high ranking officers in the PBSO, including the Sheriff.

⚬⚬⚬⚬

South Florida

Zoe held the phone away from her ear as Billy Ray Marcel yelled at her. "I thought you said it was all set, and now you're telling me she *changed her mind?* You better get her to change it back! If that doesn't work, talk to Randy. You *know* he's got the hots for you!"

Zoe felt herself blush before she said, "You're just saying that."

"It's true," Billy Ray said sweetly.

"Well, if she won't listen to reason, I'll go visit Randy tomorrow."

"Atta girl!" Billy Ray said. As he hung up the phone, he muttered, "Dumb cunt."

27

THE FIRST WHEEL FALLS OFF

South Florida

The sky was clear as the women wheeled their babies through the large glass doors of the apartment complex. As they walked, Amanda saw Randy rushing into his father's house. Hurt that he didn't come over to say hi to the baby, Amanda continued on through the door. When the toddlers were settled, Amanda walked to her job in the office two blocks away.

Bailey felt sorry for her. She knew Amanda and Randy were both miserable and too proud to give an inch. As the babies bounced in their seats, Bailey saw a familiar car pull up in front of the Carpenter's house. The yellow Volkswagen Beetle convertible could only belong to Zoe Ziegler. Zoe's blonde hair was hidden under a pink baseball cap, but she wouldn't be mistaken for a boy. The cut off Juicy Couture top barely covered her breast implants while the short shorts started below the jeweled belly button and ended high enough to show off the bottom of her butt cheeks. The four inch Juicy Couture wedge heel sandals gave her the look of a sporty pole dancer. Zoe leaned against the front fender of the Palm Beach County Sheriff's patrol car while talking to Randy, who stood in the doorway of his father's house.

She slid her ass off the car, clomped over to him and stood with her body next to his. Finally, she gave him a kiss on the cheek while moving in close to his groin.

After Zoe drove away, Randy stared down the road and watched her invisible trail. Randy looked at the ground, then returned to his cruiser and drove off in the opposite direction.

❦

Randy sat at the computer in the den of his mini-mansion. He sipped straight vodka as he scrolled through different sites. The first site he checked out had Zoe giving Billy Ray a blow job. The Palm Beach County Sheriff's cruiser was used as a prop. The next one made his heart stop. Randy didn't know whether he should cry or puke.

❦

Tiffany Gallagher opened an email from her cousin Rhonda:

> "Kiss my ass *Love and kisses from the movies in Palm Beach*. I emailed your picture around to find out about your movies. You never said you were making porn movies. You can't act for shit! What's with the bare twat? I emailed Uncle Paul. He must be so proud of you!"

Tiffany covered her face and cried.

❦

Sarah Thomas sat at her desk outside the Sheriff's office and looked at her watch. She quickly logged off the computer and yelled out "I'm leaving, I'll see you in the morning!" as she hurried out the door. Day care sucked!

Those vultures charged her for every minute she was late picking up the baby and then gave her a lecture on punctuality. Money, money, money - that's all they cared about.

As she raced down the stairs, Sarah almost ran over some of the brass on their way up to the Sheriff's office. After quick acknowledgements and head nods, Sarah sprinted out of the building wondering what the big pow-wow was all about.

28

FINGER POINTING

SOUTH FLORIDA

Bailey sat at the desk reading when Randy walked into the office. Little Riley Rose looked up, grinned and said, "Da Da Da." Randy picked her up and kissed her. but looked miserable. On seeing his companion receiving preferential treatment, the Hankster immediately looked at his mother, reached up his arms and said, "Ma Ma Ma!"

With each one holding a baby, Randy sadly looked at Bailey and said, "I have to ask you something, and I want you to swear you'll give me an honest answer."

Bailey stared at him then said, "What's the question?"

"Did Mandie talk to you about making movies?"

Confused, Bailey screwed up her face. "I have no idea what you're talking about."

"Did she tell you she was going to make movies?" he asked again, louder than he had intended.

"No! What's going on? Why are you acting so strange?"

Randy's mouth tightened, but he finally said, "This is lawyer-client confidentiality."

"If you want our conversation to be confidential, just say so. We don't need to swear a blood oath, honest!" When Randy didn't smile at her lame joke, Bailey asked, "What happened, Randy?"

After Randy told her the story of their friends making porno movies, Bailey studied him then finally asked, "What's this got to do with you or Mandie?"

"Zoe said Mandie agreed to make the movies but was waiting for me to get in on the act."

"That makes no sense! Why would Mandie agree to do something like that? If it was for the money, she went to Ann for the tax money and is working to pay her back."

"What if Ann hadn't given it to her?"

"Randy! That's beneath you! She may have spent money foolishly or mismanaged it, but now you've decided that she'd degrade herself for money. That's unfair! She's your wife!"

"Zoe told me they got drunk and Mandie agreed to make the movies."

"When did this happen?" Bailey asked.

"Monday night."

"Where?"

"At the house...our house."

Bailey considered this. "You and Mandie had a fight and you left that day. Is that right?"

Randy nodded.

"So Mandie was upset and called her friend over. They had some drinks and she suddenly agreed to make porn movies?"

Randy sighed. "That's what Zoe said. Why would she lie? She's Mandie's friend, not mine."

"With a friend like Zoe, Mandie doesn't need an enemy in the world! I believe they might have had a few drinks but nothing else."

"I drove to the house and checked. There were two empty wine bottles and two glasses in the kitchen."

Bailey studied him. "And what does that prove? It only shows that two underage women got ahold of some wine. Where did the wine come from?"

"We had the cookout on Sunday. Zoe and Tiffany brought some over."

"This bimbo brings wine to your house, comes back the next day, drinks it then signs your wife up to make porn movies. Is that what you're saying?" Bailey asked.

Randy sat down while he held the baby. "I don't know what to believe any more? She lied to me for months. I wouldn't believe a word she said."

"Who? Zoe or Mandie?"

"Mandie."

"Did she ever mention making porn movies?" When Randy shook his head, Bailey added, "Then how or when were the two of you supposed to get involved in this?"

He shrugged. "Zoe said—"

"And Zoe, being the icon of truth, must be believed?"

"Why would she lie?"

"I don't know, but I strongly suggest you think carefully about what she's saying. It makes absolutely no sense! And why is it Zoe who's coming to you and not one of your deputy friends?"

"They're not really my friends. Their fathers are high up in the Sheriffs. My dad's always pushing them on me...like we're going to create some family dynasty in the PBSO." He glanced at his watch. "I've got to be on duty..."

"Have you talked to your father about this?"

Randy nodded. "He said to stay as far away from this pile of crap as possible. I just wanted to make sure Mandie..."

"Use your head, Randy! She's working day and night. When the hell would she have time? I don't understand why these four people are so anxious to involve you and Mandie in their dirty business."

"My dad thinks it might be unraveling and he's...I guess I can tell you... he's being promoted and going over to IA."

"IA?"

"Internal Affairs. He thinks that Billy Ray and JJ already know this through their fathers even though it's top secret."

Bailey smiled. "I think that's an oxymoron, top secret and cops. It just doesn't happen!"

Randy nodded but then said, "I swear if she's involved I'll—"

"Stop it! Don't start throwing shit until you have all the facts because it sticks and never goes away."

☙

Riley Rose and Henry were asleep when Amanda returned to the house from her lifeguard duties. Bailey sat on one of the sofas in the living room waiting for her. She could see Amanda was exhausted but said, "Sit down for a minute, Mandie. We need to talk."

"I'm so tired. I'm ready to fall over."

"I'm sure of it, but I think you'll want to hear what I have to say." Bailey then told Amanda the story of Zoe and how she went to Randy and told him Amanda agreed to make porn movies.

Amanda's hand shot to her mouth. "We got drunk, and she was talking about these movies. I picked up the baby and went upstairs. I put Riley Rose in her crib and I laid down on the bed. The next thing I knew you woke me up. I thought it was just a bad dream. I can't believe this! She told him I agreed. That fuckin skank! That's a lie!" Amanda thought for a moment then said, "I've got to get some rest."

Bailey nodded, but noticed Amanda speed dialed a number as she walked up the stairs.

Amanda's voice grew progressively louder until Bailey heard her say, "The answer is no..N..O! And stay away from my husband, you filthy slut!"

When the babies woke up crying, Bailey sighed and started up the stairs.

⌒⫘⌒

Sarah sat on her threadbare couch in her shabby living room. Little Bobby Joe finally fell asleep. She loved him, but definitely wouldn't have had him if she knew how much work mothering involved. Even with her mother watching him two nights a week and Bobby Joe spending a couple of nights with his father's folks, the toddler still wore her out. She stared at the blue lava lamp as she sipped her second rum and Coke. She remembered how she had wanted to get pregnant with that fuckin Randy Carpenter. That would have been some kid with that big, blonde stud for a father. But Randy started acting like he was too good for her. then hooked up with that spoiled brat Amanda. Was it her father's money? It had to be because Sarah was definitely more experienced in the bedroom. As her self-pity subsided and the alcohol kicked in, Sarah began to feel mellow. Suddenly, the phone rang.

Sarah looked at the caller ID, pressed a button then said, "What do you want, Paul?"

Paul Gallagher, feeling dissatisfied after a young groupie only gave him a peek at her fake breasts then split, said, "I thought I might come over."

"Not tonight," Sarah quickly said. "I'm really tired and need to get up early tomorrow. Something's happening at work, and I need to find out what's going on."

"I know what's happen'n," Paul Gallagher said slurring his words. "I wanna give you a heads up. Your brother's in deeeeep shit...Bad boy... Making dirty movies."

Her mellow totally harshed, Sarah said, "Come over right now, Paul. And you better not be shitting me!"

"I wouldnnn't do that," Paul Gallagher said, dropping the phone.

29

VISITORS – WELCOME AND UNWELCOME

BOSTON

As Rose stepped off the elevator, she held the little girl's hand. A thin man wearing blue surgical scrubs walked by them and winked at Isabella. Rose and Isabella gingerly walked down the hall and had almost made it past the nurses' station when they heard "I'm sorry but children are not allowed." Rose walked over to the counter and asked conspiratorially, "Do you have children?"

When the obese woman with short, orange-colored hair nodded, Rose confided, "This is Tommie's daughter. She's been extremely upset since he was shot. I promised her she could see him for just a minute."

The nurse looked at Rose. "For a guy who has no family, he sure has plenty of visitors. I thought he was single?"

Rose gave the woman a withering look. "And that means he can't have a child?" Without waiting for a response, she whispered, "She hasn't been sleeping, and when she does, she has nightmares. I think if she sees Tommie's on the mend, it will help her."

The rotund woman looked down at the little redhead wearing a pink dress and dark glasses. When the child smiled at her, the nurse said, "In and out - fast! I never saw you!"

Rose and Isabella rushed down the hall to Tommie's room. Since he was in a private room, Rose closed the door as soon as they entered.

Isabella ran to the bed and touched Tommie's arm. When he opened his eyes and smiled at her, she took off her glasses. "I'm in disguise." She pulled herself up onto the bed and sat next to him holding his hand. She seemed unconcerned about the tubes and machines surrounding him. Isabella kissed the top of Tommie's hand. "I was so afraid for you, Tommie."

Tommie squeezed her hand as tears dripped from his eyes and disappeared into his hair.

Rose put her index finger and thumb a half inch apart and said, "We're this close to getting your computer. Don't worry about it." When Tommie nodded, she added, "We're on high alert." She reached in her tote bag and pulled out a man's brown leather grooming kit with a large zippered top. "Keep this with you at all times. You can assemble it when we're gone. Everything's in the kit." Tommie nodded again. Rose reached in her bag and pulled out a BlackBerry. "It's a gift from me and Bogie. It's the Q5 you've been admiring. You can access Outlook with it." When Tommie's face colored, Rose added, "Bogie figured out that's why you were so worried about the computer. He said not to beat yourself up over it. He said he should have realized when you were emailing Izzy from an Outlook account that you had it on your laptop."

"I'm sorry," Tommie said softly.

"No biggie," Rose said rather than reminding him that she had warned the staff not to download free accounts on the same computers that ran on the R&B secure network. "Take care of yourself. Be careful! One of the guys will be here most of the time. Coco can't come back!"

"Good!" Tommie exclaimed. "She doesn't know when to stop talking, for sure."

Rose motioned for Isabella to get off the bed. The little girl kissed Tommie's hand again and jumped off the bed. "I'll email you later," she called out, then blew him a kiss as the door opened and the man wearing blue scrubs entered the room. He smiled at Tommie and softly said, "I understand you wanted to meet me."

"Oh, Jeez!" Tommie said then grinned. "So...it's you. You're Walter, for sure! I've been following you since I was in high school..."

Isabella sighed as she and Rose slipped away. She was glad Tommie was cheered up by a visit from Walter, but Tommie would have to understand that Uncle Walter was her uncle, not his.

⌘

South Florida

Laying the babies down for their nap, Bailey looked around the room and smiled. This was once Bogie's bedroom, his sanctuary. Although he shared dresser drawers with her when she moved in, everything about it was still his room. Even two pack'n plays and a changing station couldn't hide the fact that it was still Bogie's room.

As she walked through the bedroom door and into the office, Bailey glanced out the window and saw the yellow Volkswagen Beetle pulling up to the curb in front of the Carpenter's house. With a feeling of déjà vu, Bailey watched as Zoe, dressed in a white Versace camisole top with tiny pink shorts, got out of her car. Zoe closed the car and started to walk toward the house. Randy opened the front door and stood talking to her.

Bailey pressed a key on her cell phone, and Amanda answered with "Is the baby all right?"

"She's fine. She's sleeping. I just wanted you to know that Zoe is at the Carpenters showing off her ghetto booty again."

Amanda hung up without saying a word.

Two minutes later, Bailey saw Amanda run past the window toward the Carpenter house. She had the same determined expression on her face that her father sometimes got. Bailey ran to the window in time to see the shock and fear on Zoe's face as Amanda charged toward her. Zoe's mouth flew open as Amanda's long leg moved through the air. The white Nike running shoe slammed across Zoe's jaw with a speed that stunned Bailey. Blood poured from Zoe's mouth onto her Versace top. Her eyes rolled back, and she hit the ground.

Randy looked from Amanda to Zoe and started yelling at Amanda as he talked into his phone. He continued to point down the street and yell.

Amanda stared at him then slowly walked away.

When Bailey thought Amanda was back in the office, she called her. "Are you all right?"

"I'm fine." Amanda cried then said, "That asshole!"

"What happened?" Bailey asked.

"He kept yelling at me and telling me to get out of there."

"Why?" Bailey asked.

"How the fuck do I know?"

Bailey watched as an ambulance pulled up behind a Village of Palm Springs police car. Since they were spitting distance from the municipal building, it was not surprising. "There's an ambulance there now and the Palm Springs Police. Randy's talking to them," Bailey reported.

"I hope I broke her fuckin jaw!"

"From what I saw, I think you broke something! If the police want to talk to you, refer them to me. Do not speak to them! I'd rather talk to the cops here than drag the babies to the jail to make bail for you."

Amanda started laughing then sobbing.

An hour later, she sat crying over the state of her life as she organized receipts by unit number. The office door opened and Randy walked, in carrying paperwork. They stared at each other without speaking until he tossed a sheet of paper on the desk. "Read it and sign it."

"Give it to Bailey."

"She already read it," he said.

Amanda looked over her explanation of the event: It was an accident. When she saw her friend's car drive by, she thought Zoe might have been confused and thought she was working in the other apartment complex. Amanda locked the office and ran down the street after her. Amanda ran so fast, she was unable to stop without knocking her friend over. She tried to veer to the side and somehow her leg came up and hit poor Zoe.

"This is bullshit, and you know it!" Amanda exclaimed.

Randy swallowed hard then said, "You picked a hell of a time to become self-righteous." When she glared at him, he said, "I'm sorry. That was uncalled for." After a painful silence, he said, "I'll write something similar in my report. It was just an accident."

"First, you yell at me to get out of there, then you go along with this crap. What do you want?"

Randy took a deep breath trying to compose himself. "I yelled at you to get out of there because if you stayed and said something stupid, you would have been arrested. I wouldn't have been able to stop them."

Amanda looked up at him. "I'd say something stupid? You're being stupid! Do you think that bitch won't tell anybody who will listen that I meant to do that? She used to watch me kick box in high school."

"Why'd you do it?" Randy asked.

"Because I told that fuckin skank to stay away from you, and she wouldn't listen. I told her I had no interest in making porn movies, but she wouldn't let it go. She wouldn't leave you alone."

"And you thought I was such a dumbass I couldn't tell her to get lost myself?"

Amanda shrugged. "I was just giving you a hand."

"And a foot."

Amanda smiled. "Don't lie. She'll make a big stink, and you could end up losing your job."

Randy studied her then said, "I'd rather lose my job than my wife."

Her chin quivered. She looked down at the desk. "I'm sorry. I'm really sorry. Not about her, but about the money and…"

He walked behind the desk, turned her chair to face him and helped her out of it. He held her close as she cried. When she slowed down, Randy grabbed a box of tissues and handed them to her. After Amanda wiped her eyes and nose, he held her face in his hands. "No more lies! We do the budget together. Understand?"

She nodded. "I love you," she said softly.

He held her close and brushed his lips across hers. "I love you, too." he whispered just before his kiss became passionate. His thumbs slid down the sides of her breasts, and she moaned. As her hands grabbed his ass and pulled him closer to her, his tongue glided over hers. Their movements became more frantic, and the heat between them burst into flames. Randy glanced to his side, reached over and turned the lock in the office door. They walked into the small empty room behind the office. Amanda was naked in four seconds. Randy removed his gun, equipment, shoes and uniform in less than a minute. They looked at each other and knelt down. They tried to move slowly until their animal instincts prevailed and they made love with a ferocious abandon.

30

A SAD TURN OF EVENTS

Walter watched as Bogie and Rose sat across from each other at the conference room table. Rose stared at her laptop screen while she bounced the side of her fist on the table over and over. Bogie concentrated on his screen while the fingers of his right hand quickly tapped on an imaginary keyboard. Walter thought back to when Bogie was a teenager and Rose was an adolescent. They did the same things then.

Bogie's cell phone vibrated. He answered it immediately. "Hi! This is a surprise. You're not still worried are you?" He stood up and walked out of the room while talking.

Rose looked up. "He must be talking to Bailey. He's afraid I'm going to hear some mushy, gooey shit and make fun of him. Doesn't he know I have little miss eyes and ears in there to repeat every word he says."

Isabella, her face colorless, ran to Rose. Her lips quivered and then she started to wail. "Da-dee...he's crying. Our baby! He said our baby's lost..."

Rose grabbed Isabella and held her close as she sobbed.

Walter jumped up and went into Rose's office where he found Bogie talking on the phone with tears dripping down his face.

"I'm so sorry. I should have been there with you. You've been worrying too much...This wouldn't have happened if...Have Amanda take care of the kids and...What? Where the hell is she? I'll have Carlos or John go over there. Call an ambulance! I love you!" He hung up the phone and speed dialed a number. "Carlos, get over to the big office now. Bailey's having a miscarriage, and she can't find Amanda." He hung up the phone and punched in another number. "John, this is Bogie. Would you go over to the office now? Bailey is having a miscarriage. She can't find Amanda, and she's there alone with the babies."

Walter put his hands on Bogie's shoulders. "Boghdun! Calm down. Your wife is a young woman. She'll be okay. You, on the other hand, are going to have another heart attack if you keep this up."

Bogie rubbed his hands over his face. "I should have been there with her. It was too soon after..."

"Shut up! Woulda, coulda, shoulda. Now you're God?"

Bogie took a deep breath and sighed.

Walter squeezed his shoulders and said, "I'll tell you what you should do. Go in the other room and talk to Isabella. She heard you talking about losing the baby. She thinks her little brother is gone."

Bogie got up and went into the conference room where Rose was rocking the sobbing child. "The Hankster's okay, Isabella!"

Still sniffling, Isabella looked at him. "But you said..."

"We lost a new baby who was coming..."

Isabella studied him. "Why were we getting a new baby? We already have the Hankster. We might as well keep him since he's here...and I'm almost ready to start teaching him things."

∞

SOUTH FLORIDA

As Amanda and Randy lie in each other's arms, they heard the incessant pounding on the office door. The phone rang again. Amanda sat up. "I'd better go see who's there." She grabbed her tee shirt and shorts and threw them on without underwear. Amanda smoothed back her hair and unlocked the door.

Carlos stood with his fist still in the air looking wild-eyed. "Where the hell have you been? We've been trying to get hold of you for the past ten minutes."

Randy walked out of the adjoining room wearing only his uniform trousers.

After glancing from one to the other, Carlos said, "Get back to the other office now. Bailey's having a miscarriage. She tried to call you. She won't leave the babies alone. John's on his way there, but she won't go to the hospital till somebody is there with the kids."

Without saying a word, Amanda ran out of the office and down the street. When she got to the apartment complex, John was standing in the doorway. She asked, "Is she okay?"

"An ambulance is on the way. Where the hell were—"

Amanda ran inside before he could finish. Bailey lie on the bed in the room where Henry and Riley Rose were asleep. Amanda started crying. "I didn't know you were pregnant. I'm so sorry."

Bailey put her finger to her lips. "Shhh. It's nobody's fault. It just happened. I'm so relieved you're here. I was worried about the babies."

Two EMT's walked into the room behind John Carpenter. They checked Bailey's vital signs, then lifted her and the bloody sheet. They placed Bailey on a gurney as Amanda held her hand and cried softly. "I'll come with you—" Amanda started to say.

"No," Bailey said emphatically. "If you're with me, all I'll do is worry about Henry and Riley Rose. At least now I know they'll be all right."

Amanda said, "Okay. Do you want me to call Dad?"

Bailey nodded. "Tell him I'm okay. He took this pretty hard. He's on a guilt trip because he wasn't here."

John Carpenter watched them and began to volunteer to ride with Bailey to the hospital. But Carlos jumped in the back of ambulance with her.

As they closed the ambulance doors, Amanda cried. "I didn't even know she was pregnant. She's been taking care of..."

Randy who arrived in time to hear what was going on, put his arm around her shoulder. "She'll be okay. She's a tough lady!"

The ambulance sped toward Good Samaritan Medical Center, and Carlos held her hand. He squeezed it and smiled. "Aren't you glad you have me for company rather than that cracker?"

Bailey grinned.

"You know I have four sisters. Every year one of them is having a kid. Sometimes...this happens, but they have another one," Carlos said.

Bailey smiled. "I'm sorry if I'm making you uncomfortable."

"Me? Hell no! It takes a lot more than this to make me uncomfortable. Bogie's gonna be pissed at me, though. He told me to look out for you."

Bailey laughed softly. "And what was it you could have done that you didn't do?"

Carlos shrugged. "I don't know, but one thing's for sure. It's a good thing Isabella's not here. I could just imagine the emails!"

They both laughed.

Sarah Thomas sat across from Sheriff Glenshaw as he told her about the anonymous emails received. He offered apologies to Sarah and her family for the embarrassment the Internal Affairs investigation would cause them. The Sheriff assured his assistant and confidant that he would do his best to insulate her from the press and all other demonic forces.

Numbly, Sarah walked to her desk and speed dialed her brother's number. When he answered, she said, "Tell Zoe to stand down! Do you understand me?"

Billy Ray sighed. "It's too late. Amanda put her in the hospital."

Sarah whispered into the phone, "We'll talk tonight!"

31

THOSE LITTLE HANDS

SOUTH FLORIDA

Bailey opened her eyes and smiled at Carlos, who sat in a chair next to the bed. A tanned, gray-haired man stood at the foot of the bed. He tapped keys on his handheld computer then asked, "How are you doing?"

"I'm a little groggy and..." She touched her abdomen.

"You'll probably have cramps for an hour or so. Take two Tylenol or ibuprofen and you'll be okay. The D & C went fine. You're bleeding now. That's normal. Use sanitary pads, not tampons. No intercourse for two weeks. If anything unusual happens, call the office. Otherwise, make an appointment, and I'll see you in two weeks."

"That's it? I don't have to stay?" Bailey asked.

"Not if the insurance company has anything to say about it. Take it easy for a few days, no heavy lifting," Dr. Spiegel advised.

"Sure! Tell that to the Hankster. He loves to be picked up and held."

"He's what, about a year old now?"

"In a few weeks."

⌀⟶⟶⟶⌀

As Carlos helped Bailey from the wheelchair and into his bright red Mazda Miata, she asked, "How'd your car get here?"

170

"When you were in the operating room, I went home and got it."

As she sat back in the seat, she closed her eyes.

Pulling out into traffic, Carlos glanced over and found that Bailey's eyes were still closed, but she was crying. "You okay? Are you in pain?"

Bailey shook her head and took the tissue Carlos offered her. "It's just that I think this is God's way of punishing me."

"Hel-lo! If He was into punishing people, I'd be dust on the sidewalk by now. Miscarriages happen a lot, and you've already had two kids, so you know you don't have any problems in that department."

"I didn't want to have a baby when I was pregnant with Henry. But nothing was going to end that pregnancy. And now...when I realized I was pregnant...I thought it was a good thing...maybe Bogie would have his own son."

"He does - Isabella!" Carlos reminded her.

Bailey smiled. "You're not going to get over that bride doll are you?"

Carlos glanced over at Bailey and grinned. When Isabella's fourth birthday was approaching, he had racked his brain trying to think of a nice gift. He had nieces and knew what they liked, but he had to admit Isabella was different. When Amanda moved into her own house and took all the dolls she had collected over the years, Carlos was surprised. Surely she could have shared a few with her little sister. Overhearing Isabella talk about the Bride, Carlos thought he had stumbled onto the perfect gift and bought her a Madame Alexander bride doll for her birthday. The look of horror on Isabella's face when she opened the large blue box could not be disguised. Although she thanked him after being prodded by her mother it was obvious she hated the gift. Days later, Bailey explained to Carlos that the Bride was the part Uma Thurman played in *Kill Bill,* and Isabella didn't like dolls. Amanda had offered to give her the doll collection, but Isabella refused, saying they were like little dead people.

⚛

Boston

Rose sat at her desk, listening as Coco reported by phone.

Coco pushed her long blonde hair away from her face and held the phone close. "Linda Mentor moved here after the divorce, but just before Troy Mentor disappeared, Linda started getting rid of everything. She took a loss on the house and the business. She had a boutique and seemed to be doing okay. She had about a quarter million invested in inventory, but suddenly sold it all to some liquidators for forty thousand. This woman was in a hurry to get out of town and burn all her bridges on the way out!"

"Didn't she have any friends or acquaintances she talked to?"

"From what I gathered she was one of the nastiest human beings who walked the earth and didn't go out of her way to get along with anyone."

"And she owned a boutique?" Rose asked, surprised.

"She had a couple of salespeople who took care of the customers; otherwise, she probably wouldn't have sold a thing."

"Exactly how long before Troy Mentor took off did Linda sell everything?"

Coco looked at her notes. "Sixteen days."

Rose thought. "So unless she was an oracle, Linda Mentor knew her ex-husband was going to take off. Could she have acting out of fear?"

Coco considered this then said, "I don't think so. It sounds like she was the kind of woman pit bulls feared."

"Did she change anything before she left? Hair color, wardrobe?"

"Not so that anyone noticed."

"And she cut off all her contacts in Massachusetts?" Rose asked.

Coco said, "She did that before she moved here. She had an up and down relationship with her sister. At the time of the divorce, it went down and stayed down. Linda Mentor never had anything to do with her half-brother. Parents both dead and no other family."

As Rose listened, Bogie looked up from his laptop and watched Isabella with her small fingers moving over the keyboard. He smiled then glanced at the picture of Linda Mentor on his screen. He studied the picture then yelled out, "Christ on a crutch!"

Rose and Isabella both looked up at him.

"That's it!" he exclaimed. "She's an imposter!"

Rose said to Coco, "I'll call you back in a while." She stared at Bogie. "What are you screaming about?"

"She's not Linda Mentor!" Bogie called out.

"And you know this because?"

"The hands. I knew there was something that was stuck way in the back of my mind! Remember when we met her in her attorney's office?" When Rose nodded, he continued, "She was attractive enough, well dressed and skinny. But she had these big hands and feet. It was almost like she starved herself to be thin but couldn't change the size of her hands. That's why I didn't recognize the woman on the plane: it wasn't that she downgraded her appearance; she's not Linda Mentor! This woman was thin, but her hands and feet were proportional to the rest of her body. Those are things that don't change with plastic surgery. The hair was different, but that's easy to change. She was wearing glasses most of the time, and I wasn't really looking at her that close. Now it all makes sense. He gets somebody to look like her, take over her life and then disappear with a chunk of money...his money!"

Bogie's phone vibrated. He grabbed it and looked at the caller ID. "Hello," he answered stiffly.

"It's Mandie. I just wanted to let you know that Bailey's all right. She was taken to St. Mary's. She lost the baby, and Dr. Spiegel did a D & C."

"Thanks for the update," he said coldly.

"I'm sorry. I'm sorry she lost the baby. She never told me she was pregnant, and she's been..." Mandie started crying. She sniffled then said, "And I'm sorry for the things I said. You know I didn't mean them." When he didn't say anything, she repeated, "I really didn't. I love you. I'm sorry."

"I love you too, Princess. What's going on with you and Randy?"

"We're okay now, but we're going to be staying with Bailey till you get back. She's not supposed to lift anything for a few days and that's hard to do when there's a baby in the house."

"She's out of the hospital?" he asked.

"Yep. Carlos is bringing her home now. Oh, you need to get rid of the mattress on the bed. Do you want me to take care of that?"

"Just call that 800-mattress place. Tell them to deliver a mattress and take the old one away. Get the same one that's there. Maybe for the next few days, you should work in the big office and have Carlos take charge of the small one."

"Oh shit!"

"Why? What's the matter?" Bogie asked.

"It's taken me all this time to get everything organized, and now he'll screw it up again."

Bogie laughed. "Switch the telephone over to the big office. Tell Carlos just to stop by the other office at the beginning and end of the day. He can stay at the construction site."

"Da-dee!" Isabella yelled. "Da-dee!"

"I've got to go, we have a problem here. Love you!"

"Love you more!"

Bogie looked over at Isabella. Her eyes were wide as she pointed to her laptop screen in horror. There was a picture of an old man with long white hair and a matching beard. His white eyebrows stuck out two inches from his face. The man's long hair was knotted on top of his head and held in place with a chopstick. He was truly Pai Mei. His long pointed beard was twirled around his hand. The head priest sat on a table wearing ornate robes. The caption under the picture read, "*YOU WILL DIE SOON, ISABELLA!*"

32

PLOTTING AND SCHEMING

BOSTON

As Isabella stood with her mouth agape, Bogie grabbed her laptop and typed in commands. The confused child turned to Rose, but before she could complain, Rose said. "Why don't you use my PC."

"But...did you read what that said?" Isabella asked in a shaky voice.

Rose nodded. "Do you think that we'd let someone – anyone - hurt you?"

Isabella shook her head and walked to Rose's desk.

Walter took the laptop, studied the screen and then motioned for Bogie to move into the conference room. "He had to do it, come out bragging! You said he was a show-off."

"I said he was a megalomaniac," Bogie corrected.

"Whatever," Walter muttered. "Now it's our turn to run down that bastard and find out what he's up to. Remember, sign in as Thor; I'm Zeus."

As they signed into the elite chat room, Bogie smiled. Walter had given him the name Thor, the god of war, while Walter's handle was Zeus, the king of the gods. Bogie felt like he was about to enter an online game rather than The Becks site. Less than fifteen minutes after they signed in, nine more hackers joined them. Although the group was only comprised of Walter and nine other members, they agreed to give Bogie a pass for this special project.

Eleven hackers began their work, knowing that lives were at stake and possibly something more important, money.

☙❧

SOUTH FLORIDA

Tiffany was alone on the set with Billy Ray and JJ since Zoe was too banged up to perform that night. Billy Ray finished first. He walked out of Sarah's living room and went to take a shower. Once JJ came on Tiffany, she headed for the bathroom so she, too, could take a shower.

Loud voices from the livingroom were easily heard although the shower was running. Tiffany listened as Sarah, Billy Ray and JJ seemed to be trying to out-shout each other. Billy Ray yelled, "What the fuck did he do that for?"

"He was drunk and thought he was protecting his job. His niece sent him an email telling him about the sites," Sarah answered defensively.

"Oh, that's fuckin great!" Billy Ray said. "That old horndog screws us over and we're supposed to make nice with him. We'll probably end up getting fired over this!"

"Not if you play your cards right," Sarah cautioned. "First, get your union reps lined up. Then shut up! Don't say a word until you're with your rep."

JJ pointed to the bathroom door. "What did he say about his daughter being in the movies?"

Sarah laughed. "Paul was so wasted he didn't realize Tiffany was in the movies. I think he just watched the first few scenes. He thought Zoe looked familiar, but, as of last night, he didn't recognize her either."

They all laughed until Billy Ray said, "I'll bettcha when he sobers up he'll watch the movies again. He'll recognize them for sure."

"So what!" Sarah said. "That's their problem, not ours. Just remind the girls to keep their mouths shut."

Billy Ray studied his sister. "And what about us?"

Sarah grinned. "I think we can dump this whole thing on Randy. If you're asked anything, answer it by saying 'I don't know, ask Randy Carpenter.'"

JJ said, "I don't see how that's going to help us. He'll deny everything."

Sarah nodded knowingly. "Of course, but nobody'll believe him. Besides, his old man's going over to IA, he'll be on the Rat Squad. Let Daddy Carpenter take care of this for his baby boy! That could be his first assignment, sweep this whole thing under the rug and make it go away."

"Whew!" JJ said. "You really hate that guy! What the hell did he ever do to you?"

"He dumped me and hooked up with Amanda just because her father's rich," Sarah said.

"I didn't even know you and Randy were together. When was that?" Billy Ray asked.

"A while back, when he first moved here. I had big plans for us."

JJ said, "You fuckin women are vicious! So we're supposed to say that Randy was behind this whole thing."

Sarah nodded and the men laughed as Tiffany shivered listening to it all.

⚮

For a change of pace, Paul Gallagher came straight home after work. The hangover he nursed all day had something to do with it, but he also wanted to take another look at the movies.

Paul turned on his PC then grabbed a fresh bottle of Jack Daniels and a rocks glass. He threw a couple of ice cubes in the glass and carried it and the bottle into the den.

Paul sucked down his drink as he watched one of the movies. Billy Ray and JJ with their silly blue costumes on, then off. And there she was...the blonde with the short... Zoe! Zoe Ziegler! Paul held the glass with a death grip as he watched the entire movie. The naughty schoolgirl wearing a short skirt and no underwear entered the frame. Paul's mouth dropped open. He watched his daughter giving Billy Ray a blow job while JJ fucked her up the ass. Paul felt the pounding through his head and chest as the rage consumed him. He pitched the half-empty glass through the display case of his football trophies and memorabilia. "You dirty whore! You drop your pants and take pictures fucking these useless sacks of shit. After all I've done for you, this is how you repay me? You've ruined my career! I'll kill you, you bitch."

33

DEMOLITION DERBY

SOUTH FLORIDA

Martin Ziegler glanced over at Tiffany as he drove. Tiffany sat rigidly in her seat. "It was nice of you to come to the hospital to see Zoe. I don't understand this! Her friend? Her friend broke her cheekbone and two teeth? And who the hell is supposed to pay for this? And look at her!... all black and blue and swollen. Zoe's supposed to meet somebody...next week."

Tiffany bit down on her index finger as the balding man continued. "I'm going to talk to Amanda's father, let him pay the hospital bill. That McGruder has more money than God! Not so as you'd know it by the way he lives, but he owns more real estate in Palm Springs than ten other people put together."

As they approached Tiffany's apartment complex on Kirk Road, they saw the flashing lights and police vehicles in front of the stucco building. The cops were gathered around a red Lexus outside Tiffany's first floor apartment. Tiffany recognized her mother's car. Since Dee Dee Gallagher was still in rehab, Tiffany was sure her father drove the ES350 without Dee Dee's knowledge or consent. The almost new Lexus had crashed into Tiffany's pink Hyundai and pushed it through her front door. Tiffany watched as EMT's extricated a belligerent Paul Gallagher from the wreckage. When Tiffany identified herself and ran toward the scene, Paul glared

180

at her as he was being strapped to a gurney. "You whore! You douche bag! I paid for this fuckin apartment so you..."

Tiffany's eyes welled up with tears as she watched the ambulance carrying her father speed away while he cursed the day she was born.

Martin Ziegler stood next to Tiffany looking over the scene. "What's going on here? Why was your father talking like that? Why did he do this?"

"Don't pay any attention to him. He's just drunk again," she sniffled.

34

MISERY LOVES COMPANY

SOUTH FLORIDA

After he was discharged from the Emergency Room, Paul Gallagher walked outside to hail a cab. His cell phone rang - the captain wanted to see him. Still legally drunk but running on adrenaline and survival instincts, Paul grabbed a cab, went home, then took a shower, and changed clothes while the cabbie waited.

The meeting with the captain was short but not sweet. Paul agreed to take some leave while the department sorted out the mess he created when he demolished two vehicles, one of them very pricey. And then there was all that damage to the building that housed an apartment with his name on the lease. The captain was sympathetic to Paul's situation, knowing that his wife was in rehab again and his daughter had become notorious for her acting skills. Captain Meyers would have been less understanding if he knew it was Paul Gallagher who started the whole shit storm over the PBSO porno movies.

⁊⟋⟋⟋⟍

With nothing to do and lots of time to do it in, Paul rummaged through the desk in his den and found a telephone number he hadn't used in years. The last time he called Martin Ziegler's cell phone was when Tiffany and

Zoe had been involved in a cheating scandal at the Benjamin School. And now here they were again. Paul Gallagher didn't believe that Martin could do anything about the pornography scandal, but it warmed Paul's heart to know that he could pass on some misery to another human being.

35

THE OTHER WHEEL FALLS OFF

SOUTH FLORIDA

Tiffany Gallagher looked at her wrecked car and watched as investigators tossed aside the crushed wooden door from her apartment. She knew her life was crumbling around her. The car was destroyed; the apartment was damaged, and it wasn't even hers - it was rented in her father's name and paid for by him. Tiffany had nothing...no job, a little bit of money, and lots of fancy pink clothes and shoes.

After the police left, Tiffany packed up what she could carry and called a cab. She knew Zoe would have the answers.

When the taxi stopped in front of Zoe's townhouse apartment in City Place, Tiffany got out carrying two suitcases. She rang the bell and pounded on the door for almost ten minutes before Zoe answered it. Zoe looked wretched. Both eyes were black and the side of her jaw was discolored and swollen. Zoe stared at Tiffany without speaking, tears rolling down her face. The women embraced and walked inside crying.

‿‿‿

As the deputies were falling in for their morning lineup Billy Ray Marcel turned to Jim "JJ" Johnson and said sotto voce, "There's my man, Randy the Dong?"

Other deputies snickered as Randy's face reddened.

Randy turned to Billy Ray. "Shut the fuck up!"

Billy Ray looked at JJ and said, "Do you smell something? I think I smell rat shit..."

As the last words came out of Billy Ray's mouth, he was silenced by Randy's fist. A second blow hit Billy Ray between the eyes. JJ jumped in and punched Randy on the side of the neck. Then the real fight began. It took six other deputies to separate the men as Sheriff Ron Glenshaw ran downstairs from his office. He pointed at Billy Ray who had blood pouring from his mouth and nose. "Get him to the ER!" The sheriff motioned to Randy and JJ. "Upstairs!" He glared at the group. "And no one here better tell me he didn't see anything."

⁂

With deputies on either side of him, Billy Ray was escorted into the Emergency Department of Palms West Hospital. Walking toward the reception desk, the group was almost run down by EMT's pushing a gurney with Billy Ray's father, Lieutenant William Ray Marcel, II, who had been extricated from his unmarked service vehicle after he drove it into a canal in front of his house. Reeking of alcohol, Lieutenant Marcel bellowed and cursed as he was wheeled down the hall.

Within an hour, both Marcels were heading back to Gun Club Road. Billy Ray, III, had eight stitches in his face and a broken nose. His father, Billy Ray, II, was in handcuffs and under arrest for suspicion of drunk driving. As they drove toward the barracks, an ambulance carrying Billy Ray's grandfather, Captain William Ray Marcel, I, was racing toward Palms West Hospital where Grandpa Marcel would be treated for a heart attack.

Lieutenant Marcel was placed on administrative leave with pay pending an Internal Affairs Investigation. Billy Ray and JJ were also placed on leave with pay pending an Internal Affairs Investigation. Randy was suspended without pay for starting the fight. He, too, was made part of the Internal Affairs Investigation into the porn movies.

36

SOCIAL MEDICINE

Bogie parked the black SUV in the tiny parking lot adjacent to 15 North Beacon Street in Allston. As he and Isabella climbed the stairs to the front of the building, she looked apprehensive. Bogie held her hand. "It's okay, Pumpkin. We're just going to visit Mr. James and Mrs. Trudie." The now retired couple had served the McGruder family in their Beacon Street home for more than forty years. When thirteen-year-old Boghdun Uchenich was thrust on his father, it was James and Trudie who showed the boy the only compassion he'd ever know in that house.

Bogie was aware of Isabella's fear of this building. This was the same building where she and Bailey had stayed when their bodyguard was shot and Isabella was abducted. Isabella tried to smile, but Bogie knew she was still uncomfortable.

When the old woman opened the door to the second floor condo, she grinned as she studied Isabella in her black martial arts costume. The short, round lady hugged Isabella then embraced Bogie. James, frail and barely able to stand, made his way off the couch and did the same.

"You're so lovely!" Trudie exclaimed. "And a black outfit now, oh my goodness!"

Bogie went back to the Escalade and retrieved bags of groceries and wrapped packages. "Our house warming gifts for you," he explained. Bogie helped James back to his seat on the couch and handed him a large brown bag. "For those cold nights!"

The old man smiled. "It's really comfortable here summer and winter. I use my cane and we walk out onto the street and visit the small shops. There are quite a few little restaurants here too. We're very grateful—"

Bogie waved him off. "It was Ann—"

"With your help...we truly appreciate it. You don't have to send money..."

Bogie dismissed him again as Isabella explained that they had to come to Boston to visit Tommie and find the bad man who was trying to ruin their computers. "And we lost a baby, but not the Hankster...a new one nobody told me about. We're still keeping the Hankster. He's going to be one year old."

The old couple beamed as they listened to Isabella chattering away. "I could email you and tell you things all the time if you give me your email address."

Confused, James looked at Bogie.

Bogie asked, "You don't have a computer, do you?"

The couple shook their heads simultaneously. Bogie turned to Isabella. "You'll have to communicate the old fashioned way. Write down Mr. James and Mrs. Trudie address and send them letters."

"She reads and writes?" Trudie asked.

"Of course! I read to Grandma all the time," Isabella answered for him.

James asked, "How's she doing?"

Isabella answered again, "Grandma likes when I read to her, but she calls me Jennifer. That's okay because she calls the Hankster *Bud* and holds him and kisses him."

When the couple stared at Bogie, he said, "That just about sums up how she's doing!"

"She's still in the apartment?" James asked.

Bogie nodded. "She needs twenty-four/seven care now, but she's happy enough. She sees the kids every day, and now I understand that they've added a new member to the children's afternoon tea group, little Riley Rose." Bogie reached in his pocket and took out his cell phone. He showed them pictures of all the children.

"Oh, goodness!" Trudie exclaimed. "Riley Rose looks exactly like Amanda. She was a bit older when you first brought her to Boston, but Riley Rose has the same sweet face and big black curls. Oh, how beautiful! And Henry! What a handsome little boy!"

Bogie appreciated that she didn't mention that Henry looked just like Bud as a baby. He already knew that from looking at Bud's baby pictures.

James smiled at Bogie. "I'm very happy for you. You look good and content."

Bogie nodded. "I'll be a lot happier when I find the guy who shot Tommie and is messing with our system.

⌒⟋⟋⟍⟍⟍⟋

As they drove away from the building, Bogie's cell phone vibrated. He glanced at the caller ID and turned onto Washington Street. He made a right turn onto Henshaw Street just before the Brighton Police Station. Ken Nguyen walked on the sidewalk in front of the large older houses facing the back of the police station, a backpack slung over one shoulder. Bogie stopped, and Ken jumped in, and sat in the passenger seat. Ken looked back at Isabella in her bumper seat. "Hi, Izzy. How are you doing?"

"Hi, Ken! Isn't this wonderful! We just visited Mr. James and Mrs. Trudie, and then we found you. Now we can all ride together."

"Yes, it's wicked wonderful!" Ken said and winked at Bogie.

⌒⟋⟋⟍⟍⟍⟋

Rose held Tommie's large bruised hand. "How much longer are they going to keep the IV's running?"

Tommie shrugged.

"Are you eating anything solid?"

"Yeah, red Jell-O and green Jell-O," he said petulantly.

"Well, maybe this bit of news will cheer you up! We got it back!"

Tommie studied her then smiled as she nodded. "Where is it?"

"In the safe. When you're out of here..."

"But I thought—"

"Tommie! Think about it! Anybody could take it while you're sleeping."

He nodded.

Rose smiled at him, wondering how such a brilliant guy could have the street smarts of a three year old.

"So the EMT guy gave it back?" Tommie asked.

Rose shook her head. "Not quite. I told you that George and John Washington met with both EMT's. Each guy denied having the laptop, but George and John figured it was the dude who lived in Brighton. When the first signal came from Brighton, Ken went into his snatch and grab routine. It wouldn't have been my choice, but he got the job done."

Tommie smiled. "He likes doing that stuff."

Rose nodded. "Unfortunately, he does. Any movement in the legs?"

Tommie closed his eyes and looked away.

As Rose turned to leave, she almost bumped into a small man wearing a white shirt with a pocket protector filled with pens. The Chinese man glanced at her then smiled at Tommie. "Hi, Tommie," he said, hesitantly.

Tommie beamed. "Dr. Wang. I'm so glad to see you!"

"When I heard my favorite student had been hurt, I wanted to come here immediately. But the hospital..."

Tommie smiled. "I was in the ICU for a while and couldn't have visitors. I tried to reach you the day before I was shot. I actually fell asleep waiting for you to get back to me."

"I'm sorry, Tommie, I had a death in the family and had to fly home," Dr. Wang said.

"To China?" Tommie asked.

Dr. Wang laughed and shook his head. "No, Chicago! If you told me you had a family emergency and flew home, do you think I'd ask you if you went to Sweden?"

Tommie's face flushed. "I hope not," he said softly. "I don't know anybody there."

While Tommie and his professor chatted, Rose slowly backed out of the room sure that neither would notice she was gone. Rose walked toward the elevator and was greeted by the man with salt and pepper hair, grinning at her. He was wearing a gray suit, white shirt, and maroon tie. Rose wanted to smile, but forced herself to keep a neutral look on her face.

"May I buy you a coffee?" Detective Michael Wislowski asked.

She studied Wislowski. "Is this a social encounter or an interrogation?"

"Neither, just an offer to buy you a cup of coffee."

She gave him a 'what the hell' shrug then said, "Well, you cleaned up nice! The last time I saw you, you looked like an unmade bed."

"Wow! You're brutal! I'd been working sixteen hours straight," Mike Wislowski said.

As he led her toward the cafeteria, Rose quickly said, "Outside. I hate hospitals and their cafeterias. Besides, I want a cigarette with my coffee."

"A woman after my own heart!"

As they walked down the street, Mike Wislowski said, "I know you're Darryl's daughter."

"So?"

"He's my man! He looked out for me when I was the new Polak on the block."

"And now you're the old Polak, The Great Mike, so what?"

"The Great Mike" Wislowski repeated then smiled.

"My father talked about you all the time. 'And Mike did this and Mike did that'... yada, yada, yada."

Mike Wislowski smiled. "And you were never curious about The Great Mike?"

Rose thought for a second then said, "Not with Pop pushing you the way he did. I figured you were another Dot Rat who was stuck in the hood for life."

Mike Wislowski laughed. "I like *Dawchestahh*. My family lives there. Your father lives there."

"But I don't. I've moved on."

Mike grinned. "I guess you did! Anyway, Rose, I just want to let you know you can trust me."

Rose studied him. "To do what?"

Mike shrugged. "I'm not looking to make trouble for you or Tommie Jurgenson. I just want to find out who shot him."

"And I don't?" Rose asked quickly.

"But you see, Rose, that's my job, not yours."

"Maybe that's your problem, Wislowski. You don't know what my job is, and it's not defined by what you think I should or should not do. I'm running a security business. It doesn't look good if I can't keep my own people safe."

"Why would someone want to gun *him* down?" Michael gestured with his thumb toward the hospital.

"I have no idea. He's the sweetest..." Rose's eyes teared up, and she looked away.

Mike studied her then said, "The techs finished going through the limo, the one that tried to run your father down."

"Any prints?" Rose asked almost knowing the answer.

Michael clicked his tongue then said, "Wiped clean! The driver must have been wearing gloves. We still haven't found the real driver. He seems to have disappeared."

"Who ordered the limo?" Rose asked.

Mike Wislowski looked at her. "Why does that matter?"

Rose shrugged. "Somebody ordered a limo then the driver disappeared. You'd think somebody would be running down the person who ordered it."

Mike sighed then said, "It's strange. The limo was ordered for someone at the Four Seasons, but a call came in just after the driver left. They wanted the pickup moved to the Devonshire. The dispatcher called him and told him to go the Devonshire."

"He was supposed to pick up the same person?"

Wislowski nodded. "But there are no guests or residents at the Four Seasons by that name."

"And the Devonshire?" Rose asked.

Mike Wislowski shook his head. "They used a phony name and credit card. Even the phone wasn't registered...probably one of those throwaways."

As they approached a Starbucks, Mike grabbed Rose's elbow and said, "Wait here! I'll go inside and get a couple of coffees so we can drink them out here and enjoy a cigarette. How do you take yours?"

"Cream, no sugar."

Michael Wislowski smiled, lightly thumbed his fist against his heart and pointed his fingers *gangsta* style at her then himself. "I think we've got something going on here! Smokin paper...drinkin coffee..."

Rose looked at him, incredulous. "Sure, Snoop Dogg!" Her deep throaty laugh filled the air.

37

OUT WITH THE OLD

SOUTH FLORIDA

Tiffany tossed her cell phone on the coffee table.

Zoe studied her, then asked, "What did your grandmother say? Will she give you some money?"

Tiffany shook her head. "I guess Billy Ray's mother called her and told her about the movies. Grandma said she has to help my mother because she's a Page but since I'm not, she doesn't have to do anything. Would you believe she's still bitching about me getting expelled from the Benjamin School? God! How many years ago was that? She said I'm a liar and a cheat just like my father, and she's glad I'm a Gallagher so everybody can laugh at the Gallaghers and know they're nothing but white trash." Tiffany sighed deeply, pushed back into the soft couch, and studied the ceiling.

"I'll call my father and see if I can get money from him," Zoe said. "He can't say no to me."

After she finished an unpleasant conversation with her stepmother, Zoe closed her cell phone, lit another Marlboro, and inhaled deeply. Taking a gulp of wine she turned to Tiffany. "I don't believe this! My father found out about the movies, and now he won't talk to me. That fuckin Annette said I'm dead to him."

Tiffany choked on her wine. "What?"

"He pulled the same shit six years ago. My sister was hooked on heroin and wouldn't go into rehab. Essie almost died of an overdose. But rather than having her committed or something, he said Essie was dead to him. He sat shivah for her. Three months later, Essie was dead. She really overdosed that time."

"What's shivah? Is it a curse or something?" Tiffany asked.

"No. When somebody dies, you sit shivah for a week praying and stuff. It's mourning for the dead."

"He did this before she died? Why?"

"Because he's a flaming asshole! If he's displeased with you, that's it, you're dead to him!"

"What are you going to do?"

Zoe stubbed out her cigarette and put down her glass of wine. "I'm going to visit him and get some money!" Zoe studied her face in the mirror. Most of the swelling was down and the light smears under her eyes could easily be covered with makeup.

"You don't think that Billy Ray or JJ could help us out?" Tiffany asked hopefully.

"Forgetaboutit! Billy Ray told me to shut up and stay away from him. He said not to say a word to anyone about who was involved or how we got paid. He said if I did, he'd slit my throat. Does that sound like someone who wants to help us?"

Fifteen minutes later, Zoe pulled her Volkswagen Beetle out of its parking spot in City Place and headed for the white stucco mansion her father liked to call home, although the true owner was his second wife, Annette Goldstein Kuperstein Epstein Ziegler. Annette had acquired the mansion and lavish lifestyle through good marriages and better divorces.

Zoe wondered if they would let her through, but when she saw a black Mercedes Benz approach, she knew she had her chance. The driver spoke into a microphone attached to the white wall. The double gates opened wide. Zoe accelerated and drove in almost kissing the bumper of the Benz.

When the Mercedes stopped at the front door, a tall, bald man wearing dark glasses emerged. He wore a black long-sleeved shirt and black slacks. The front door opened, and a small woman of indeterminate age walked toward him. They embraced, though Annette had no expression on her face. After several surgical procedures and years of Botox injections, Annette's eyebrows were frozen in place and her mouth looked like it had been stretched from ear, neither smiling nor frowning.

As Annette and the man spoke, Zoe jumped out of her car, dashed up the two wide front steps and ran into the house. Standing in the main hallway, Zoe heard the sounds coming from the back of the house. She dashed down the hall and quickly opened the door to the library. Zoe watched as ten old men wearing yarmulkes prayed and moaned, "*Yisgadal v'yiskadash..*" along with Martin Ziegler, who was unshaven with his shirt torn, sitting among them. "What the hell are you doing?" Zoe screeched.

The prayers stopped and the old men gaped at Zoe and gasped. They stared at Martin in horror. "You said she was dead!" one of the men choked out.

"She is dead to me," Martin said stubbornly. "I have no more daughter. She's dead!"

"Just like Essie was dead to you, Papa?"

"Yes!"

Zoe studied her father and his friends, then glanced to the side as the man in black held Annette's upper arm as if to hold her back. The man had his head cocked and a slight smirk on his face. Zoe took a deep breath and said, "I'm dead to you? Well you're dead to me! You've got a lot of chutzpah judging me! You've cheated more people than Bernie Madoff! You've fucked over business partners and family members. You cheated my mother so you could hook up with this despicable bitch!" She pointed to Annette. "No one in their right mind could live with her! Her ex-husbands would have paid anything to get away from her. You didn't have to try so hard. Nobody else wanted her! You think you're better than me because you have some money? You've got the curse that comes with it...this paskudnika!" She pointed at Annette.

Annette gasped and tried to lunge for Zoe, but the stranger held her back.

Zoe looked at her father and her eyes filled with tears. "Don't pray for me, pray for yourself! You need it worse than I do!"

Zoe pushed past Annette and ran from the house. The man in black followed her and caught up with her as she was about to open her car door. He stuck out his hand. "I'm Moshe Rabin. I've come from New York to meet you. I must say, that was the most unusual introduction I've ever had!"

Zoe studied him then smiled. "You don't sound like you're from New York."

"I'm actually from Israel. I came to New York about six months ago, and I've had every relative in this country trying to fix me up. But you were special. I saw your picture, and asked to meet you."

"Oh...You're her relative," Zoe said disappointed.

"Distant cousin," Moshe said.

Zoe shrugged. "Well, now that you know that I'm dead and can't stand your distant cousin, you might as well head back to New York so you can get fixed up with a real prospect."

"I think I've just met her."

Zoe laughed. "Hardly! If you hang around with me, your relatives will probably hold an intervention or have you shipped home until you come to your senses."

"I don't think so; I'm with the Israeli Consulate. Let's go somewhere so we can talk," Moshe said when he saw Annette glaring at them from the front door.

"Follow me. I'll take you back to my place while it's still mine." When Moshe smiled, she added, "Don't get too excited. I've got my friend staying over. She's already homeless."

⚇

Randy lay on the queen-sized bed next to Amanda. She was asleep and making funny noises with her lips. He stared up at the ceiling in the darkened room and thought about his baby daughter sleeping in the nursery. Riley Rose and Henry were happy to be together, but Randy worried that neither child would be overjoyed when the Carpenters returned to their own home. Thinking of his house, Randy felt sick. How could he afford to keep up that house now that he wasn't bringing home a paycheck? They could end up losing the place. Amanda probably wouldn't understand, and then he could lose her too. Nobody would believe Randy was the victim, not even his father.

38

MOVIE NIGHT

Quincy, Ma

When Jack and George Hampfield told Bogie that they were having some friends over to watch the HBO movie *Behind the Candelabra*, Bogie could tell the men were uncomfortable. George apologized, saying they had planned the get-together long before Bogie and Isabella arrived. When Bogie offered to go to a hotel, Jack and George were adamant that he should stay. Bogie didn't argue because R&B was already stretched thin, using investigators for security on Bogie, Darryl and Rose. Checking into a hotel would force R&B to keep two people in Quincy and add two more to a hotel.

George tried to downplay the whole event saying it was just part of their social networking, interacting with potential clients.

Listening to the men discussing the guests coming to the house, Isabella believed she would be at the center of the party, greeting everyone as they arrived. If cajoled, she'd demonstrate a few of her new kung fu moves for the group.

Understandably, Isabella was quite upset to learn that she and her father would not be attending the party. Unhappy at being cast aside, she interrupted Bogie every few minutes as he worked on his computer. Isabella rolled on the bed practicing her moves, sang every song she could remember and read out loud from her kindle. Bogie ignored her and continued

working on the laptop. At some point, Isabella wore herself out, and fell asleep splayed over the bed making sure there was no room for him.

Bogie sat on the floor in the darkened bedroom trying to figure out Troy Mentor's reasoning. Bogie believed Mentor was a madman. There was little rhyme or reason to what he did. And the addresses...Troy had used the Devonshire address on his business card and then had a limousine stop there. Was he trying to draw them a map to his location? It couldn't be that simple, or could it? While Bogie obsessed over Troy Mentor, he followed strings that took him to unusual sites, if not Mentors IPO.

While Isabella lie across the bed sound asleep, Bogie looked up and smiled as he thought, "What a spiteful little witch!"

Bogie was startled when his cell phone vibrated. He was even more surprised when he saw the caller ID. Bogie answered by asking, "Is everything okay?"

After a moment of silence, Randy said, "Not really. I need to talk to you."

"I'm listening," Bogie said.

"Did you hear about what happened...to me?"

Bogie spoke in a low voice but with a bit of an edge. "I heard your friends were making porno movies and you got in a fight with them while you were on the job and got suspended. Is that about it?"

"Yes," Randy said softly.

"How can I help you?" Bogie asked.

"I don't even know if you can. Mandie always says you're good with... sort of a genius with computers and..." His voice cracked and he took a deep breath then started crying.

Listening to Randy cry, Bogie said, "Hold on. I've got to go to another room so we can talk." Bogie muted the phone, picked up his laptop, and left the room. He walked down the hall toward a bedroom that George had turned into a home gym.

As he sat down in the darkened doorway, Bogie listened as Jack, George, and their friends laughed and made bitchy comments about Michael Douglas as he portrayed an aging Liberace about to take Matt Damon as his young lover. "What is this fuckery?" one of the men called out.

Bogie smiled when he remembered George's excitement as he decorated the living room with a candelabra and candles. Bogie set his computer down and released the mute button on the phone. "I'm back," Bogie said.

Composed, Randy said, "I've got a problem, and you're the only one I know who can help me." When Bogie didn't respond, Randy continued, "I found my pictures...naked pictures...on one of the porn sites that Billy Ray and JJ were on. But I swear to God I didn't pose for those pictures or get involved with their movies. Zoe asked me to, and I said no."

"Why was it Zoe who asked you?"

Randy thought then said, "Billy Ray or JJ probably put her up to it. Maybe they figured I'd agree if she..."

"Why, do you have a thing for her?" Bogie asked.

"No! Absolutely not! It might be the other way around. She always sort of flirted with me, but Zoe flirts with everybody."

"So these pictures of you...are they stills? Streaming?" When Bogie received no response, he asked, "are they just pictures or are they movie clips?"

"Just pictures," Randy answered.

"You're sure they're pictures of you?"

"Yes."

"Is it a full body shot? Your face? Wait a minute! Just give me the name of a site and I'll bring it up." After he looked at Randy's pictures, Bogie asked, "When were these taken?"

"About four years ago. I had just moved to Florida and was dating this woman...Sarah. She's Billy Ray's sister. It was one of those things where everybody was pushing...my father, her father, Sarah...but it just didn't feel right. She was too *advanced* for me...if you know what I mean."

"No, I don't. What do you mean? She was too old for you or into some kinky shit?"

"Kinky shit," Randy said softly. "One weekend she had a party. She had a couple of her girlfriends over. I was there and so were Billy Ray and JJ. There was some serious drinking going on then somebody put out a small bowl. At first, I thought they were M&M's but they turned out to be pills...all different kinds. There were lines of coke on the coffee table. It got really wild and pretty soon everybody was screwing everybody else. It was like an animal farm. After a while, I crawled into the bathroom, puked my guts out and passed out on the floor. I was glad to get out of there alive. After that, I made up excuses not to see Sarah and then I met Mandie."

"Who was taking the pictures?" Bogie asked.

"I don't know! I never knew anybody was taking pictures. I never saw a camera."

"How do you know it was that weekend?"

Without hesitating Randy said, "I never had another weekend like that...ever!"

"Are you sure this Sarah didn't take pictures of you in a motel room somewhere?"

"No, if you look at the background you'll see a living room. That's hers. She had this blue lava lamp on the end table."

Bogie studied the picture of Randy next to the lava lamp. Randy stood naked looking to his left sporting an enormous erection.

"How long has this site been up?" Bogie asked.

"I don't know. Zoe gave me the names of some of the sites, then I found others. I have no idea how long they've been up or who's in charge of them."

"Did you get paid for these pictures?"

"No!" Randy said incredulously. "Do you think I'd pose for this crap?" He sighed deeply. "What a nightmare! When are you coming back?"

"I'm not sure. We're working on pushing this rat into a corner," Bogie said.

"Is it going to take long?" Randy asked.

"I don't think so. We've got several people working on this. Maybe a few days," Bogie said. When Randy sighed hopelessly, Bogie added, "If Zoe or Tiffany call you, talk to them. If they don't, let it go. Whatever you do, don't speak to the guys. You're in enough trouble. Just hang tight, and we'll get to the bottom of this. I could...I know somebody who could...take these sites down, but whoever is running them could throw them right back up again. Do you want them taken down?"

"I don't know. If somebody could put them back up, it won't do a lot of good."

"Like I said, I'm hoping to get out of here in the next couple of days...if you can hold out that long," Bogie said.

"I guess I'll have to," Randy said dejected.

After an uncomfortable silence, Bogie said, "And talk to your father."

"He's really gonna be pissed at me," Randy said.

"He'll get over it. John and I don't usually agree on much. But I know one thing for certain; he's always on your side."

"Yeah," Randy said then sighed. "See ya." Randy disconnected the phone and sighed again.

"You could have told me," Amanda said from behind him. Startled Randy turned around from his seat on the couch in the family room and looked at his wife. "I thought you were sleeping. How long have you been there?"

"Long enough to know how scared you are," Amanda answered.

As Bogie studied the computer screen, the door to the guestroom flung open. Isabella, looking wild with her eyes opened wide and her mouth twisted, stared at her father while he sat on the floor. Isabella's lips began to quiver. She ran to Bogie and sat down beside him.

Bogie studied her then asked, "Are you okay?"

Isabella shook her head and looked down. Her shoulders trembled. "I thought you left me," she finally said half-crying.

Bogie logged off the computer and closed it. "Why did you think that?" he asked.

She shrugged then said, "I don't know. Maybe you thought I wasn't a good girl." When Bogie didn't respond, she continued, "I try."

"I know you do," Bogie said and put his arm around her shoulders.

Isabella nodded. After a moment she said, "It's not easy being good, you know."

"I know," Bogie agreed. "Let get some rest."

⟩∭⟨

While Bogie slept, Walter Beck sat on the bed in Rose's guestroom typing and receiving messages. After they compared data, Walter and the Becks agreed on their next course of action. He sent off his last message for the night: "FOLLOW THE MONEY."

⟩∭⟨

Dressed in black, Troy Mentor opened cardboard boxes and spread the contents over the couch and coffee table. He organized ropes, spikes, a hammer and other equipment he would use in his climb to the top of the world.

39

BUDS AND SUDS

John Carpenter parked close to the front door of The Place. Recognizing some of the pickups in the gravel lot, he knew it would be a good night to pound back a few brewskies. When John opened the door of the noisy bar, a wave of silence descended over it like the Black Plague. The music still played, but the patrons all looked away. No one remembered his name. John walked toward a table where he recognized some of the guys. As he approached, all the men stood up, threw bills on the table and walked toward the door. Feeling the heat of anger and humiliation rising inside him, he followed them out the door and got in his car.

John remembered the cookout at Randy's house and how he sat at the end of an empty semi-circle of chairs holding his granddaughter when the Johnsons arrived. He invited Johnson to sit next to him, and they talked. But less than five minutes later when the Marcels arrived, Johnson stood up, offered his seat to one of the Marcel women so all the women could sit and gossip. Johnson walked away leaving John sitting alone at the end of the semicircle. Remembering the piss poor treatment he received at the hands of the Johnson and Marcell men, he quickly drove out of the parking lot unconcerned whether he ran over buddies or brass.

40

THE KNIGHT WORE BLACK

The man in black entered BB King's Blues Club in City Place with a blonde on each arm. The bar was packed and noisy, but the threesome was finally able to make their way to an empty table. As they sat down, a battered looking Billy Ray Marcel approached them. He motioned for Zoe to come to him. Moshe felt her body stiffen, so held her hand, and studied Billy Ray. He continued staring until Billy Ray looked away, glared at Zoe, then walked to the bar. Moshe glanced from Tiffany to Zoe and studied their frightened faces. He smiled at Zoe. "I thought we came out to have a good time! Where's that famous Zoe smile!" Moshe grinned as she forced a smile.

Moshe didn't mention Billy Ray again and acted like he wasn't in the club. When Billy Ray went into the men's room, Moshe excused himself and followed him. A few minutes later, Moshe came back to the table and looked at his watch. "If we're going to make that movie, we'd better go."

Although they had twenty minutes to spare, Zoe and Tiffany didn't argue with him.

As they walked on the upper level of the plaza toward the Muvico IMAX cinema, Zoe heard a commotion behind her and stopped. Two police cars with their light bars flashing were parked below BB King's. Uniformed cops raced up the stairs, and Zoe stopped and leaned against the outside railing to watch. The cops escorted a man out the door. That man had nothing but a white tablecloth wrapped around him.

Tiffany gawked and did a quick intake of breath. "That's Billy Ray!"

Moshe smirked. "How about that!"

Zoe squeezed his arm. "My hero!"

Moshe smiled. "Always!"

41

LET THE WAR BEGIN

The room was quiet as Bogie and Walter worked on their laptops as Rose studied the screen on her PC. Without Isabella in the cramped office, the silence was deafening. They finally heard her giggles from the practice room, and Bogie looked up and asked, "How's Pop doing?"

Rose moved her hand from side to side, indicating he wasn't much better.

"Did he go to the doctor's?" Bogie asked.

"Surprisingly, he did," Rose answered.

"He must be in a lot of pain."

Rose nodded. "The doctor thinks it's sciatica. No wonder! He sits on his ass from one end of the day to the other, either watching TV or doing crossword puzzles. That little excursion with Isabella did him in. That's pathetic! Pop worked all those years, most of them on his feet, and now he can't even spend a few hours walking without falling apart. He said he wrenched his back when he pushed into Jacob Wirth's. I told him that was bullshit!"

Bogie smiled. "So now he's pissed at you?"

Rose nodded. "He can stay pissed as long as he gets up and walks around while he's cursing me out."

"The Washingtons still watching the Devonshire?"

Rose nodded. "Since it's the address on Mentor's business card, the place where someone called for the limo pickup, and there's an apartment leased to Black Hat Elite Entertainment, I figured it wouldn't hurt to see what was going on over there. So far, it's quiet. Neither one of them has left that apartment.

"He's goading us. He wants us to come over there!"

"That bastard!" Walter shouted.

Rose and Bogie stared at him.

"That bastard!" Walter repeated. "He stole my program. That bastard! That's my program! He copied it." Walter took a deep breath then sighed. "I designed a program to go into certain sites...financial institutions. It removes small amounts of money – nothing big, just two dollars and thirty-five cents from each customer's account. The money is transferred to another account, my account. If the bank has seven hundred thousand customers, a million dollars is out of the bank in seconds."

Bogie tilted his head. "I think your math is a bit off."

Walter shook his head. "It only goes into accounts where there's enough money to hide a small transaction. I don't want to take two dollars and thirty-five cents from an old lady who has forty dollars in the bank. And if an account is overdrawn, obviously that account gets a pass."

Bogie smiled. "You're a real humanitarian, Walter."

"I was, until this bastard came along. My Becks have been following his movements for the past forty-eight hours. Three of our people are good at histories; they're the ones who picked up on his bank accounts. He used my program to go into financial institutions in Hartford, Connecticut, about six months ago. He pulled over sixteen million dollars out of accounts all at one time. Troy Mentor is greedy and stupid, or at least not as smart as he thinks he is. All my work could have been destroyed if he'd been caught."

"How do you know it was him?" Rose asked.

Walter jabbed his finger at entries on the screen. "These are his accounts, he has the numbers listed in a special email file in his computer – one of those emails that sits in a draft form but never gets sent."

Bogie studied Walter who seemed to be aging before his eyes. "So? That doesn't mean he copied your program. He might have come up with his own."

Walter shook his head. "This!" He pointed to the screen again. "This proves he stole my program because he doesn't know the last part. I was the only one who knew the final step. My final commands have the money leave those dump accounts and go off into new accounts without leaving strings."

"You could do that?" Bogie asked in amazement.

Walter puckered his lips and nodded. Bogie shuddered as he realized that was the same expression Isabella wore when she proudly acknowledged one of her achievements.

Rose bounced her fist lightly on the desk then asked, "How did you design the program when you were inside?"

Walter nodded. "When Beethoven was deaf, he still composed symphonies."

"How did you get the coding to your friends?" Bogie asked.

Walter looked at him and rolled his eyes. "A little bit at a time… TracFones, computer parts…lots of ways."

Bogie stared into space then said, "So one of your Becks betrayed you, sold you out."

Walter nodded. "And I know who it was; Diogenes."

Bogie laughed. "He sold you out in his search for an honest man?"

"He was always trouble - too idealistic, too political. I voted against having him in the group, but the others wanted him. That's the downside of a democracy. Sometimes you get too many people with the wrong answer running the show."

"So what happened to him?" Rose asked.

"He was upset about things happening in Syria and uploaded documents showing the Syrian government gassing their own people. The American government grabbed him and tried to connect him to Anonymous or WikiLeaks. Both of those groups denied he was a member. Then he started bragging about being part of the Becks. We went silent immediately. All communication stopped for thirty days. Passwords were changed and the chat room was relocated. So Diogenes was swinging in the wind until somebody heard his pleas and made his bail, a million bucks. After that, he disappeared."

"So you think Troy Mentor paid the bail for him?"

Walter nodded. "It wasn't anybody in our group. Diogenes was out. When he started dragging the Becks into his mess, I told the others it was him or me. Besides, none of them had that kind of money because we hadn't run the program yet."

"When did you run the program?" Bogie asked.

"We didn't. I was putting the final touches on it when Darryl called and said Rose needed me. Since I was speaking at DEFCON, I was able to meet some of the Becks in person in Las Vegas."

"Where were you going to run it?" Bogie asked.

"LA," Walter said without hesitating. "Haven't you ever heard 'All the gold in California is in a bank...'"

"'In Beverly Hills in somebody else's name,'" Bogie and Rose finished for him.

"Remember when we used to sing that?" Rose asked the men. They smiled and nodded.

"What about Mentor? Where do you think he's planning on running it?" Bogie asked.

Walter considered this then said, "Boston. I think Hartford was a dry run for him. If that blew up, he could still run away with a lot of money.

If it worked, he could get ready for a bigger pay-off because he obviously doesn't care about having a long term thing...he just wants to take the money and run."

"Do you think he picked Boston so he could kill us, then get a big pay day?"

Bogie shook his head. "I don't know. He was originally from this area so he knows it. He obviously wants to kill us and isn't too concerned about making it look like an accident. As far as the money, that shit bird could do that from anywhere."

"Da-dee!" Isabella exclaimed laughing as she entered the room. "Remember what Mommy said about..." She stopped and giggled. "Shit bird."

It was apparent that Isabella was ready to entertain the group who still had hours of work ahead of them. Bogie smiled at Isabella, then pushed a button on his phone. "Jack, I'm sorry to dump on you, but I was wondering if Isabella..." He listened for a minute then said, "Thanks, Jack!" He looked at Rose and Walter. "Jack and George are going to pick her up. I want Ken to follow them home and stay inside the house."

Rose shook her head. "He's at the hospital with Tommie."

"Jesús?" Bogie asked.

Rose shook her head again. "He and one of the new guys are with Pop."

"And the Washingtons are sitting in the Devonshire. This really sucks! Everybody's scattered around the city because of this asshole Mentor. How about Benjamin or Rodney?"

Rose nodded. "They're not our most experienced, but they're available and they can shoot."

Bogie laughed. "Maybe we could add that to the profiles we send to clients. *NOT THE SHARPEST KNIVES IN THE DRAWER, BUT GOOD SHOTS.*"

⌘

The thin man with wisps of light hair covering his head looked at his computer screen in disbelief. "Fuck! Fuck! I should have annihilated them before that fuckin Walter got here!"

The woman, now sporting short, blonde hair, came up behind him and asked, "What's the matter?"

"That fuckin Walter has taken money from three of my offshore accounts."

"How do you know it's him?"

"No one there's as good as he is! It has to be him."

"So what? After tomorrow, we'll have—"

Before she could say another word, Troy Mentor pushed back out of his chair and punched her in the mouth. "I'll decide what to do and when to do it! Understand?"

The faux Linda Mentor held her hand to her bleeding mouth and walked into the bathroom. She knew better than to try to speak. The mood would pass, then he'd be back to normal. He was under too much pressure now.

Troy returned to the computer and started typing in more commands. He was going to leave a trail of bread crumbs for these lemmings, and let them drop off a cliff while he got rich!

After working months on this project, he was ready to launch it...just twelve more hours.

Troy liked being in the center of the city, surrounded by five major banks, three investment houses, and the Boston Stock Exchange.

Troy's program was scheduled to empty accounts indiscriminately, so at some point, alarms would surely sound. But R&B Investigations was going to cause such a spectacular diversion that no one would pay any attention to the bank alarm systems' squeal.

Troy laughed at his own genius.

42

NOW I LAY ME DOWN TO SLEEP

BOSTON

Walter rubbed the bridge of his nose as he studied the computer screen. The accounts in the Bahamas, Barbados, and Switzerland were empty. The others would be closed out in the next few hours.

Bogie stared at Walter and furrowed his brow.

Walter looked up. "What?"

"You look like hell," Bogie said. "How about you get a few hours rest and let the Becks earn their keep?"

Walter sighed. "I'll have plenty of time to rest when I'm dead."

"Not the way you look now, that might happen in the next ten minutes. Come on, Walter, let's call it a night."

⟨⟩

Exhausted and bleary eyed, Bogie, Walter and Rose stood in the elevator in her building at four o'clock in the morning. When they arrived on Rose's floor, she turned to Bogie and asked, "Are you sure you want to stay in Tommie's place? It's kind of messy, and I know how you are about—."

"I'm too tired to care! I just want to crash!" Bogie said.

Ten minutes after they said good night, Bogie called Rose. She grinned when she looked at the caller ID. "Yeees?"

"What the hell's the matter with that kid? He's a pig! Do you have any clean sheets? I can't find any here."

"Go to the door, and I'll hand you some." Rose laughed as she removed sheets from the linen closet and brought them to her front door. Handing them to Bogie, she said, "I told you so!" Rose would have been surprised if Bogie hadn't noticed the mess. Bogie grew up with nothing and was always taken aback when anyone treated their possessions with negligence and indifference.

⚭

At four-forty-five that morning, Troy and Linda took an elevator down to the underground garage in the Devonshire. They moved swiftly through the garage carrying a suitcase and his equipment, and stopped next to a black Corvette Stingray. Linda removed the keys from her pocket and opened the trunk. After tossing the suitcase and his climbing gear inside, Troy walked to the passenger door. "You drive. Take me over to their building."

Linda, with her mouth swollen and sore, didn't need to ask which building. She simply removed the parking pass from the glove box. On their way to Lincoln Street, Troy said, "After you drop me off, drive over to MGH and park in the garage. Stay in the car until nine-thirty, then go inside and finish off Ten Ton Tommie. When you're done, drive to Darryl Jones' house and take him out...you'll have to get rid of the bodyguard too. Park the Corvette at the T station and grab a cab to the airport. I'll meet you at Terminal B. They'll all be dead by noon, and I'll be rich and outta here with nobody left to look for me."

43

THE BATTLE OF BOSTON

BOSTON

Troy sat in the dark on a rooftop, studying his laptop. He cursed Walter Beck, but cursed himself more for underestimating that old man. Walter had emptied all the off shore accounts and burned the money trails behind him. He muttered, "You're going to burn too, old man, as soon as you give me back my money."

⁂

By eight-thirty in the morning, Bogie, Rose and Walter were on their way to the office. "...and I put plastic bags under my feet just to take a shower..." Bogie continued his tirade on the filth in Tommie's condo. Rose and Walter just glanced at each other.

The group arrived in front of the R&B Investigations building almost at the same time as a blue BMW and a black Escalade. As Walter and Rose entered the building, Bogie walked over to the BMW and the windows rolled down. Jack and George looked exhausted; Isabella, refreshed. She grinned. "Guess what I had for dinner last night?" Her little mouth almost puckered in a kiss, and her eyes glistened. Before Bogie could answer, she said, "McDonalds! The Happy Meal!"

Bogie nodded then shook his head while looking at Jack and George. "I don't need to say anything. I'm sure you've suffered enough."

George sighed. "She never used to be like that."

"But now that she's not living on that junk, it's like a nuclear explosion when she does eat it."

Jack said, "Don't worry; we've learned our lesson. Tonight, tofu!"

Isabella giggled. "Oh, Uncle Jack, you're so funny!"

Bogie and Isabella entered the building along with Benjamin and Rodney, guns drawn. Benjamin and Rodney were big boys, not mental giants, but nice guys who liked guns and especially the CZ75 automatic pistols they toted. The men were members of the Pilgrim Church where Darryl served as a deacon. Benjamin and Rodney were not merely referred by Darryl; they were placed on the job by him. Neither Rose nor Bogie believed it was prudent to challenge Darryl.

Walter had his laptop opened and was staring at the screen. He ran his finger down rows of numbers in his small spiral notebook before looking up at Bogie. "Where's Isabella?"

"Ken is showing her some new moves. Maybe she'll work some the McDonalds toxins out of her body."

Rose looked at the schedule. "John Washington's at Mass General. Since nothing's happening at the Devonshire, it didn't make sense to leave both John and George there." Rose turned and yelled out, "Ken! You're due over at Mass General to relieve John."

Bogie cringed as she shouted.

Rose looked at him. "What?"

"What's that, the Dorchester whisper?"

As Walter laughed, Rose said, "Hmpf! Somebody's crabby. What's wrong? Not enough sleep last night."

Bogie nodded. "You got that right."

When Rose's phone rang, they all looked up. She looked at the screen and read a text message from George Washington. "URGENT. MENTOR APT VACATED. BODY INSIDE. COMPUTER RUNNING. COME SOONEST."

Rose showed the message to Bogie and Walter.

After staring at the screen for several seconds, Bogie told her to call George and get more details.

Rose tried several times, but her calls went straight to voicemail.

Bogie walked over to the safe and unlocked it. He took out the newly cleaned 9mm Smith & Wesson semi-automatic gun and a spare clip, then walked to a supply cabinet to get a box of cartridges. He slid on his black nylon shoulder harness and placed the gun into it. As he pocketed the spare clip, he looked at Walter. "If Rose and I run over there, are you going to be okay here?"

Walter laughed. "I have Darryl's boys with their big guns to protect me. And if that's not enough, I've got Isabella. You go ahead...just...be careful."

When Ken walked past the office with Isabella trailing behind, Rose called out, "Ken, how about dropping me and Bogie off at the Devonshire on your way to Mass General?"

Ken Nguyen looked at them. "Sure, no problem. You going now?"

Rose and Bogie nodded.

"Where are you going, Da-dee?"

"Aunt Rose and I have to go check on something," Bogie said.

"And you need to take a gun?" Isabella asked, her bottom lip quivering. She wrapped her arms around his legs. "I'm scared, Da-dee!"

"I know, Pumpkin, but I'll be okay. We'll finish this up, and then we can go home. Okay?"

"But why do you have to go?"

"It's my job."

"You do your job at home without a gun." When Bogie said nothing, Isabella wiped a tear with her sleeve and pointed to her face. "Does this look like a happy face?"

"No, it doesn't, but you and Uncle Walter will stay here and guard the office till we get back."

She nodded as he hugged her and kissed the top of her head. "You know I love you and Mommy and the Hankster and Mandie."

"What about Riley Rose and Randy and Pop Pop and..."

Bogie continued to nod as the list went on.

As he jumped into the back seat of the SUV, Bogie said, "I got a bad feeling about this."

Rose glanced back at him. "You and me both, Kemosabe."

"Now you're my faithful Indian companion?" Bogie asked.

Rose smiled. "Fuck you!"

44

VENGEANCE – SWIFT AND THOROUGH

BOSTON

As they travelled up State Street, Rose held her phone and tried to reach George Washington again. She turned to Bogie and said, "At least he's entered the twenty-first century and sends text messages. Not like—"

"Since when?" Bogie interrupted. "Washington's a retired cop. Who's he sending text messages to?" As they came near a narrow street on their left, Bogie called out, "Drop us off here rather than going all the way around the block." He pointed to his left. "The Devonshire's right there. We'll just scoot up the driveway."

Bogie and Rose rushed into the lobby and looked from the concierge to the large man with curly gray hair sitting in the reception area. Rose ran over to George Washington and said, "I got your message."

George looked up at her and asked, "What message?"

Rose stared from Bogie to George Washington. "Have you been upstairs?" she asked Washington.

George shook his head.

"And you didn't send me a message?"

He shook his head again.

"Somebody wanted us here in the worst kind of way," Rose said as she bit down on her knuckle.

"Or they wanted us out of the shop," Bogie said as he pressed keys on his phone. He held the phone to his ear and asked, "Is everything all right there?"

Walter Beck answered, "Yes, everything's fine. What happened?"

"Nothing. It was a hoax. I think Mentor hijacked George's phone service."

Walter sighed. "They've been in the same area long enough. That's possible. Have you gone up to the apartment?"

"Not yet."

"Be careful. You can't believe he'd leave his computer there for you to find! If there is a computer in the apartment, it's not the one he's using."

Bogie nodded to himself. "You're right. Have your friends keep close tabs on him. He's doing something or is about to do it."

When Bogie ended his call, he listened as Rose spoke on her phone. "I'm telling you what he texted. If you're not interested, I'll talk to a real detective." Rose was silent for a moment then said, "I'll see you in a few minutes."

"Who was that?" Bogie asked.

"Mike Wislowski. He claims he's trustworthy. We'll see."

⁂

In the wee hours of the morning Troy sat on the roof across the street and trained his binoculars on Bogie, Rose and Walter as they left. When the SUV pulled away, Troy went into action and got onto their roof. All that rock climbing had paid off!

He knew Walter and the kid were inside. They'd probably have one of the black guys watching the front door, but the element of surprise would be on Troy's side. He couldn't wait to get back at Walter! His nest egg accounts were empty. The strings seemed to evaporate after a few bounce points. That old fool was going to pay for this!

The R&B Escalade had barely driven away when he moved over the roof. From his perch above, he looked at the front of the building. No one was there. He duck-walked across the roof and checked the back. There was a large black man leaning against the wall in the alleyway carrying what looked like an automatic pistol. Mentor attached a silencer to his .45 Smith & Wesson, reached down and shot Benjamin through the top of head. Benjamin lie in a bloody heap on the ground with his finger still resting near the trigger.

Troy Mentor removed the insulated pliers from his pocket and gingerly snapped a cable. He checked the spike that secured a long rope ladder, laughing softly to himself. The fools hadn't even checked their own building before driving off, falling for his con.

☙

Isabella sat turned away from her workstation and studied Walter. When he looked up from his computer, she said, "I'm very worried, Uncle Walter."

Walter nodded slightly and motioned for her to come over to the desk. "Bring your laptop with you," he instructed.

Isabella signed off and carried the laptop to Walter and handed it to him. Walter studied it and pointed to an icon on the screen. "What's this?" he asked.

Isabella glanced at the screen and said, "Oh, that's Angry Birds. Mommy put it on my computer. She said I'd like it."

"And you don't?" Walter questioned.

Isabella shrugged with one shoulder. "I'd rather play Mortal Kombat, but she won't let me."

Smiling Walter typed commands onto her computer as he copied information from an index card. "There you go!" he said as he showed Isabella the screen. He pressed the Angry Birds icon. When the game appeared on the screen he clicked on the red bird. Isabella's eyes opened wide as she watched another world open up. Her favorite movies were listed: *Kill Bill Volume 1*, *Kill Bill Volume 2*, *Rush Hour 2* and *Rush Hour 3*. "These are on your special cloud, Isabella. When you think you deserve to watch one movie, you can click on the bird. But you must promise me that you will only watch one movie a week."

The grinning child nodded.

Walter continued. "If you spend too much time watching movies, you'll be caught and then..." He made a slicing motion with his finger across his throat.

Isabella continued to nod. "Thank you, Uncle Walter. I love you."

Walter smiled. "You are a very special girl, Isabella. You will do great things. You must promise me that you will study everything you can."

"I promise," Isabella said solemnly.

Walter pointed to a fifth item in the list. "This is not for you. These are passwords for a special website. When the time comes, I will have you share them with someone. Do you understand?"

Isabella considered this. "I think so. Do I have to let them use my computer?"

Walter shook his head. "No. At the proper time, you will memorize the passwords." He pointed to the lines on the screen. "Then you will pass them along and delete them."

"Okay," Isabella said, still confused.

When Walter glanced at the security monitor, the screen was blank. Sitting at Rose's desk, Walter reached in the bottom drawer and removed a 9mm Smith & Wesson semi-automatic and a box of shells. As Walter loaded the clip he said, "You should never put too many bullets in the clip" as if he were teaching Isabella how to prepare hot cocoa. When Isabella nodded, Walter inserted the clip and jacked a round in the chamber. "The gun could jam with too many bullets. Fewer is better." When Isabella nodded again, he rested the gun on the desktop between stacks of paperwork. Walter studied Isabella, then asked, "Do you know how to shoot?"

She shook her head.

"Look away from me then look back and point your finger at my chest."

She did.

"That's it!" he said. "Don't think, just aim for the chest and pull the trigger."

Isabella looked from Walter to the 9mm gun. "It's big," she said softly.

He nodded then took a small .25 caliber Beretta from the same drawer. Walter loaded the small bullets into its clip and pulled back the slide. He placed that gun in his waistband at the small of his back. Walter heard Rodney's cell phone ring in the reception area followed by the sound of glass shattering. Walter reached over to grab Isabella, but Troy was there before Walter could get out of the chair.

Standing in the doorway to the conference room across the narrow hallway, Troy pointed his gun at Walter and said, "Hello, Walter! We meet at last! I've admired your work for years!"

45

LENDING A HAND

Still pale with dark circles under his eyes, Tommie was propped up in bed with a chess board and pieces on the tray table in front of him. A nurse with a stethoscope around her neck walked into the room. Nurse Linda Mentor's shoulder length black hair seemed to emphasize her swollen lips and blackened chin. Wearing blue latex gloves, Linda Mentor lightly pushed the end of the syringe allowing a fine stream to exit the needle. Without speaking, Nurse Mentor walked toward the bed. Studying her, Tommie Jurgenson produced a small handgun. "Stop!" he shouted. The gun was almost lost in his large, shaking hand. The woman ignored him and continued to walk to his side.

John Washington, who was in the middle of relieving himself in the patient bathroom, heard Tommie, grabbed the bathroom door and opened it. Washington watched Tommie trembling while Linda Mentor, holding a syringe in her right hand, moved closer to Tommie. Still peeing, John Washington moved behind Linda Mentor and grabbed her arm with both his hands. Enraged, she spit and squirmed to get free of him. John twisted her arm with such force that the sound of her bone snapping filled the room. But Linda would not stop. She yanked her broken arm away from John Washington and tried to plunge the needle into Tommie. John covered her hand with his and moved it until the needle was facing her. He

225

continued to push until the needle went into Linda's stomach. Linda looked and sounded like a wounded animal as she dropped to the floor.

Ken Nguyen and a nurse ran into the room. They stared at Tommie, who was crying as he held something in his large hand. Ken and the nurse moved toward Linda Mentor who was twisted on the floor with her black wig next to her. The nurse looked away from John Washington. Ken smiled at John and said, "Your junk drawer's open."

John Washington looked down and realized that in the commotion, he had urinated on himself, left his pants unzipped, and exposed his penis.

46

EXPLODING THEORIES

Washington and Devonshire Streets were cordoned off. Residents of The Devonshire plus a group of half-naked people from The Sky Club fitness center and all surrounding occupants were herded down to the next intersection. When the building was evacuated, the bomb squad moved into the fifth floor apartment. They saw nothing out of the ordinary, but three minutes after the cops entered the fifth floor apartment, a thunderous explosion filled the air and the windows blew out onto Washington Street.

After several seconds of stunned silence, pedestrians who were still standing looked up while those who had hit the ground started getting their bearings. "Get off of me!" Rose yelled as she pushed Bogie's shoulder.

He got up on one elbow. "Are you all right?"

She thought for a second then nodded. "Thanks for the rescue, Sir Galahad! I never could figure out why guys liked to play football. I don't like getting knocked to the ground."

"Nobody does. But I'd rather knock you down than explain to Pop how I let you get hurt."

Mike Wislowski reached down and offered Rose his hand. As she stood up, she asked, "A bomb?"

Mike nodded. "It looks like Mentor had the computer on a timer. These guys were going through the apartment and nothing happened. Then suddenly the whole place blew up. What a shit show!"

"Anybody..."

Mike Wislowski nodded then looked around as police cars with light bars flashing and sirens blaring jammed into the area. Washington, State and Devonshire were packed with people and police going nowhere.

Bogie's phone vibrated as Rose's rang. "Oh, my God!" they said together. Rose stared at Mike Wislowski. "Somebody just broke into our building. Bogie's daughter and my uncle are in there!"

As they turned to get away, police cars with sirens wailing blocked all the streets.

47

CHILD'S PLAY

As Troy Mentor stood in the doorway, Walter studied him then said, "Let the child go! She can't hurt you."

Mentor laughed. "I know all about Isabella! I even watched your favorite movie."

The little girl stared at him without expression.

"What's the matter, the cat got your tongue? All you ever do is talk. Talk, talk, talk like a friggin wind-up toy! You gave me a headache! Oh, I almost forgot. I brought you a present." He reached behind his back with his left hand and produced a small plastic sword. He held it out to her, but she didn't move. Finally, he tossed it on the hallway floor near his feet and yelled, "Pick it up!"

Isabella remained frozen in place.

"Leave the child alone! You can see she's frightened," Walter pleaded.

Troy glared at him then turned back to Isabella. "Pick up the sword or I'll shoot Walter."

Isabella moved toward the sword, and watched as Troy Mentor started to lift his right leg. Isabella swerved to the side then jumped, landing on his left foot. She reached up and quickly moved her hand over his chest trying to perform the Five-Point-Palm-Exploding-Heart technique. Unfazed, Troy Mentor seized the front of her outfit and flung her into the back wall.

Isabella hit the wall with a thud and dropped like a rag doll. "This is what *really* happens when you try to outwit a superior force. You got lucky once - dumb luck - but it won't happen again. I just wanted you to learn one valuable lesson in your short little life!"

Half-propped against the wall, Isabella's eyes were glassy, and she didn't speak.

Troy turned to Walter and pointed the gun at him. "Now, Walter, you're going to go in and reverse all the damage you've caused."

"I don't..."

The sound of the gun firing in the enclosed space was deafening. Walter seemed to lift up in the chair then slump over as a large red circle appeared at his waistline. His face turned colorless as the circle grew. Walter clutched his abdomen and his head fell back.

"Sit up and work on the computer, old man! I'm not going to kill you right away, I'm going to keep shooting parts till you wish you were dead."

Walter opened his mouth to speak when Isabella shook her head to clear it and ran to him crying. She wrapped her arms around Walter's waist. "No! No! Don't hurt Uncle Walter!"

"Get that kid away—"

Before Mentor finished speaking, Isabella turned and fired at his heart. One of the five shots missed the heart and hit his head.

Bleeding, Troy Mentor aimed the gun at Isabella as Walter reached over the papers on the desk, grabbed the 9mm and emptied the gun into Mentor.

"Dial 911, Isabella," Walter instructed as he held his arm over his stomach.

Neither of them heard the front door crashing in or the sirens in the distance.

48

CLEAN UP

Mike Wislowski moved his car out of the area with Bogie and Rose riding in the back seat. Brian Freeman, Wislowski's partner, was in the street redirecting other police vehicles to allow Mike to get out. Wislowski called ahead for police and medical assistance at Lincoln Street.

Mike, Rose, and Bogie arrived on the scene seconds after the first black and white. More police cars and an ambulance followed.

Bogie jumped out of the car before it was fully stopped. He glanced at the destroyed front window, then dashed through the open door and saw a uniformed cop looking down at Rodney. The young man's eyes were open wide; he held a cellphone in one hand and his pistol in the other. The bullet hole in his neck didn't seem large enough to do the damage Bogie knew it had, ripping the veins and arteries to shreds leaving Rodney to suffocate on his blood. "Ah Jeez," Bogie muttered as he walked into the hallway where another cop was standing over Troy Mentor's bullet-ridden body. Bogie kicked Troy Mentor and ignored the cop when he said, "Hey!"

Isabella sat on the floor holding Walter's head in her lap, stroking his hair as she cried. "Don't let him die, Da-dee."

Bogie started CPR before the EMT's entered the building. As they were wheeling Walter out, Bogie called out, "Take him to Mass General!"

Rodger Mason, one of the EMT's, said, "We can't bring anyone there. There was an incident inside the hospital. It's on lockdown."

Bogie looked at Rose who was already speed-dialing John Washington's number. "How's it going, John?" She listened then said, "Don't talk to anybody. Tell them your lawyer is on his way." Rose hung up and dialed another number that would soon be put on speed dial. "Hi, George, this is Rose. Is Jack available? No, I don't need to talk to him. Just tell him to get over to Mass General. There's a dead body on the floor in Tommie's room." Rose paused and listened then said, "Yes, we know who it is. Linda Mentor."

Bogie held Isabella close as he carried her through the reception area trying to shield her from the carnage. When he stepped outside, he was greeted by Catie Christenson, the tall, blonde Channel 7 News Anchor. The carefully made up woman looked at him and smiled for the camera. "This is the hot hunk who rescued the little Girl in White Pajamas. Now I see she's the Girl in Black Pajamas. What happened in there?"

Bogie stared at her then watched as the ambulance took Walter away. Police cars blocked Lincoln Street, but the Channel 7 News van was outside the cluster of vehicles. Rather than telling her to get out of the way, Bogie motioned to the news van with his head. "Give me a ride to Floating Hospital with her." Catie quickly walked beside him to the van. "I get the exclusive!"

49

KISSING A BOO BOO BY PHONE

Boston

On the way to the Floating Hospital for Children, Isabella whimpered in her father's arms as she stared at the blood on her hands and clothing. Isabella didn't want to talk, just cry. Since it was only a few blocks from the office, they arrived quickly. Before exiting the van, Bogie removed his shoulder rig. He wrapped the straps around his gun and placed them under the seat. "I'll talk to you when we get out of there. Don't come in with us!"

After registering Isabella, he carried her to a corner of the large waiting area where he could speak softly while he held her on his lap. "Tell me everything that happened, Pumpkin, from the beginning."

Isabella told Bogie of the events that led up to Walter getting shot and the shooting of Troy Mentor.

Bogie held his daughter tight, realizing that Troy Mentor destroyed the invincibility that only a child could feel. Trying to comfort her, Bogie said "I'm sorry you were hurt." When she seemed to relax, he said, "Walter was injured, too...he was shot..."

Isabella nodded.

Bogie studied her then said, "You don't want Walter to get in trouble, do you?"

Isabella shook her head.

"You know it's not good to tell a lie, Pumpkin?"

She nodded.

"But sometimes we have to tell a small lie so we don't hurt someone."

"Like when you told Mommy that yucky stew was delicious?"

Bogie smiled and nodded. "You see, Pumpkin, Walter is not allowed to have a gun."

"Why?"

"It's a long story...I'll go into it another..."

"Is it because he was in prison?"

Bogie nodded. "So you see...if the guns were in the drawer already loaded, and you and Walter found them and defended yourselves, that would make it better for Walter."

"What about me?"

"Nobody's going to do anything to you. You're a child!"

She thought about this and nodded. "He hurt me, Da-dee. That bad man...he threw me at the wall..." She started crying again.

Bogie reached in his pocket, grabbed his phone and pushed a button. As soon as Bailey answered, he said, "I have to talk fast." Before she could speak, he continued, "I'm okay, Isabella is safe. Do you understand?"

With a death grip on the phone, Bailey asked, "What happened?"

"There was a shooting. You'll probably see it on the news. Remember, we're okay!"

"Isabella! Let me talk to her," Bailey demanded.

Bogie held the phone for Isabella while she cried into it.

⌘

They left the hospital assured that the bump on the back of Isabella's head was not a concussion, and confident that she had soft tissue injuries with no broken bones. Catie Christenson stood near the entrance signing autographs for adoring fans as the sweat-soaked cameraman moved to the side. The tall blonde looked a bit wilted after standing in the sun for more than two hours, but Bogie gave her points for persistence.

The cameraman shot some footage of Bogie and Isabella with the real hero, Catie Christenson. Bogie turned to Catie and said, "Walk with me over to Boston Medical Center, I need to check on Walter."

Catie Christenson held up her hand to stop him. "Listen, Ace, my dogs are killing me! I've been here in the hot sun schvitzing all over myself for the past two hours. Hop in the van, and we'll talk on the way over there. This time, I'm coming in!"

Bogie nodded.

50

AUF WIEDERSEHEN

BOSTON

Walter lay in the bed hooked up to an IV drip with a clear oxygen tube under his nostrils. The old man was the color of death. He held Rose's hand as Darryl stood behind her with glistening eyes. "These are some good drugs! I should have known about these in my misspent youth," he said softly.

Two men in dark suits stood on the other side of Walter's bed. Both of the non-descript men had short brown hair and brown eyes. The older Federal agent asked, "Are you sure you don't know how he got into those banks or the stock exchange? If you help us, we are authorized to offer you immunity from prosecution."

Walter laughed then coughed. "You're offering a dying man immunity. That's beautiful! Next you'll offer me a free TJ Maxx credit card with ten percent discount off my first purchase!"

The younger agent grimaced and asked, "How did you know he was targeting those institutions?"

Walter sighed. "I didn't. All I knew was that someone was harassing my niece and trying to kill my brother-in-law. Someone with strong computer skills was trying to take over their system. I was only helping Rose try to figure out who was causing problems, that's all. We figured out it was Troy Mentor. He had a grudge against R&B going back to his divorce."

"What's that got to do with him breaking into all those institutions and removing seven hundred million dollars in under ten minutes?"

"I've already told you. I don't know. He had a program set up to run at the same time his apartment at The Devonshire blew up. I assume he wanted to cause enough havoc to hamper anyone from manually stopping the flow of money until it was gone. He was good. He was a computer genius."

"But not like you," the older agent said trying to goad Walter.

Walter shook his head. "My computer days are behind me. I'm an old man, a sick old man."

"And what about the Becks?" the agent asked. "They don't know anything about this guy?"

"*The Becks!*" Walter scoffed. "There is no such thing! Who makes up this stuff? It was probably Troy Mentor who started the stories so people would stop looking for him." Walter looked up and watched Bogie and Isabella, her clothes still stained with his blood, walking into the room with a tall blonde woman.

Catie Christenson smiled at Darryl. He gave her a slight nod. Her smile to Rose evaporated when Rose sneered at her. Isabella pulled away from Bogie and nudged the federal agents until she was standing in front of them. Isabella placed her small hand on Walter's arm and watched the IV drip attached to the front of his hand.

The older agent said, "Who are these people? How did they get in here?"

Walter looked at him. "They are my family. They stay. You can go if you don't like it."

The agent pointed to Catie. "She's not family. She's the woman from Chanel 7 News..."

Catie extended her hand. "How do you do! I'm here at Bogie McGruder's request. He said that Walter Beck would tell me what happened."

The agent protested. "This is classified…"

She looked at him. "Bullshit!" Catie turned to Walter. "Hi, Walter, It's a pleasure to meet you. I Googled you on the way over here. You've had quite a colorful career. They say you're the greatest!"

Walter smiled. "Flattery for an old man! You can stay." As they listened, Walter told how his niece contacted him because someone had shot one of her employees and was trying to sabotage the R&B Investigations computer system. Since he knew a little about computers, he came to help Rose. During the course of their investigation, they learned that Troy Mentor had probably killed his divorce attorney, his ex-wife's divorce attorney, the forensic accountant and possibly the judge in their divorce case. He most likely killed his ex-wife and hired an imposter to pose as Linda Mentor. He then started gunning for R&B Investigations since they were the first to discover that he funneled his ill-gotten gains into offshore accounts, and started the investigations that brought him crashing down.

In tracking his activities, R&B investigators came to believe that Troy wanted to destroy them. But R&B had no way of knowing Mentor planned to siphon money from major banks and investment houses in the area.

As Catie's eyes opened wide, the older agent glared at her and said, "This is all off the record. National Sec—"

She looked at him and laughed.

Walter smiled. "What does it matter now? Everybody knows! Troy Mentor made a plan to drain hundreds of millions of dollars from those places on a Sunday when everyone was home resting. He had gained access to all of their servers and re-routed the money…CNN said seven hundred and sixty million dollars…into accounts all over the world." Walter didn't mention that Troy Mentor didn't believe R&B Investigations would get the police involved, fearing their own illegal activities might be uncovered. Mentor was sure they would be the ones blown up in the Devonshire apartment.

Catie stared at the agents. "Mentor was a cyber-terrorist, yet you came in here to brow beat this old man! Leave Walter alone, he's not the one who did this. How many more Troy Mentors are out there plotting and scheming while you're standing here trying to shoot fish in a barrel? Go do your job, and leave him alone!"

The older agent said, "He killed..."

"Thank you, Walter! You performed a great public service!"

Walter smiled as the agent shouted, "This is no laughing matter! He and this little girl..." He pointed to Isabella and continued "...shot that guy full of holes..."

Walter looked at Catie and said, "Isabella and I were in the office with two nice young men. He murdered Benjamin and Rodney like that!" Walter snapped his fingers. "I had enough time to grab a small gun from Rose's desk. I stuck it in my waistband...in the back. I just brought out a 9mm gun when he charged into the room with a gun. The 9mm was lying on the desk, but he didn't seem to notice it. He hurt the child!" Walter choked up, but Isabella smoothed her small hand over his arm. "He threw her against the wall. Then he shot me. Isabella ran to me and flung herself over me to protect me. She reached behind me, took the small gun, and shot him. She's a superhero!" Walter stopped and smiled at Isabella. "Mentor was shot but the bullets were small. He was still standing and aimed his gun at Isabella. I reached over, grabbed the 9mm and fired." Walter smiled at Catie, "I'm very tired now and want to say good-by to my family. So if you'll take these gentlemen with you..."

Catie nodded, gave him an air kiss and motioned for the agents to follow her out.

When they were gone, Walter looked around. "My family! Rose, Darryl please take Isabella down the hall. I want to speak to Boghdun. Five minutes...then come back with Isabella...okay?"

After they were gone, Bogie stood next to Walter and held his hand. He half-smiled and softly said, "Valter!"

"Boghdun, it was more than thirty years ago...I got to have my own children for a summer. That was the best and the worst summer of my life. Gretchen was dying, but I got to spend time with my Rose and meet you. You were like an animal that had been kicked too many times. I grew up in Germany after the War, it was tough. I'd seen that look before. But I also saw that when you were with Darryl, you were like a puppy looking for a new owner. I think if he asked you to jump out a window, you would have, without even asking why."

Bogie nodded and wiped a tear off his cheek.

"Then I realized you were a brilliant boy." When Bogie started to protest, Walter held up his hand. "We don't have time for false modesty. That summer you and Rose became the children I never had. After Gretchen died, I followed your activities. When I didn't see you for long stretches, I always asked Darryl how you were doing. You made a few mistakes, but you turned out to be a decent man...a bit more conservative than I would have expected. But you were raising a child, beautiful Amanda. And then you gave me this special granddaughter I never had. Oh, Isabella! What a jewel! She is so smart and brave...I know you cherish her like you were never treasured. That monster wanted to destroy her, don't let him win! Make her understand I was a dead man when I came here. The doctor's gave me three months to live six months ago. I already overstayed my welcome, but I got to say goodbye to my family and meet Isabella. The Becks have moved. I have the new website and passwords that—"

Bogie shook his head.

Walter shrugged slightly then said, "I'm leaving a gift for Isabella and the babies so please don't insult my memory by refusing it. Now, Boghdun, we say goodbye. No more tears! Bring me Isabella! When we're finished, take her out of here and go home. She doesn't need to watch an old man dying. She's seen enough."

Bogie squeezed his hand and turned as Isabella came into the room. Rose placed a chair next to the bed for Darryl who was in obvious pain, but Isabella assumed it was for her. The little girl jumped onto the chair, knelt down on the seat and held Walter's hand.

Isabella's lips quivered then she said, "Please don't die, Uncle Walter."

"Liebchen, this is my time! I'm an old man and very sick. I just stayed this long so I could meet you...the wonderful Girl in Black Pajamas..." As the child cried, her tears dripped onto their joined hands. Walter brought the tear stained hands to his lips and kissed them. "You are a very special girl with great power..."

"But he said..."

"He was wrong, Isabella. He was an evil man who wanted to destroy you because you are so special. You are a very smart little girl. Promise me you will continue studying everything." When she nodded, he said, "And always watch out for the babies. You should protect them from those kinds of fiends." When she nodded, he softly said, "Tell Tommie about the website but only face to face, no emails."

Isabella nodded sadly.

"Goodbye my precious Isabella."

The child kissed Walter's cheek and cried as her father lifted her up and carried her away.

51

A HERO'S WELCOME

South Florida

Bogie and Isabella walked through the jetway at Palm Beach International Airport. Isabella was no longer in disguise; she wore her now famous black martial arts outfit. They were greeted by John and an ununiformed Randy. Amanda held Riley Rose, and Bailey sat in a wheelchair holding the Hankster. On seeing his father, the little boy pushed off Bailey's lap and stood up. He took two wobbly steps before sitting down. He looked up and said, "Da-dee!" clearly. Bogie wiped a tear off his cheek, picked up the baby, and hugged him. Isabella ran to her mother, sat on her lap, and they both cried as Bailey rocked her.

Not to be outdone, Riley Rose started crying. Randy took her from Amanda. He held Riley Rose and kissed her while Amanda went to her father and put her arm around his waist and kissed his cheek. "Welcome home!"

John Carpenter shook his head. "You're the cryingest family I ever saw!"

Bogie nodded then walked to Randy who was holding Riley Rose. Bogie kissed the baby then softly said, "Come to the house, we have work to do."

52

LOVERS AND OTHER STRANGERS

SOUTH FLORIDA

As Moshe stood on the mini-balcony on his cell phone, Zoe looked at Tiffany. "I think this is it!"

"What?"

"I don't know what he's saying, but I don't think it's 'Having a great time, wish you were here.' Did you notice how he gets that strained look on his face when he's talking in Hebrew?"

Tiffany shook her head.

"Well, he does. Super-serious. I have a feeling he's going to be on the next flight out of here."

"Are you going to miss him?"

Zoe thought about it then said, "Yeah. I will. I'll really miss him. It's been a lot of fun...this week...like a vacation...but it's over. My Palm Beach vacation."

Moshe stood behind her studying her. "Are you throwing me out already?"

Zoe looked at him and her eyes filled with tears. She shook her head and reached down for the pack of cigarettes. Moshe took her hand and held it. When he glanced at Tiffany and realized she wasn't going to move off the couch, he led Zoe back to the balcony and closed the door. "I have to go back," he said softly.

Zoe only nodded.

Moshe took both her hands. "I spent more than twenty-five years in Sayeret Matkal. I told you about that, special forces. I've been with many women, but never married, never had a family. I'm forty-five years old and want to have my own family. When I saw your picture, I knew..."

Zoe started crying. "People...your family..."

Moshe smiled. "What's that you say? 'Fuck them.' You have a past, I have a past. How about we have a future together?"

Zoe wrapped her arms around his neck and cried. Finally, she sniffled, "I've done a lot of crazy things, but I've never been in love before."

Moshe pulled her closer and kissed her long and hard.

As Tiffany watched them, from the couch, she knew that soon she was going to be all alone.

⁂

As Isabella sat on the couch telling her mother, sister, Randy and Grandpa John all about her adventures in Boston, Bogie brought the large toy basket into the living room and placed it on the floor. Henry and Riley Rose crawled and toddled to it in their quest to empty their contents as quickly as possible.

Bogie motioned for Randy to follow him. When John and Randy got up, Bogie didn't protest since it was obvious Randy had spoken to his father.

After they were seated, Bogie asked, "Did Zoe or Tiffany call you?"

Dejectedly, Randy shook his head. "I even tried to call Zoe, but she wouldn't answer the phone."

Bogie opened his desk drawer and took out a yellow legal pad. He clicked the pen in his hand. "Let's do a chart of all the players." Bogie produced an organizational chart showing the three generations of the Marcel family in the Sheriff's Office and two generations of the Johnson

244

family along with the two generations of Carpenters. "Anybody else in either family work for the PBSO?"

"Sarah. She's Billy Ray's sister," John Carpenter offered as he pointed to an empty space next to Billy Ray's name.

Bogie stared at him, when John added, "She's the administrative assistant to the Sheriff."

Bogie put down his pen and glared at Randy. "Why didn't you mention that before?"

Randy shrugged. "I didn't know it was important. I haven't been thinking too clear lately. I still don't understand this whole thing."

"Is she the one who was at your cookout?" Bogie asked recalling the hefty brunette who flirted with Randy then huddled together with Zoe and Tiffany.

Randy nodded. "She's the one who had the party...the pictures."

Bogie considered this then said, "We need to find out who set up the websites? Who did the photography? Who handled the money?"

Randy shook his head and said, "I have no idea. The only people who would know are the ones involved, and they're not talking."

John added, "Johnson and Marcel want nothing to do with me now. I tried to talk to them at work and they're too busy for me."

Bogie looked at John Carpenter and said, "They were always too busy for you. You just didn't know it. Now they're trying to figure out how to put up a unified front after their sons showed their asses all over the internet. You're the one who should be avoiding them."

John Carpenter nodded.

Bogie looked at his watch and tapped some keys on his computer. "Wow! Zoe lives in City Place? That's kind of pricey for a girl with no reportable income."

"It's her father's place. He lets her live there. His wife and Zoe don't get along so he has her live there while he and the wife live in a mansion on South Ocean Boulevard," Randy said.

"This guy's living in a mansion? He called me and gave me shit demanding I pay his daughter's medical bills!" After a pause Bogie pointed at Randy and said, "Let's go for a ride! John, stay here. If too many of us show up, we'll spook these girls."

John smiled, glad not to be publicly involved.

∽⟋⟋⟋⟋⟍

Bogie had to park in the City Place garage since Zoe not only had her Volkswagen in front of the town house but also a Mercedes parked behind it. Bogie banged on the door and Randy rang the bell. It was finally answered by a tall muscular man wearing black.

After Moshe and Bogie studied each other, Bogie said, "We'd like to speak to Zoe."

"She's not taking visitors right now," Moshe said.

Bogie continued to study the man. "Tell her it's very important that I speak to her. She knows me."

Zoe came to the door and stared at Bogie and Randy. "What do you want?" she asked coldly.

Bogie said, "We'd like to ask you some questions."

"I don't..."

"Please...!" Bogie implored.

Startled by his supplicating manner, Zoe waved for them to come in. As they entered the living room, Tiffany sat up from the couch where she had been watching the Kardashians taking Miami.

Bogie continued to study Moshe, then pointed at him. "Moses!"

Moshe stared at him, then exclaimed, "The Ukrainian!"

The men punched each other's shoulders playfully. Moshe studied Bogie and moved his arms out. "You used to be this big. Now you're skinny."

"I'm lean and mean. You used to have a full head of hair!"

246

Moshe shrugged. "I asked after you, but nobody ever knew who I was talking about."

"Probably because you were the only person who ever called me The Ukrainian."

Moshe nodded. "I heard you got out. I thought maybe you went to the dark side."

Bogie studied him. "Russia?"

Moshe nodded again. "Well, you spoke Ukrainian…"

Bogie shook his head and laughed. "Looking back I think it's funny. We were all playing war games, getting ready for the big attack from Mother Russia while the rag heads were painting bulls eyes on our backs."

"Didn't I tell you that?"

Bogie considered this then said, "Yes, but you qualified it. You said if the Arabs ever got together, they'd wipe Israel off the map. But you said Israel was safe because the Arabs hated each other almost as much as they hated Israel."

"Well, they found a new way of coming at us. Jihad!"

Bogie nodded.

Moshe asked, "Why'd you get out? It couldn't have been Clinton's 'Don't ask, Don't tell.'"

Bogie laughed. "I had a child to raise. It was tough on her."

"No mother?"

"Not really. Anyway, my daughter's grown up now. This is her husband," he said pointing to Randy.

Moshe shook Randy's hand. "Wow, I feel very old now!"

Zoe quickly said, "He didn't tell you he has a new wife who isn't much older than we are…and two small kids…"

Moshe studied Bogie and grinned. "So what do you want from Zoe?"

"Some answers."

Moshe held Zoe's hand. "Do you feel like answering some questions?"

Zoe shrugged. "What the hell! But that fuckin Mandie..."

"I'll take care of your hospital bill," Bogie said quickly.

"What about my pain and..."

Bogie took a folded check out of his shirt pocket and handed it to her.

Zoe studied the check. "Is this like a bribe?"

"Yes," Bogie answered.

"Okay. What do you want to know?"

After telling them everything she knew about their movie business, Zoe ended with, "...and Billy Ray said if I talked to anybody he'd slit my throat..."

Bogie and Moshe looked at each other as if to say, 'that's not going to happen.'

Bogie studied his notes. "Randy! Why are they involving Randy in this?"

Zoe shook her head, looked at Randy and smiled. "I'm sorry they did this to you. All I know is that they wanted him and Mandie in the movies in the worst kind of way, but I really don't know what the real story is. If Billy Ray ever told the truth, his teeth would fall out."

Bogie nodded. "So Sarah Thomas handled the money and did the photography. Who set up the websites? Who maintained them?"

Zoe shrugged. "I don't know. I assumed Sarah did, but then again she's got a kid...and she's such a cokehead. I don't think she'd have the time..."

They all looked up when they heard the incessant pounding on the front door. Moshe, Bogie and Randy stood and walked to the door. A messenger had a letter for Zoe Ziegler. She had to sign for it. The letter of eviction was signed by the owner, Martin Ziegler.

Bogie looked over the letter and then at Zoe. "Your father's giving you a Three Day Notice. After that, he'll have the Sheriffs serve you a Five Day Summons. You've got about a week to get out of here."

"Moshe and I are leaving tomorrow morning. We're flying to New York."

"We're getting married," Moshe added.

Bogie's eyebrows shot up. "Wow! That was quick!"

When Tiffany blew her nose, they all looked at her. Zoe sat down on the couch and hugged Tiffany. "I'm sorry, Tiff, I didn't know he'd do anything so fast. It's probably that fuckin Annette..." She stopped suddenly remembering that Annette was Moshe's relative no matter how distant.

Randy opened his mouth, but Bogie shook his head then looked at Tiffany. "You'll come to my house, Tiffany."

"But Mandie."

"Mandie doesn't live there. We have a guest room, and you can stay there."

As Tiffany cried and packed, Bogie took the cellphone out of his pocket. Moshe made a gesture toward the balcony. "The private phone booth."

Bogie smiled and walked outside. After telling Bailey about their new house guest, he listened as she said, "You can't save everybody. You know that, don't you?"

"Yes."

"I know you feel bad for this girl, and I'm sure she's grateful. But just make sure she understands that gratitude in the form of sexual favors is strongly discouraged by the management. That's me! Got it?"

"Yes, ma'am."

When Bogie came back into the living room laughing, Tiffany, teary eyed looked at him. "What did your wife say?"

Bogie smiled. "She said, 'mi casa es su casa!'"

Moshe and Randy rolled their eyes.

53

LIAR, LIAR PANTS ON FIRE

South Florida

The sun was shining and the air was clear, but Paul Gallagher was in an ugly mood. Still out on leave from the Riviera Beach Police Department, he felt like he was losing his edge. Guys on the job weren't going out of their way to meet up for drinks. Although he had the pickup lines and moves down pat, the police groupies were looking through him and shaking their booties at the younger guys. Even that fuckin Sarah changed her telephone number.

While sitting at home alone drinking, Paul Gallagher began to realize that his problem was Tiffany. She humiliated him, then moved into the McGruder house. But what really galled him was seeing her riding around in that yellow Volkswagen Beetle like she didn't have a care in the world. Everyone knew that was Zoe Ziegler's car, and now Tiffany was driving it all over Palm Beach to remind them she was a hardcore porn queen.

Paul Gallagher riffled through his desk until he found a telephone number. For the second time that month, Paul made a call to Martin Ziegler.

Martin did not seem particularly glad to hear from him, so Paul got to the point. "I wanted to talk to you about Zoe's car."

"My daughter is dead to me."

"Yeah, well she might be dead to you, but her car is still moving around Palm Beach."

"I believe your daughter is the one who is driving it."

"Exactly! What right does she have to drive that car? It's in your name, isn't it? Aren't you paying the insurance on it?"

"Yes," Martin answered. "I was thinking about getting it back."

"How much do you want for it?" Paul Gallagher asked.

"Why? Do you want to buy it for her?" Martin Ziegler asked.

"Hell no! I want it off the road. It's an embarrassment to me and my whole family. I'm sure you feel the same way."

"What do you have in mind?" Martin asked.

"If you don't want too much for it, I'll buy it from you and drive it up to Jacksonville to my niece. She's a good kid, hard-working...not the kind of girl who makes her parents ashamed."

"How much did you have in mind?" Martin asked.

"Three thousand," Paul said quickly. "That's all I have."

After a long silence, Martin Ziegler said, "I paid twenty and some change for it...a graduation present for...her. What the hell! I don't want it, I don't want to look at it every time I'm driving on I-95. I'll call McGruder, and tell him to have her leave it at your house."

"What the hell's McGruder got to do with this?" Paul asked his voice raised.

"Nothing," Zeigler answered. "I was going to call him anyway to thank him for paying Zoe's hospital bill...and I heard Tiffany's staying with him and his family."

"That's right," Paul said not trying to conceal his agitation. Paul was certain that more than half the population of Palm Beach County knew Tiffany was living in the McGruder house. "I used to think he was an okay guy, but now I know he's just a self-righteous prick. He's so glad his daughter's not involved in those movies that he treats mine like she's some orphan he found on his doorstep."

∽⟋⟍∾

After ending his conversation with Martin Ziegler, Paul punched in a number he knew by heart. When Orlando Garcia answered his phone, Paul asked his friend, "Do you still want that yellow Beetle for Mary Lou?"

"Marcy Jo," Orlando, a fellow swordsman, corrected. Orlando Garcia, a West Palm Beach cop with dark hair and a deep tan painted over a heavily muscled body, believed he was just too much man for one woman. His first marriage ended in divorce. He was separated from his second wife while his baby momma, Marcy Jo, was now bitching that she needed a decent ride for their soon-to-be-born son. Marcy Jo didn't care if he was paying alimony and child support, her baby was not going to suffer. Orlando asked, "How much?"

"You know the car is a year old and in mint condition. It sold for twenty-two—"

"How much?" Orlando Garcia interrupted.

"You could get it for ten," Paul said conspiratorially.

"No can do. That's too rich for my blood! I don't think I could get financing...my credit sucks," Orlando said.

"Too bad," Paul said. "I thought this was Marcy Jo's dream car."

"It is, it was. But that little sun bunny's gonna halfta lower her sights."

"Well, I just wanted to give you first crack at it," Paul said. "There are a couple of other—"

"What about you? Could you help me, take some paper on the car. I could get five together if you'd take a note for the other five."

"Do I look like a fuckin bank?" Paul asked irritably.

"Your wife's—"

"In rehab...again! The insurance company won't pay for the Lexus. They claim I was drunk. Her old lady's pissed and said she'll only replace the car when Dee Dee's well enough to drive. Tell me again about how much money I have..."

"Sorry, dude, I didn't realize..."

Paul sighed audibly. "I shouldn't do this, but I like you. And, fuck it, it's only money. You get the five together and I'll draw up a note for the other five. But there's one condition."

"What?" Orlando asked skeptically.

"You have to help me get the car."

54

A YOUTUBE STAR

Bogie and his construction manager, Carlos Aragon, were inspecting a property that had been vacated for two years. Bogie shook his head and grabbed a switchblade out of his sneaker. He made a quick circle in the rotted wood and pulled out a plug, finding termites. "If they were giving this place away, I wouldn't want it. The first thing we'd have to do is level it. We don't need that headache. There are a lot other—"

Bogie stopped suddenly when his cellphone vibrated. He looked at the screen and answered it. "Hi, Randy. What's going on? Did any of the sites come back up yet?"

"No," Randy said dejected. "I don't know if they're going to...anyway, if you could have taken them down when..."

"It didn't seem like a good idea at the time," Bogie said remembering Randy's tearful pleas for help while he was in the middle of a crisis in Boston.

"I'm sorry," Randy said. "And that's not even why I called. Either go on Youtube or Gossip Extra...Jose Lambiet's already got it up on his blog."

"What am I looking for?" Bogie asked without enthusiasm.

"A video of Tiffany's father beating the crap out of her in the Walmart parking lot while a West Palm Beach cop stands there watching."

❦

Trying to make herself useful while staying with Bogie and Bailey, Tiffany offered to go to Walmart when Bailey was working in the office and Isabella was practicing her kung fu.

After purchasing twelve white towels and twenty-four washcloths, Tiffany stepped outside the Walmart Supercenter that sat on a chunk of Belvedere Road and Military Trail. Tiffany walked to the yellow Volkswagen, tossed the large bag in the back and sat in the driver's seat. Suddenly a black and white patrol car stopped behind her t-boning her into the spot. The cop turned on the light bar but not the siren. He spoke into a cellphone then slowly got out of his vehicle. Orlando Garcia moved to the driver's side window and tapped on it. As the window rolled down, he said, "License and registration."

"This car is registered—"

"License and registration," Orlando Garcia repeated not giving her a chance to speak.

Tiffany reached over and grabbed paperwork from the glove box and sorted through it. Then she went into her small pink handbag and pulled out her wallet. She retrieved her driver's license and placed it and the registration on the window ledge with shaking hands.

Garcia slowly read the registration then asked, "This isn't your car?"

Tiffany shook her head. "No, but I have permission—"

Garcia walked away before she could finish. He sat in the patrol car and waited until a banged-up red Lexus pulled into the parking lot. Paul Gallagher stopped in the middle of the row, blocking other cars from entering or leaving. He opened his door, walked over to the patrol car and handed Orlando Garcia a sheet of paper. Garcia signed it and returned it to Paul Gallagher with a check and Tiffany's license.

"The keys should be in the ignition. I'll get the title to you as soon as I get it," Paul Gallagher said.

Orlando Garcia nodded as Paul Gallagher walked to the Volkswagen and motioned for Tiffany to unfasten the seatbelt. As soon as she did, Paul opened the door, grabbed her by her long, blonde hair and dragged away from the car screaming. When she continued to scream, Paul slammed Tiffany's head against the trunk of Garcia's patrol car. Garcia got out of the car, walked to the Beetle, rolled up the window, removed the keys and locked the car before returning to his black and white then slowly driving away.

Paul Gallagher shoved Tiffany toward the Lexus. She screamed, "Help! Help!" A crowd of Walmartians, who had been taking video of the event with their phones, moved toward Paul. Paul reached in his pocket and produced his ID. "I'm a cop!" he shouted as he held his identification in the air for the crowd to see.

Tiffany screamed again. Paul punched her on the back and pushed her into the passenger seat of the Lexus. He got in and drove away as the damaged car coughed and sputtered while the crowd took close-up shots of his license plate.

Bogie and Carlos watched the video without speaking. When it was finished, Bogie muttered, "Motherfucker!" He took a deep breath then turned to Carlos and asked, "You wanna go for a ride?"

"I thought you'd never ask," Carlos answered and smiled.

∽∞∾

When the black Dodge Ram truck pulled up a half a block away from the Gallagher home, Bogie glanced at Carlos then said, "Remember, the kitchen door is right off the carport. It has a glass window in it."

"You're sure about this?" Carlos asked.

Bogie nodded. "It was like that three or four years ago when the girls were in high school. The mother was passed out in the house, Tiffany didn't have a key and Paul was nowhere to be found. I broke the glass in the kitchen door, reached inside and unlocked the door."

"What if he has the alarm on?" Carlos asked.

"Who gives a shit! It should be over by the time anyone responds."

"Hmmm!" Carlos said. "You be careful! You're going to that front door unarmed. He could just shoot you through the door."

"I'm counting on my charm and personality to get me through," Bogie said.

"That's what I'm afraid of," Carlos said. "I'm the one who should take the front door."

Bogie shook his head. "He doesn't really know you. You've got a greater chance of getting shot through the door than I do."

Carlos pushed back his dark hair with both hands then reached down and picked up his new Century Arms pistol. As he opened the passenger door, Carlos said, "Be careful, bro. Don't forget you got a couple of small kids to support."

Bogie smiled. "At last count, so did you."

After they bumped fists, Carlos slammed the truck door and headed across a neighbor's front lawn. When Carlos disappeared into the next door neighbor's driveway, Bogie slowly got out of the truck and grabbed a large white plastic bag.

He walked on the sidewalk then turned into the Gallagher's front walkway. The smashed Lexus sat with its front half in the driveway and the back half still on the street, steam pouring out of the hood. Tiffany's mangled, pink Hyundai lay in the carport like a dead horse.

Bogie sauntered up to the front door and rang the bell. He listened to Tiffany moan as a strap struck her flesh. Bogie knew the sound well, having been brutalized by his father when he was a teenager. When there was no answer, Bogie rang the bell two more times, trying not to push the bell too hard and appear anxious. He knocked on the door, restraining himself from pounding too hard. Finally, he tried to turn the knob and called out, "Paul! Paul, are you there?"

Paul yelled through the door, "What the fuck do you want?"

"I brought Tiffany's clothes here since she's moving back home."

"What!?" Paul asked confused.

At that moment, there was the sound of glass smashing inside the house. Believing Paul would turn toward the sound, Bogie stepped back, stood sideways and kicked the door below the doorknob. The door stayed in place, so he kicked it again. This time, the frame splintered and he pushed the door in.

Paul Gallagher stood in the middle of the living room aiming his gun at Bogie. "You think you're so fuckin smart, don't you?" Paul said contemptuously.

Bogie looked at Tiffany lying in a bloody heap on the rug. Her clothes were ripped and shredded. "You trying to kill her?" Bogie asked.

Paul smirked. "She's not worth killing. She's moving to Jacksonville, and you're leaving here in a body bag. You broke into my house, asshole. Ever hear of Stand your Ground?"

Bogie gave Paul Gallagher one of his smiles as the corner of his mouth moved. "You think you're George Zimmerman now?"

"Fuck you!" Paul yelled.

"No, fuck you!" Carlos said from behind Paul. "I have a 45 aimed at the back of your head, shit bird. Put down the gun!"

"You gonna make me?" Paul asked as he stared at Bogie. Bogie smiled again. "I'm not armed, Paul."

"I don't—"

"Drop it!" a uniformed cop said from behind Bogie.

Paul glared at Bogie then the cop. "He broke—"

"Put the fuckin gun down, Lieutenant!" the broad cop demanded.

When Paul lay the gun on the floor, Carlos moved in from behind him and kicked the gun toward the front door.

"He's got a gun!" Paul shouted.

"Irregardless, you were trying to shoot this dude with no gun," Carlos answered. "We just came here to get Tiffany before this loco shit bird killed her."

Officer Flores nodded as Bogie walked over to Tiffany and lifted her off the floor. "I'll call for an ambulance. And, Lieutenant, the captain wants to see you now."

Paul looked away and muttered, "I'm busy right now."

"Lieutenant Gallagher! He wants me to bring you in now! He's waiting for you in the chief's office," Officer Flores said through his teeth.

⸙

Bogie jumped into the back of the ambulance with Tiffany, and Carlos watched as Officer Flores slammed the passenger side door of cruiser. Carlos walked over to the cop and said, "Hey, bro, thanks for not making a big deal out of our breaking into this dude's house."

Juan Flores stared at Carlos. His face was expressionless. "Just because you knocked up my sister that don't make you my bro. And if I dragged your sorry ass in, you'd be sitting in jail. Then you wouldn't be working and making money to pay your obligations. Yazmin wouldn't have enough money to take care of your kid, and she'd be coming to me. I've got four kids of my own to feed, I don't need to be supporting yours. And, besides, this guy's a super asshole."

⸙

As Bailey, Randy and Mandie sipped hot chocolate, Bogie drank herb tea. Bogie started his tirade. "Between Martin with his dead daughter routine and that fuckin Paul Gallagher, it's no wonder those girls acted out. Tiffany should sue him, the Riviera Beach, and the West Palm Beach Police Department!"

"What Tiffany should do and what she's going to do might be two different things. She's badly beaten and very frightened," Bailey said. "Tiffany wouldn't even stay in the hospital overnight, and we all know she should have."

⌒〰〰〰〰⌒

As they lie in the dark listening to the monitors in the children's rooms, Bogie's eyes opened as he heard muffled crying, then someone speaking softly. He slid out of bed.

"Put your robe on! No walking around in underwear with a guest in the house," Bailey admonished him.

"Yes ma'am," he said then smiled.

Bogie walked down the hall and saw Isabella's bedroom door wide open. His heart skipped a beat until he saw the guestroom door was also open. He peeked inside and watched Isabella sitting on the bed stroking Tiffany's head. "Don't cry, Tiffany. Everything will be okay. Da-dee can fix anything. You know he's a hero, don't you? If you're scared, I could lie down here with you and hold your hand. Even I get scared sometimes and Mommy and Da-dee let me sleep in their bed. When Uncle Walter died, I got to sleep with them for two days." Isabella continued to stroke Tiffany's hair.

"Thanks, Izzy. You're very kind. Sure, you can sleep here."

Bogie returned to the master bedroom, hung up his robe, and slid in bed next to his wife. He held her hand and beamed. "What are you grinning about?" Bailey asked.

"I think Isabella's a kinder soul than we realized," Bogie answered.

Bailey smiled. "Let's not get crazy now."

55

KEY TO THE PUZZLE

As the family ate fruit, yogurt, and whole grain toast, the Hankster decided he wanted to feed himself. He pushed Bailey's hand away and tried using the spoon. The result was a mess of yogurt over his hair and face with some berries stuck to his cheeks. He grinned with his four teeth and bit into a piece of toast. Bogie laughed, took out his cell phone, and snapped a picture. "We'll see who's laughing in twenty years when I show that to all your girlfriends."

Isabella giggled. "Would you really do that, Da-dee?"

"Sure. That's half the fun of being a parent. You get to embarrass your children."

"Like..." Isabella looked toward Tiffany then looked down at her plate. "I'm sorry," she said softly. "I shouldn't say that."

Tiffany patted the little girl on the shoulder. "That's okay, Izzy. You didn't say it to be mean." She turned to Bogie. "I need to talk to you when you have a chance."

Bogie nodded.

After they ate, Tiffany helped Bailey clean up the kitchen while Bogie grabbed the Hankster and carried him upstairs saying "We've got to hose you off, Henry my boy." Tiffany looked at Bailey. "You have a very nice family."

Bailey only nodded.

When Bogie brought the baby downstairs bathed and wearing fresh clothes, he looked at his watch then at Tiffany. He pointed to the home office. "Why don't you go in there? I'll be right in."

Bailey and the children headed for the large apartment complex. Bailey could work in the office while the Hankster and Riley Rose played and Isabella received lessons from Master Lim.

Bogie sat behind his desk. "What's up?"

"I want to thank you for bringing me to your home and treating me...so...well."

Bogie only nodded.

"I want to help you."

When Bogie raised an eyebrow, she added, "I wasn't going to say anything because...because...I was hurt...Everybody acts like I'm stupid. Even when you came to Zoe's place and asked her all those questions, you never asked me any questions. Did you think I was so dumb I didn't know anything?"

Bogie shook his head. "I assumed that Zoe was the only one who had contact with Billy Ray and JJ as far as the business was concerned. That was my mistake. It's like the tired old saying 'Assume something and you make an ass of you and me both.'"

Tiffany smiled. "I never heard that."

"That's because you're so young. Anyway, I apologize for not speaking to you about this whole movie business. Is there something you know that can help?"

"I know who sent the emails to the Sheriff and the others that exposed the movies."

"Who?"

"My father."

"Why would he do that?"

"My cousin Rhonda sent him an email telling him about the site with the Palm Beach County Sheriff's deputies. My father was drunk when he got it and recognized Billy Ray and JJ right away. He sent emails to Glenshaw and other top brass. He wanted there to be a big scandal. I think it had something to do with the Sheriff's Office taking over the policing in Riviera Beach. He wanted everyone to know that they couldn't police themselves, let alone Riviera Beach. Then he told Sarah what he did. She talked to Billy Ray and JJ and told them to blame everything on Randy...to say he was the one behind the movies."

"Why Randy? Why's he being blamed for everything?"

Tiffany considered this then said, "Sarah's got a grudge against Randy. I heard her talking to Billy Ray and JJ when I was in the bathroom in her house. They were saying something about Randy's father going over to IA and how he'd get to fix everything for Randy. The guys said they'd spread the word that Randy gave them up to save his own ass. Billy Ray said nobody would believe Randy didn't have anything to do with the movies. Sarah really liked that - she's a bitch! She was really pissed when Randy dumped her and went after Mandie. Even at their wedding Sarah was saying crap like 'he only married Mandie because he knocked her up' and 'it'll never last, Mandie's just a spoiled kid.'"

"Did you think Randy was part of this?"

Tiffany shook her head. "No! If he was, why was Billy Ray telling Zoe to push Mandie to get him involved? If he was already in, they wouldn't have to do that, would they?"

Bogie shook his head. "Did you know Randy was on one of these sites?"

"He wasn't, was he?" Tiffany asked.

Rather than answering that question, Bogie said, "I don't understand the connection between Sarah and your father."

"She's one of my father's..."

When Bogie stared at her, Tiffany added, "Oh, yeah. When Sarah was pregnant, there were rumors that the baby was his. But then the kid turned out to be black so she figured it belonged to some captain. The only thing everybody knew for sure was that it wasn't her ex-husband's. It seems Sarah slept with everybody except him. Anyway, when my father sent the emails, he had no idea Sarah was behind it. Maybe he still doesn't know."

Bogie tapped his fingers on the desk. "So Sarah was running the whole thing?"

Tiffany nodded. "It was Sarah's show all the way! She's the one who called the shots! She set up the sites, took in the money and everything."

Bogie asked, "Where did Sarah maintain the sites, in her house?"

"Mostly. But some of the stuff she did right at her desk in the Sheriff's office."

Stunned, Bogie sat staring at Tiffany.

56

HARD DRIVES DON'T LIE

At five o'clock, Sarah Thomas quickly backed out of her parking spot, late to pick up her son from daycare. As soon as her car cleared the property, John and Randy Carpenter, driving the white Escalade, entered the lot. They were both visibly nervous but determined. Randy glanced at his father. "Are you sure he'll see us?"

"Why not? Bogie said the sheriff plans on being here till six. He's got some kind of fundraiser and doesn't want to bother driving home. I don't even want to think about how Bogie got all this information, but I'm grateful he did. Don't tell him that, though, he's already got an ego that won't quit."

Randy only smiled, knowing his father was more than a little jealous of Bogie.

After entering the Sheriff's office and presenting him with a memo of their findings along with an affidavit signed by Tiffany, they watched as Ron Glenshaw slumped in his chair. "This can't be true!"

"It is, sir," John Carpenter said. "If you turn on her computer, you'll get all the proof you need. But before you do that, you might want to have witnesses so no one can accuse you of tampering with it."

⌒॥⌒

At ten o'clock that night, Ron Glenshaw was still in his office. Sarah Thomas was under arrest, her home computer confiscated, and her son turned over to the Department of Children and Families. Billy Ray Marcel, III and Jim "JJ" Johnson were issued letters of termination. Billy Ray vowed to fight the wrongful termination. The Sheriff swore he could fight till hell froze over, but Billy Ray would not return on his watch.

57

CAREER ENHANCEMENT

Tiffany walked down the stairs and studied Bailey who was curled up reading a book in the corner of a large couch. Tiffany sat on the opposite couch. "Don't you have a TV?"

Bailey looked up and smiled. "There's one in the room where you're sleeping. The wardrobe opens up and there's a TV inside."

"But what about you? Don't you watch TV?"

Bailey considered this then shook her head. "I'm on the internet every day. I read a lot so I don't have time for TV."

"Oh."

Bailey studied her. "What's the matter, Tiffany?"

"I just saw a news report and they said my father was being investigated by Internal Affairs from the Sheriff's Office. That doesn't make any sense."

Overhearing this, Bogie walked into the living room from the hallway. "Yes, it does. When there's a question of how a high ranking officer in a police department handled a situation, sometimes they have another department or services investigate to make sure there's no collusion."

Tiffany studied the floor. "I'm so sick of this. I don't want to get dragged back into this same crap over and over. Let the guys get their pictures taken and be humiliated the way Zoe and I were."

Bogie smiled. "So you think it's their turn up at bat?"

Tiffany nodded.

Bogie sat down on the couch next to Bailey. He stretched his arm around her shoulder. "Have you given any thought to what we talked about?"

Tiffany nodded.

"I think I'll go for it. After all, what have I got to lose?"

"But you know, Tiffany, if you want to go somewhere else and start all over, you don't advertise your location to the world. You stay off Facebook, close your email account and stop text-messaging people. You keep your head down and don't call attention to yourself. After a while, you'll be living in a whole new world."

She nodded again. "Do you think I'll like Boston? I know it's cold."

Bailey smiled. "There are a lot of young people there. Don't forget, there are more colleges per square mile in the Boston area than any other place on earth. The winter weather sucks! It's cold. You have to dress warm. But you'll meet new people. Remember the mistakes you made and try not to make them again. You'll work. Rose will have you do a lot of clerical work while you're training."

"What will I wear?"

"No problem," Bogie answered. "Everybody at R&B wears black tee shirts and black cargo pants with black army boots. If you're good, you'll even get your own R&B jacket."

"No pink?" Tiffany asked softly.

Bogie and Bailey shook their heads.

"Where will I live?"

"I'll rent out the ground floor apartment in Pop's building for you. You'll be paid up for six months. After that, it's up to you."

They looked up when the doorbell rang. Bogie glanced at his watch. "Who the hell's coming here at nine o'clock?" he muttered as he went to the door.

Holding a sleeping baby, Randy and Amanda stood there.

Bogie gestured for them to come in. "Why didn't you just walk in?"

Randy grinned. "Probably because your door's locked."

Bogie hugged his daughter, kissed the sleeping baby, and gestured for them to sit down. After an awkward silence, Tiffany stood up and went to Amanda. "I'm sorry for all the trouble." She started to sniffle, and Amanda hugged her.

Randy looked at Bogie. "I need to talk to you."

Bogie gestured toward the home office.

They walked down the short hallway. Bogie closed the door, sat down and asked, "What's up?"

"Based on my report to the Sheriff and the fact that I pointed out all the connections between the sites and Sarah Thomas' computers, I was offered a job in the Computer Crimes Unit." When Bogie smiled, Randy scowled. "It's not funny! If I take it, they'll know for sure what a dumbass I am and that I don't know shit about these things. Do you think you could show me?"

Bogie shook his head. "It would take months and even then you might not get it...most people don't understand what's really happening in a computer. They just turn it on and expect it to work."

"But if I turn them down, they'll wonder if I really found out all that stuff myself or somebody else did."

"It's better to let them wonder than for you to go in and confirm it. Besides, it's tough to live a lie. Every day, you look around and wait for the other shoe to drop."

Randy nodded. He sighed. "That's how I felt, but Mandie thought..."

"Randy, if it would help you, I'd do it in a second. But I don't want to be a party to you making a fool of yourself."

Randy shrugged and grinned. "You know what really impressed the hell out of the computer guys?"

Bogie shook his head.

"Telling them how they could get the time frame on those pictures of me since she kept pictures of everybody at that party on her computer. That was embarrassing! That's one party I'll never forget."

"At least it proved she took those pictures of you long before she set up the websites. You could take action against her for selling them."

Randy shook his head. "I had enough of that whole business. The site's down now. That's all I want. Let somebody else sue her. I'm just worried about what I'm going to tell the brass."

"You might tell them you have a problem with your eyes, you just can't see yourself working on computers all day."

EPILOGUE

The party was held in the reception area of the large apartment complex so Grandma McGruder could easily attend. Margarita, looking lovely in a yellow ruffled dress, pushed the wheelchair through the door as Jorge, the young, buff pool man held it open and winked at her. Carlos smiled at her and nodded. The machismo was gone, and he looked a bit sad. Margarita gave him a curt smile and wheeled Elizabeth to the table. When the old lady saw the children, she beamed. "Oh, my babies! You're all here."

John Carpenter, still in uniform, walked through the front door. Isabella ran to him. "Hello, Grandpa John!"

"Hi, Isabella," he responded in a quizzical tone. "What's happening?"

"Today is the Hankster's birthday, and we're going to eat cake and ice cream!"

John laughed, knowing Isabella's parents always monitored her sugar intake. He stopped when he found her studying his holstered gun.

Isabella looked up at him and smiled. "I was just wondering if it was loaded."

John nodded. "Wouldn't be much sense carrying it around if it wasn't."

The child nodded in agreement then asked, "How many bullets do you put in the clip?"

John studied her. "Why?"

"I just want to make sure you're not overloading it. The gun can jam with too many bullets in the clip. Less is better!"

John grinned then stopped. "Surely you're not going to start asking for a gun, are you?"

Isabella shook her head. "I'm too young, but I want to be prepared."

John wondered if she was getting ready for the day when she ruled the world, but asked, "No Aunt Rose?"

Isabella shook her head. "She's busy nego-she-ating for our building and hiring more people. We got.." After considering this, she said, "Publicity! That's what she said, but she promised to come for my birthday. But Pop Pop is here." She looked around then noticed the office door was closed. "He's probably still talking to Da-dee."

John nodded as he thought of the unfairness of being a studly man who was being called "Grandpa John" not only by his own granddaughter but by Bogie's two children. Bogie, on the other hand, was called Da-dee by his own children and his granddaughter. Da-dee might be strange, but didn't conjure up images of an old man.

John studied Isabella who was a virtual fountain of family gossip. "I don't suppose your Aunt Ann is coming for the birthday party?"

Isabella shook her head. "She sent the Hankster a present, and she talked to Da-dee last night." She whispered conspiratorially, "Da-dee said she's very needy."

John studied her. "He told you that?"

Isabella shook her head. "I heard him talking to Mommy..."

As John continued to study her, Isabella added softly, "When I was sleeping."

"Maybe we'll just keep that between us."

Isabella nodded.

∞

As Darryl and Bogie sat at the desk, Darryl hung his cane on the edge, took a piece of paper from his pocket, and handed it to Bogie. "These are account numbers. There are three accounts with the kids' Social Security numbers as the passwords. One for Isabella, one for Henry, and one for Riley Rose. Isabella's is four million. The others are two million. He said she's a special girl and should always know it. He predicted she'd be in medical school by the time she was fourteen or, if she chose another path, she could use the money to post bail. Walter said you promised to respect his wishes."

Bogie shook his head. "Did he give me a chance to refuse him?"

Darryl shrugged. "Is she seeing that new counselor?"

Bogie nodded. "For all the good it's doing. It's pretty much the same shit. 'She has an IQ of almost two hundred and should be in a special school.' Isabella's already getting bored with her...Isabella's not some freak! This woman can't seem to get off the IQ train and deal with the fact that the kid's been through some serious shit!"

"Did you catch Catie Christenson's special report on Isabella and Walter?"

Bogie grinned. "CNN picked it up. I think Fox did, too. Jack emailed me clips. *Baby Einstein aka The Girl in Black Pajamas and the Greatest Hacker of the Twenty-First Century* teamed up to stop the cyber-terrorist who was trying to destroy our financial system. Serious as the situation was, Catie sure knew how to sensationalize it. He was no cyber-terrorist; Troy Mentor was a thief and a psychopath."

Darryl sighed. "Speaking of psychopaths, that apartment where Mentor and woman lived was strange to say the least. The place was filled with costumes, wigs, makeup...it was like the dressing room in a theater."

"All the world was their stage," Bogie said. "They certainly cursed it with a lot of heartbreak and destruction."

Darryl nodded. "Those two boys!" Darryl's eyes filled with tears. "Benjamin and Rodney were so excited to have real jobs...I could hardly speak when I met with their mothers. They'll never get over that...I'll never get over it..."

"It wasn't your fault!" Bogie said with a bit too much force.

Darryl shrugged. "Two cops were seriously hurt when that apartment blew up, but nobody mentions them. Mentor and his girlfriend killed their neighbor in the Devonshire just to be able to use his Corvette, but that was buried in the story somewhere. I still don't know if there was any follow-up on all those people he killed. All the focus is on the money! Did I tell you who Linda Mentor was?"

Bogie shook his head.

Darryl thought then said, "I can't remember the name now...she was an administrator in that computer company's Palo Alto branch. I heard they had a thing going on whenever he flew out to California. Nobody knows if she was aware that he had a woman in every port. Anyway, this one quit her job before his trial began. Mentor could see it coming and started getting ready for action."

Bogie sighed. "There are more like him out there. Maybe someday the people who are supposed to be monitoring these sites will be able to distinguish their asses from their elbows."

"Maybe you and Rose..."

Bogie laughed. "The government would tie our hands behind our backs, send in about six people to oversee us, and then explain what we were not allowed to do...under the law...that would be fun!"

"You know Walter bought the condo from R&B for Tommie?" When Bogie nodded, Darryl added, "Tommie's there now with nursing care and everything he'd get in a rehab center. His medical bills are going to be astronomical. The Walter Beck Foundation is paying for everything insurance doesn't cover. With the proceeds from the condo and another chunk from Walter, Rose's been looking at small buildings. But now the owner of the building R&B leases is making some sweet sounds about selling it cheap. The whole building would have to be revamped for underground access and security."

Bogie nodded. "You could be the general contractor and oversee it."

"I'm too old for that."

"That's bullshit! Either come here for the winter and work, or oversee that project. We're not going to let you sit on the couch watching TV. Which reminds me, Isabella is excited to take you for walks while you're here. She said you love to walk with her. Maybe you'll be able to get rid of that cane by the time you leave."

Darryl scowled then sighed. "You're as big a pain in the ass as Rose is."

Bogie nodded. "Your choice! And about the money... I've heard that about seven hundred and sixty million was siphoned from accounts in Boston, but they've only recovered six hundred and eighty million. I get the feeling they're never going to recover the rest. I'm thinking the Becks took a finder's fee."

Darryl laughed. "You had to expect that. They certainly wouldn't work for nothing."

Bogie considered then said, "They got sixteen million from Mentor's offshore accounts. So if you throw that in the pile and ten people shared the loot, the math is off."

"How so?" Darryl asked.

"Running the numbers quick and dirty, I figured the money he left the kids, the condo, Tommie's medical bills and the million he left the church we're already over his share of the loot. And he left Rose enough to buy a building. What am I missing?"

Darryl laughed. "You were always good in math. Who said they shared the money equally?"

Bogie feigned shock. "You mean there's not even honor among thieves?"

Darryl shook his head.

"So you're okay with Tiffany going back with you?" Bogie asked.

"It's fine with me, but she's not going to become another Patzo."

Both men smiled as they remembered the white dog.

After considering Darryl's remark, Bogie said, "After Momma was gone, I couldn't go back there anymore."

"I know," Darryl said. "But I can't take Tiffany for a walk or a ride in the car. This girl's got problems I can't begin to handle."

"She's the one who has to deal with them. We'll give her the tools. The rest is up to her."

Darryl looked at Bogie. "What's up with Randy? Is he okay now?"

Bogie nodded. "He was able to show them how Sarah used old pictures of him on the website without his permission. The pictures had been in her computer for four years...long before she started the whole porn business."

Darryl grinned. "It's a good thing he's such a whiz with computers so he could point out these things."

Bogie smiled and nodded again. "Yes, it is. What blows my mind is that Billy Ray! He's fighting this whole thing tooth and nail, demanding a termination hearing and threatening to sue the department. Billy Ray's grandfather had a heart attack and hung it up. His father put in for retirement just when they were about to nail him to the wall for his drunken exploits. Even JJ's father took his retirement. Yet Billy Ray is holding his head up high saying his First Amendment rights have been violated. JJ took off. Nobody's sure where he landed."

"What about Sarah?"

"She's taking the route of everyone else who gets caught with their pants down - she's in rehab. She could be looking at jail time, but I doubt it'll come to that. She was the Sheriff's personal assistant and confidante while she was running a porn business right under his nose. So much for employee loyalty!"

"And Zoe's in New York?"

Bogie nodded. "She emailed me a picture from their wedding. I've never seen such a little wedding dress. It looked like something Isabella could wear. She wrote that she bought it with the check I gave her. I hope she was joking. If she paid that much for the dress, she got robbed!"

"Why'd you give her a check?"

"First, so she'd tell us what was going on. Second, I wanted the whole business to end there. I didn't want her getting lawyers involved and her and Mandie getting in a pitched battle. The only ones who would make out would be the lawyers."

"Does Mandie know you gave her a check?"

Bogie shrugged. "I never said anything. I don't know if Randy did. She knows better than to confront me with that. I didn't have to give Zoe anything. But I remembered when we first came here, and I didn't know if I was going to make it. Amanda was a scared kid in a strange place. The other girls already had their little cliques and groups in place. The only ones who went out of their way to make friends with her were Zoe and Tiffany. They may not have been my first choice for her friends, but they were hers. All in all it would have been cheaper for me to pay the friggin taxes, but Mandie was really spinning out of control with her spending."

Darryl nodded. "It's tough saying no. It's a lot easier being a yes man."

"Amen. Let's go celebrate my son's birthday!"

As they walked into the reception area, Amanda, deeply tanned, came through the front door. Bogie took her arm. "Are you using enough sun block? Do you cover your head?"

Amanda's eyes rolled. "Yes, Grand..ma!" She hugged him. "You always worry no matter how old I am!"

"Of course, that's my job! Where's...?" Bogie glanced across the room and beamed at Riley Rose being held by her father. The baby looked at Bogie and grinned. "Da-dee!"

Amanda smiled and walked over and hugged her husband and baby. Thanks to Bailey, Amanda was able to keep working and not worry about

Riley Rose's care. Bailey claimed there was a fair and equitable schedule, but Riley Rose and the Hankster seemed to spend quite a bit of time together.

When the two men wearing shorts walked in from the pool area, most of the adults teased them. Jack's skin was so white it seemed translucent. George was half a shade darker. Their hopes of getting a nice tan in the forty-eight hours they were spending in Florida were diminishing as the hours ticked away.

Looking boyish with his dark spiked hair, George glanced at his watch then looked around for Isabella. He spotted her and winked. She came to him and they walked down the hall hand in hand to her practice room. When the door opened again, Isabella called out to her mother. Bailey shushed the crowd and announced, "George and Isabella are performing the upcoming number for Henry in celebration of his first birthday!" She gave a signal to Tiffany who started the CD player and the webcam. As Freddie Mercury and Queen sang: "We are the champions." George, wearing only white shorts with a red bandana around his neck, strutted down the hall with Isabella wearing a white tee shirt, red bandana and shorts. They danced, lip synced and moved around with their arms raised repeating

We are the champions..
We are the champions of the world...

The babies joined in singing and raising their arms. For the finale, everyone but Grandma, who was confused, had their arms raised singing when George dropped to his knee with one arm in the air as Isabella dived over him, rolled and also dropped to one knee. When the music stopped, they bowed to the profuse applause from the adults and babies. Even Grandma McGruder smiled.

The performance was picked up on Rose's computer as she, Jesús, Ken and Coco sat in her office laughing. Grinning, Mike Wislowski stood behind Rose with his hands on her shoulders.

Tommie Jurgenson and Catie Christenson stopped their follow-up interview to watch the song and dance on Tommie's extra-large HD monitor.

As Elizabeth held Henry, Bailey walked to Bogie and put her arm around his waist. "You and Pop were in there a long time. Is everything okay?"

Bogie nodded. "I'll tell you all about it tonight." He slid his hand down her back and rested it on her buttocks. "Late tonight!" and the corner of his mouth twitched into a Bogie smile.

THE END

ACKNOWLEDGDMENTS

With heartfelt thanks to those who made the story better and brought the characters to life:

Editorial:

Robert Marx
Maureen Moley
Mauricia Darvish

Artwork:

Original artwork: Catherine Christenson Stenhjem

Graphics: Ashley Haines

ABOUT THE AUTHOR

I am the author of the Pajama series. The Girl in Black Pajamas is the second book in the series.

I was born and raised in Pittsburgh, Pennsylvania. After graduating from high school, I did a four year stint in the Middle East. When I returned to the States, I settled down in the Boston area and became a true Bostonian by collecting college degrees while raising my family.

For more than twenty years, I did investigative work for Boston law firms. Being an avid mystery fan made me either fearless or foolhardy while working in rough neighborhoods and housing projects. I know how it feels to have a gun stuck to the back of my head…and that was in a courtroom. I know how it feels to have an angry client walk in my office and point a small gun at me saying, "I want my money!" That was when I opened my desk drawer, removed a large gun and drew back the slide while aiming it at him. "Have a seat!" I said.

There is no substitute for experience.

I live outside of Boston with my husband. We also have a place in Palm Beach where we escape to hide from the snow.

Made in the USA
Charleston, SC
27 July 2014